The Solomon Scandals

By David Rothman

Twilight Times Books
Kingsport Tennessee

The Solomon Scandals

This is a work of fiction. All concepts, characters and events portrayed in this book are used fictitiously and any resemblance to real people or events is purely coincidental.

Paladin Timeless Books, an imprint of
Twilight Times Books
P O Box 3340
Kingsport, TN 37664
http://twilighttimesbooks.com/

First Edition: January 2009

Library of Congress Cataloging-in-Publication Data

Rothman, David H.
  The Solomon scandals / by David Rothman. -- 1st ed.
      p. cm.
  ISBN-13: 978-1-60619-042-5 (trade pbk. : alk. paper)
  ISBN-10: 1-60619-042-3 (trade pbk. : alk. paper)
  1. Reporters and reporting--Washington (D.C.)--Fiction. 2. Investigative reporting--Fiction. 3. Landlords--Fiction. 4. Washington (D.C.)--Fiction.
I. Title.
  PS3618.O8687S65 2009
  813'.6--dc22
                                    2008056117

Photo credit Robert Farber

Cover design by Ardy M. Scott

Printed in the United States of America

To my wife, Carly, and sister, Dorothy,
and in memory of my parents,
Harry and Hortense.

Praise for The Solomon Scandals

"...We get to relish his chatty first-person narrator spinning characterizations of D.C. with the same dark zeal Hammett held for Frisco or Chandler had for Los Angeles."
Ted Scheinman, Washington City Paper

"At times, *Scandals* reminded me of a good Robert B. Parker mystery novel. At other times, such as during the party when socialite celebrity gossip columnist Wendy Blevin meets her ultimate demise, the book reminded me of the elegant prose of F. Scott Fitzgerald in *Tender is the Night...* Will I recommend this novel? Yes, in a heartbeat!"
Brad's Reader

"The book's women are especially likable: they radiate that screwball-comedy pizzazz a la Roz Russell's Hildy Johnson in the film *His Girl Friday.*"
Michael Pastore, ePublishers Weekly

"*The Solomon Scandals* is a mordantly entertaining book that broadens the cast of the standard Washington novel beyond spymasters and politicians to include real estate barons and federal contract officers."
James Fallows, author of *Breaking the News.*

"David Rothman's bright, breezy, face-paced, and funny novel shines a merciless spotlight on greed, skulduggery and fraud within government... Stone's fictional struggle to write and publish his expose is more than a shadow of the truth."
Bettina Gregory, former ABC New Washington correspondence.

Acknowledgments

My appreciation to Lida Quillen at Twilight Times Books.

We found the cover photo in the wild via Google Images™. The photographer turned out to be none other than Robert Farber (farber.com), a prize winner whom Doubleday published at the suggestion of Jacqueline Kennedy Onassis. Thanks Robert. And the same to Janelle Gibson-Haerle of Corbis Images™ and Pam Nicholson of Corbis and Veer for making use of the photo possible.

Also thanks to Gordon Batson (Clarkson University) and M. Kevin Parfitt (Pennsylvania State University) for vetting the details related to building safety.

James Polk, honored for Watergate reporting for the much-missed Washington *Star*, offered Pulitzer-level encouragement and advice when *Scandals* most needed it.

Blame me, not anyone else, for errors.

Major Characters

Rebecca Kitiona-Fenton: Great-grandniece of Jonathan Stone, the narrator. Tireless student of "previrtual media," the inky old paper kind.

Jonathan Stone: A reporter whose curiosity might kill his career and maybe him. Sees Washington as a white-collar factory town. Covered the Kent State massacre's aftermath while working in a blue-collar town. Known to have protested an early-morning meeting by showing up to work in his pajamas.

Sy Solomon: The real estate tycoon in the title—a massive ex-bricklayer with two missing fingertips and a huge, rickety building housing IRS and CIA bureaucrats. Friends with **President Eddy Bullard** and the *Washington Telegram's* top editor, George McWilliams.

George McWilliams, the editor: An embittered politician named a baby shark after him at a VIP hangout. Friends depict Mac as a priest in an editorial cathedral. But why is he at the *Telegram?* Made a fortune outsmarting the Brahmins of Wall Street and beyond.

Wendy Blevin: Vassar-educated gossip columnist and multimillionaire socialite who may or may not be sabotaging Stone's investigation of Solomon. Years earlier helped Saul Alinsky flesh out two of the thirteen *Rules for Radicals*. Owns an Afghan Hound named Thackeray.

Ezekiel Jerome Rawson: Jon Stone's direct boss—E.J. for short. Fled to D.C. from West Virginia Gothic.

Rexwood Garst: Stone's resume-obsessed rival at the *Telegram*. "Serbo-Croatian, that's the key. I know how to speak it."

Lew Fenton: Construction union leader and source of the few negative quotes about Solomon in the *Telegram's* library. Not the biggest fan of Solomon's construction practices.

Donna Stackelbaum: Stone's lover and old family friend who leaves him for a corrupt Lamborghini owner. About to get caught up in a nuclear scandal connected in some ways with the Solomon Scandals.

Margo Danialson: B.A. in Medieval Studies, now a junior bureaucrat at the General Services Administration (GSA). Helps Jon Stone circumvent **Larry Zumweltnar**, a PR sleaze. Points Stone to **Lucky O'Brien** at GSA. Although a drunk hoping to make a mint as a tabloid tipster, O'Brien may actually offer some useful information.

Fred Green: Muckraking congressional aide. Deep Throats on the Alexandria-to-Mount Vernon bike path.

Herb and Lydia Stone: Jon's parents. Herb works for a PR and lobbying firm that is in cahoots with a bank financing Solomon's projects.

Foreword by Rebecca Kitiona-Fenton, Ph.D., of the Institute for the Study of Previrtual Media

Just what to make of my great-great-uncle's *newspaper* memoirs? When Aunt Erica first told me of them, I did not know what to anticipate—they might, for all I knew, have been about whaling. I almost expected to read of harpoons and blubber boilers.

Typewriters existed outside museums back then. And those quaint old chronicles known as blogs had yet to bewilder and horrify the elite.

Washington, D.C., in skin color, was not so multihued. Rich, pale ladies born in the 1800s, the very century of *Moby Dick*, lingered on in gargoyled apartment buildings. Civil War widows still breathed.

Even before first seeing Uncle Jon's memoirs about the Solomon scandals, I had known of George McWilliams. He had been Jon's editor at the *Washington Telegram* and lorded over the most skilled of harpooners. Then one day his Ahab-like captaincy ended with a bloody dénouement in the parking lot.

No matter where Uncle Jon is these days, and regardless of the usual academic strictures against sentimentality, I wish him the happiest and most accurate of harpooning.

—Rebecca Kitiona-Fenton, Ph.D., of the Institute for the Study of Previrtual Media, Washington, D.C., January 4, 2081

Chapter 1

Wendy Blevin's obituary in the *Telegram* ran only 578 words—a notably miserly length. As much as anyone, she was a natural for a long feature in the "She had everything to live for" vein. I say this despite the Solomon scandals.

She was thirty-three, slender, and WASP-pretty, with pale blond hair that matched the coat of her Afghan hound. She earned $75,000 a year, as one of Washington's best gossips in print and in person. She'd been president of her class at Sidwell Friends School while leading an un-Quaker-like social life. She won a short-story contest sponsored by one of the snobbier women's magazines. She edited the yearbook at Vassar and was the first columnist on the student newspaper to use the F-word with impunity.

Wendy marched against the Vietnam War. She lobbied for the environment, a cause made all the more attractive when a ticky-tacky development encroached on her family's mansion in Potomac, Maryland. She was as highly pedigreed as her dog; she was eccentric rather than crazy. She jumped to her death off a balcony at the Watergate.

The day before her suicide, she was the subject of an exposé in her own paper—one, I am pleased to say, I had no part in writing.

And having said that much, I'll stop. The Blevin obituary was a cover-up, all right, but no more than the *Telegram's* treatment of the scandals that preceded it. I'll never forget how George McWilliams wavered on his way to journalistic immortality, how McWilliams the editor warred with McWilliams the friend.

ᎦᎤᏨ

Inside the glass booth in the middle of the newsroom, I saw a wrinkle-faced man in a dowdy plaid jacket.

Mac was small and had a sloping forehead and receding chin. But when he started speaking to you, quizzing you, trying to outmaneuver you, you felt as if he were a shark, preparing to steal dinner off the flesh of a larger fish.

I'll always remember the glass shark tank that one of Mac's foes suggested for the Sans Souci restaurant on Seventeenth Street, a VIP-gawker's Eden. An embittered politician, he wanted the tank's occupant to be named "Little Mac." The Sans Souci originally threatened to banish the man to Little Tavern hamburger shops, but McWilliams caught wind of the customer's malice and was captivated. Mac said he would only lunch at the Sans Souci *if* it brought in the baby shark.

‘’„

Frowning, McWilliams lit up a Corona and leaned back in a plushly padded swivel chair.

My immediate boss and I sat on hard seats. E. J. Rawson—"E.J." around the office, not just in his byline—was a national editor. He wore bifocals and had fled to Washington eons ago from a gothic-grim railroad town in West Virginia.

"Stone," Mac said, after the third puff, "I hear you want to go after Seymour Solomon."

"Not go after him. Investigate him." Officially, the *Telegram* was objective—Mac kept his shit list only inside his head. "Jeez, he's got fifty percent of the leases locked up in the D.C. area. A little payback for political donations?"

Vulture's Point, Solomon's rickety complex, housing no small number of IRS and CIA employees, never really came up in the beginning. I had yet to learn of the cracks in the slabs, the sexual blackmail from the Oval Office, the Papudoian connection, Wendy's role in the scandals, or the other heads of the Hydra. The white-sheeted corpses existed just within the realm of the unthinkable.

Mac glanced at his gold Rolex, with which he personally timed reporters writing stories or pumping news sources on the phone. After six months on the job, you were safe from the more lethal aspects of the Rolex Treatment, although the watch served the entire newsroom as a reminder of the *Telegram's* role as a high-speed word mill.

"I know Seymour Solomon—he's a good friend." McWilliams puffed an "O" and, with his fierce, dark eyes, stared at me as if hoping he could elicit a good flinch. "What I'm driving at, pal, is he's not the sort to steal from anyone."

So Mac had Solomon hooked up to a polygraph twenty-four hours a day?

"Including the government," McWilliams blustered. "Especially the government."

I was touched. "Government" included President Eddy Bullard, Mac's fellow OSS alum who, like him, had majored in French literature. At Burning Tree Country Club, they gleefully forsook regulation shoes for ragged sneakers. I could just imagine them in private, jabbering away in obscenity-laced French about Rousseau and putt shots.

"Do you know how much Solomon gave Washington Stage last year so they could build that new children's theater in Reston?" McWilliams asked me. "Two million. Now *that's* Sy. How many millionaires do you know who drive 1970 Mavericks?"

Mac himself drove a nondescript gray BMW. His job, Rolex, and the antiques in his mini-Versailles provided enough dazzle in his life to suit him; well, those and the Power People he'd befriended outside his word mill.

"Take it from me, pal," Mac said, as if auditioning for a Humphrey Bogart movie, "Sy is a regular guy. Look, isn't Judge Philips one of his investors?"

"That's reassuring," I said. "I'll remember that next time he rules in a zoning case."

Not once did E. J. Rawson—Ezekiel Jerome Rawson back in Thurmond, West Virginia—speak up for me. He was in his fifties, with crew-cut white hair, a weakened heart, and prudent decency toward his reporters despite fits of boss-man rhetoric. We had met through one of my parents' neighbors in northern Virginia, when I'd returned for Passover from my newspaper job in Ohio and accepted an invitation to E.J.'s home.

The first thing that struck me was his excessive formality before he knew you. "I would like," he said, "to discuss your career in the newspaper business." No contractions, no "I'd." Even in the ivy-covered brick Colonial he shared with his wife—a short, buxom Mississippian who had turned the basement into a seven-thousand-book library with thirteen dictionaries—he wore a white shirt and tie. It was as if he were distancing himself from the dust and grit of Thurmond.

I don't remember drinking Scotch as E.J. went on about Dostoevsky, Melville, Faulkner, and the editor of the *Saturday Review*, and some odd but logical parallels among the four. Still, I could not imagine any other beverage in his off-hours life.

By the time E.J. was through, a dozen writers later, having discussed George McWilliams in the same reverent tones, I hadn't the least doubt of my future as Mac's successor.

My own father, a "public affairs" man for a PR and lobbying firm on K Street, toiled in a bazaar, not an editorial cathedral.

"Well?" I asked the priestly shark in the plaid jacket.

"I'm not a regular guy, I'm a bastard, and I'm just enough of one to turn Stone loose on my friend Sy"—McWilliams glared at E.J.—"at your direction, pal."

I wished that just once Mac would gulp down a tranquilizer or reach for some ulcer medicine or do anything else that would confirm his mortality.

As if dismissing a pair of menials, McWilliams waved us out of the booth, the Shark's Cage, as everyone called it, and I decided I was confusing mortality with humanity.

ഇൻഇ

Rexwood Garst, renter of a converted carriage house in Georgetown, filled in for me on the national housing beat. He had a penchant for pipes and attaché cases and the other impedimenta of Washington stereotypes.

Garst knew he'd soon rise beyond his beat in Prince George's County. "Serbo-Croatian," he had told me, "that's the key." Pause. "I know how to speak it."

"So?"

"It's how I'll become Eastern European Correspondent."

"Why not Polish?"

"Because Serbo-Croatian's more unique."

I'd shaken my head. "The real future's in Korean."

"How do you know?"

"Suit yourself," I'd said, "but you'll never make it big here if you don't know Korean."

McWilliams rejoiced in assigning two people to one task and seeing who'd come out on top. If Garst dug up too much at the Department of Housing and Urban Development while I was away, I might have to share my muck with him in the future.

⊗ભ

The *Telegram* was that kind of a place—a whole newspaper remade to reflect Mac's ambitions for himself and the rest of us.

Mac had been born sixty-three years ago, the only son of a Scot and a Jew, and he'd put himself through Columbia University while reporting murders for the *New York Daily News*.

He had graduated summa cum laude; he had gone on to awe the dons of Oxford. In his thirties, after his days as a *Herald Tribune* prodigy and time in Washington with two secretive spy agencies, he had made a fortune as a bond and currency trader, outsmarting the Brahmins of Wall Street and beyond.

Mac's econo-Versailles on the fringes of Maryland hunt country dwarfed his publisher's Victorian mansion on the Chesapeake Bay.

No one could fathom why Mac had returned to newspapering as a flunky rather than doing the genteel thing and buying Knopf or *The New Yorker*. He might still be alive today if enough people had gotten curious and saved him from himself.

When McWilliams blew up at an underling, he might take a catcher's mitt from his battered wooden desk and smack a baseball against it. The object of his temper would inevitably recoil, as if convinced McWilliams were about to bean him. Mac didn't use the mitt that often but kept it on a shelf behind him, so that you might as well be a horse looking at a whip.

The Rolex, too, had inspired a few stories. McWilliams had bought it just a few years out of Columbia, an ever-ticking, ever-gleaming assurance that he had left Brooklyn behind.

His parents, a warehouseman and a nurse, were long dead, but his sister, crippled from polio, still lived in the old neighborhood. As divulged by a six-thousand-word profile of him in the Sunday magazine of the *New York Times*, she could barely support herself as a seamstress doing piecework—relentlessly paced by a dime-store watch.

Mac's ambitions and quirks were fodder for the diligent ladies at The Elephant, the big-eared gossip column of a rival paper, which mailed its victims quarter-pound bags of Virginia peanuts. The Elephant sounded off enough about McWilliams for him to amass enough bags to feed half the denizens of the Washington zoo.

ಐೞ

Driving home, I could see my obsessions all around me. Up and down Connecticut Avenue, the buildings of Seymour Solomon and associates loomed—each reaching Washington's commercial height limit, each grabbing every dollar of space in the sky, each looking as if a giant George Babbitt had been at work with Scotch tape and an Erector Set.

Bureaucrats occupied Solomon's buildings, along with stockbrokers, trade associations, and other staples of the local rental market. Every now and then rumors wafted about. The drones next to Barb's Secretarial Service—were they Agriculture or CIA? Was another Manhattan Project aborning above Menkov's Ladies' Wear?

At Dupont Circle, I saw half a dozen couples playing catch, just as Eddy Bullard did with his wife. A policeman strutted near the fountain there, his walkie-talkie squawking in some mysterious mix of cop lingo and Citizens Bandese. I remembered Dupont when it had been the territory of beats and hippies and junkies: an Allen Ginsberg poem writ in life on Connecticut Avenue.

In recent years, however, it had become too expensive to be degenerate close to the Circle. Sy Solomon's crowd had bulldozed away many of the cheaper rooming houses in the area, and they had priced the new apartments for the upper-level civil servants and lobbyists who worked in his office buildings. Washington was a veritable white-collar factory town run for management.

My own apartment building was a jumble of sooty red brick, a semislum named Cambridge Towers. I wondered how many years would creak by before Solomon's crowd tore it down in favor of their kind of ugliness.

I tried to envision myself a competent white-collar criminal. The closest I normally came to Dynamic Executivehood, the local robber barons' most common guise, was when I donned my suit from

Garfinckel's to infiltrate the stockholders' meetings of the companies I exposed in my articles.

Never could I have passed for Solomon himself, and not simply because he was older by several decades. We were both tall, but I was reporter-thin, as I liked to style myself, and he was business-man-heavy. He had wide shoulders and thick limbs and looked as if, by sheer bulk, he could bully the rest of the world. I remembered the huge hands I'd seen in newspaper photographs. Both physically and financially, Solomon struck me as a born grabber.

Chapter 2

"We've talked to you mothers already, and we're tired of your bullshit. You know about Solomon's fucking dime, don't you?"

Lew Fenton, a union leader and source of the only critical quotes about Seymour Solomon in the *Telegram*'s library, was eager to add to his distinction.

Solomon had quarreled with Fenton's construction local over paying the men a dime more an hour. The upshot was a federal case, going up to the Supreme Court and inspiring editorial-page apologia for Sy along the way.

"Well," Fenton jabbed at me over the phone, "that's about it, mister, except one of his buildings'll fall down. He's just as cheap with his materials as he is with us. The floors—Vulture's Point."

I remembered that fifteen hundred clerks and bureaucrats worked for the Internal Revenue Service there. But I spoke not a word back to Fenton. More than once in my days as a reporter, I'd heard false alarms, whether about impending earthquakes likely to topple the Washington Monument, or anthrax in the mashed potatoes at the Kingswood Elementary School cafeteria.

"The slabs," Fenton said. "He cheated on the rebars. It's the difference between a building that'll stay up and one that'll fall. And the difference of a million bucks to put the mother up. And that's just one thing—the concrete, the girders, you name it, mister, he cut it cheap all the way around."

"But why," I asked, "would Solomon gamble with human life?"

I was lost in my work, unmindful of the evening ahead with Donna Stackelbaum, an old friend with charms beyond the anatomy suggested by her name.

"The banks," Fenton said. "His loans. The interest rates went up just before the loan, and he had to cut it real close."

"How do you know?"

"The suit, mister. Buried in the middle of the trial records. All I know is that there's cracks on the seventh floor, and a lot of fat-assed bureaucrats are gonna fall on their behinds. One of our guys knows someone in maintenance. At GSA."

GSA was the General Services Administration, the government's business and recordkeeping agency. It had doled out so many leases to Solomon that I suspected President Bullard of being his silent partner.

"You want another Skyline?" Fenton asked.

Not far from Vulture's Point, in Fairfax County, the next county over, the center section of a huge condo building had caved in after the collapse of the twenty-fourth floor and a domino-like effect below. Many blamed the weight of a construction crane. Whatever the case, the official story was that a subcontractor had removed the concrete's shoring too early.

Fines had added up to just $300 for the shoring problem and $13,000 for violation of worker safety codes. Manslaughter charges hadn't stuck against the manager who had overseen the shoring at Skyline Plaza. Crimped by a local court ruling, prosecutors could not hold Skyline's owner criminally responsible for the lapses of subcontractors.

I remembered a line from *A Prairie Home Companion*, one of my favorite public-radio programs: "Welcome to Lake Wobegon, where all the women are strong, all the men are good-looking, and all the children are above average." Yes, yes—welcome to Fairfax County, Virginia, where all the buildings are strong *enough*, and the business climate is always superior.

Skyline had killed fourteen workers and injured thirty-four. But could another collapse happen, in the adjacent county and the same decade? When it came to bad luck on such matters, northern Virginia had already exceeded its quota.

"How come the people in the building aren't bitching?" I asked about Vulture's Point.

"Because GSA and Solomon have a cover-up going," Fenton said, "a real cover-up. A little reinforcement, pour more concrete, and plop down a carpet. Problem gone, and your upstairs storage area looks prettier. Just a little routine maintenance."

I was getting much closer to being shocked, and I remembered the smashed corpses I had seen after a mine collapse in Sloansville,

Pennsylvania—the bloodied, blackened men identified by their dental work and wedding rings.

"You disappoint me," E.J. said when I shared Fenton's alarm. "We had Swinburn check it out."

"Before or after he went to the Real Estate section?" Or became a PR man for the Chamber of Commerce?

"You remember Skyline, don't you?" I asked.

"Come on, Jon," E.J. protested in the informal language he used with the already-hired, "that was a construction accident. A different animal altogether."

"Maybe there's some interbreeding," I said. "Cracks are cracks."

I recalled an essay that E.J. had written about growing up in Thurmond, where, as a foreman for the Chesapeake & Ohio, his father had bossed the Coaling Tower crews. Like father, like son? I wondered what either would have done as a company man in Sloansville.

"Nothing to worry about," E.J. persisted. "Routine stuff. Your story, it would fall apart long before the building did."

༂༄

Arriving in my apartment that night, I took off my Dynamic Executive suit, then headed toward the shower, where I could hear the water already running. Behind the steamed-up glass stood a tall, auburn-haired woman with enough curves for the most demanding of blackmail work. General Motors might well have used her as bait against Ralph Nader, in the Safeway cookie aisle, to try to drive him off his Corvair exposés.

"Sweetie," said this fantasy come to life, my life, "your mom called. Seven-thirty Sunday: dinner with the Maxwells."

No blackmailer, no slimy operative, private or public, needed to lure me into bed with the corporate sector or its government stooges. I'd already been there—on and off, between other affairs—for years.

Donna Stackelbaum and I had gone to elementary and high school together, and religious school and the University of Virginia, too, or UVA as most referred to it. Nowadays she was a rising young lawyer-bureaucrat with an almost orgasmic eagerness to do the bidding of the nuclear power industry.

Our parents had always hoped we would marry someday. They were touchingly unaware of the ballots her friends had stuffed to elect her as treasurer of the Student Government Association at Langley High.

Donna drew me against her, and we hugged enthusiastically, both of us, while I enjoyed the voluptuousness around me, my hand gliding over the well-defined waistline, then squeezing her gracefully rounded backside. Its firmness hinted of regular workouts at the health club that one of Seymour Solomon's real estate partners owned a few blocks away.

I smelled Donna's freshly shampooed hair, nuzzled into her generous breasts, and almost didn't care if sex with her kept me out of Muckraker's Heaven. How could I have resisted her good intentions? Donna's future had been as palpable to her, ever since high school, as the ripe nipple I'd just tickled. If a prospective husband did not make enough money, and she was talking millions, not just upper-middle-class respectable, then she would do so herself without the hassles of sugar daddies.

Nothing mercenary impelled *us*, however, just a carnal fondness for each other in defiance of a values gap dwarfing the Mariana Trench.

At the Nuclear Regulatory Commission, Donna radiated a sunny obtuseness toward moral complexities—she regarded her work there as just a warm-up for her future lobbying duties for Corporate America. But she was more Civil Service-smart, more exam-smart, than brilliant in the Machiavellian style of energy lobbyists. The stuffed ballots were child's play by Washington standards. With my job and worldview, I never could understand why she had chosen me as a confidant, except for our families' propinquities, her lust for extratall, skinny men, and a bizarre and endearing appreciation of my quirks.

"Heard the latest on Papudo?" It was the setting of America's latest oil-driven exigency.

"Sweetie, you're running out of soap." This response from a woman juggling a budget of tens of millions!

I rubbed the shrunken bar all over her, and she returned the favor while I silently reflected on her urge, off the job, for domesticity.

Putz! I scolded myself—don't let Papudo distract you. The bedroom awaited us. But even amid the ecstasies in the shower, I couldn't help asking myself if Donna was criminal-brainy enough to reach a sleazy pinnacle as a lobbyist rather than slip off a cliff and into a prison cell.

My father, by contrast, had come by his public-affairs job honestly, the result of sheer canniness and diligence. No bribes need he dispense or receive. Most of his routine consisted of simply tutoring the guilty to avoid indictment—he might as well have been working in one of the cleaner jobs in a stockyard. He didn't slaughter or clean up after the animals. Rather, he just herded the cattle along, except that his mission actually was to steer them away from the blades.

If Donna wanted to be a realistic sellout, then she should work for my father's well-lawyered firm, a nice, safe pseudo–Civil Service, so to speak, for careerists keen on abetting the more obnoxious of the corporate profiteers.

Heated pleas from me notwithstanding, Donna failed to acknowledge her limits as a potential influence-peddler. And so in time we became simply "love buddies," as she euphemistically called us—still good friends and happy with the joys of the moment but not looking far beyond. That was even *before* I learned of her preemployment deal with Quad-State Atomic.

Risky career move. For the deal to fly, Donna had to enlist the help of enough compatibly ambitious coworkers to "adjust" federal oversight of Quad. At least for now, though, as with the stuffed ballots, Donna was getting her way. No one had squealed yet. Fish kept dying in hot discharges from Quad, while antiradiation precautions slackened to the level at which I expected the people nearby to be glowing a bright green.

To Donna's horror, I glommed more on to the hazards of nuclear meltdowns and cooked fish than the crinkly kind of green destined for her three-hundred-dollar handbag. So we agreed to clam up about each other's work, all the less for me to have to share with a grand jury someday, and all the more chance for her to retreat into pseudodomesticity. Though she had the key to my apartment, I warned her that it was not her fate to be forever domestic with *me.*

Despite our friendship, and despite her Mensian IQ, the crippled golden retriever she had rescued from the D.C. pound, the volunteer duties for the Humane Society, her prowess as a sailboater on Chesapeake Bay, the stamina both on the Appalachian Trail and in the bedroom, the curly auburn locks, the milky complexion, the little snub nose, the high cheekbones, the strong but feminine chin, the endless legs, not to mention the twin wonders so artfully hidden under the well-cut suits she affected at the Nuclear Regulatory Commission—despite all her assets, I just could not stand the prospect of someday limiting my sex life to conjugal visits.

—›✣‹—

After our first trip to my bedroom that evening, Donna warmed up some lasagna in the kitchen while I watched President Bullard lie away on CBS News. He had shaggy gray hair, thick eyebrows, and deep wrinkles that looked as if a cartoonist had drawn them after too many martinis. The *Telegram's* editorialists had marveled at the compassion and concern for us all that the president's furrowed forehead bespoke; I myself suspected the wrinkles were whiskey lines.

Walter Cronkite announced that the president was flunking the Gallup and Harris polls—the election was next year—and the Republicans were pouncing on him for being too soft on some on-again, off-again Reds in Papudo. Of course, Bullard was reacting like most other practically liberal Democrats in the White House. His latest speech had been bellicose enough to please the owner of a tank factory.

I was ingesting microwaved lasagna, and Walter's latest on stocks, tumbling because of Papudo, when our publisher suddenly came to mind.

Victoria Simpson owned the *Telegram*, but the real objects of her affections were a concert pavilion in suburban Maryland, the American Vivaldi Foundation, and invitations to the White House. She'd originally had a few misgivings about Eddy Bullard, a cocky commoner from Chicago, until he'd shown up at a picnic benefit for her pavilion. When one of the official White House photographers snapped a picture of the president that somehow made it seem as if he were rakishly leering her way, vanity overcame snobbery.

Mac had gone through eight music critics in five years, and I rejoiced that Bullard's GSA was not a concert pavilion.

Chapter 3

Larry Zumweltnar, chief PR man at GSA, was a relic from the Nixon days with a stentorian growl and a fleshy, pouty face—the look of a fat teenaged bully turned bald and dressed in a dark blue suit and tie.

Briefly avoiding his dourness, I sneaked past his Maginot Line, the agency's inept central switchboard, and eventually reached a junior bureaucrat named Margo Danialson. As a rule I mistrusted Margos; too many seemed to be man-hating preppies or hookers. But this Margo pleased me, the way she was "really" sorry for having to buck me back to Mr. Pouty. So I indulged in the hunch that the voice belonged to a nice, rounded woman with long hair of the kind that delighted men. I hoped her postgovernment ambitions were sufficiently innocuous.

"I don't mean to be nasty," Margo said, "but why are you asking all these questions? You're not quoting me in the papers, are you?" I told her I'd stick her name at the end of one of the letters in the lonely hearts column.

"Let's just say we're doing a story on certain real estate trends," I said. That was no lie: There could be a trend—more and more leases going to Sy Solomon.

Margo and I bantered a little more, promising each other a celebratory lunch after GSA coughed up the leases. I couldn't believe my luck. A sympathizer in the Augean Stables? So I wanted to think. With all the guile lurking within the mounds of shit, I might never know for sure.

I was about to dial another call when a news aide walked up with panic on her face. She looked as if she'd just heard McWilliams smack his mitt.

"You poor woman," I said, knowing who must be on the line. I reached into my pocket for two quarters. "Here—buy yourself a Coke and drink up to the fact that neither of us works for him."

I picked up the phone, wishing I'd had time to sneak in a martini at the *Telegram* Tavern across the street.

"Stone, what are you doing harassing our people again?" Most "information directors" at least feigned friendliness with trouble-some newspeople, but Zumweltnar was forthright enough to let you know from the start that he hated your guts

"You should talk, Zumweltnar. You're the most accomplished bully of secretaries on the East Coast."

"I'm getting tired of this, Stone. How many times have I told you—if you have any questions, just work through me, and I'll do everything I can to help you. Okay?" Zumweltnar spat out the "Okay?" as if he were kicking me karate style in the groin.

"Look," I said, "maybe I feel masochistic enough to see you in person today. Three o'clock?"

"All right," Zumweltnar said in his gloomy way, "but I'm doing this only because I believe in the free flow of information."

I hung up, typed out a final copy of my request for the leases, stating where and how they were stored, and left for the GSA build-ing at Eighteenth and F, one of the uglier legacies of the Wilson administration.

☙ଔ

In the world of corruption, this neoclassical blight was a land-mark. Once the building had housed Interior and a good number of those involved in the Teapot Dome scandal. GSA had been in existence and in the building only since the late forties. The Public Buildings Service and various supply agencies had been consolidated then, so that as much of the pork as possible was in one barrel. A huge agency plaque covered half the door of Zumweltnar's office. I saw in bronze a public works project of another time, a pyramid, and it reminded me of many of GSA's creations—imposing and wasteful.

The office itself was appointed in standard GSA executive mod-ern; it looked like a cross between a Howard Johnson's and the inside of an Amtrak Metroliner. Room C900 was long and narrow, with reddish orange cloth partitions. I wondered if they could ever muffle Zumweltnar enough when he was chewing out inquisitive reporters.

I winked at Zumweltnar's deputy, a Southern-polite blond wom-an with a better disposition than he deserved. As she greeted me, I peered into her pencil tin and saw an empty bottle of tranquilizers.

Her boss was typing away on his own IBM, and that tickled me. It was a reminder of the grubby work he'd left for $49,000 a year and the privilege of lying as an official spokesman. Zumweltnar had actually been a newsman once, a bureau chief for one of the second-tier chains that were always boosting themselves in promotional ads in *Editor & Publisher*.

"All right, Stone," he said. "What's the smear you're working on now?"

"Who says it's a smear? Maybe I'm writing a man-bites-dog story about your agency doing something right."

"I'm told you want to see every lease in the Washington area."

I nodded—I wanted to find out how much Solomon and friends might be ripping off the taxpayers compared to the competition.

"You're talking three ninety-seven, okay?" said Zumweltnar, and happily informed me that the "professional and clerical fees" would come to $2,000.

ଠଉଓ

My mind wandered as I drove back to the *Telegram* from GSA. It was midspring in Washington, a blessed break between the March monsoons and the summer mugginess. I saw myself taking a little time off to hike on the Appalachian Trail south of Snickers Gap with my old friend Al Bergmann of the Associated Press.

E.J. had proposed me for an assistant editorship on the National Desk, and I felt as smug as any flunky in an insurance company. George McWilliams paid me $24,000 a year, which in those days was more than I could have earned at any paper other than the *New York Times* or *The National Enquirer*. I wasn't money-mad, but I'd grown up in McLean, Virginia, where the Kennedys lived, and while I didn't run with that crowd, I wasn't ready for a tumble to Beltsville.

Paradoxically, the Solomon investigation might propel my career forward, given McWilliams's fondness for chutzpah within bounds. If I didn't make too much of a nuisance of myself about Mac's friend Solomon, I'd be showing just the right amount of brashness.

Chapter 4

Wendy Blevin—a fount of Solomon-friendly adjectives on the People Page, totally out of character for someone of her usual acuity—was perched atop Rexwood Garst's desk. Just what were they doing? Gossiping about a female congressman's new lover?

I was about to interrupt to ask Garst about a housing story when ten chattering schoolchildren walked up, led by a *Telegram* tour guide and a plump, schoolmarmish woman in a loose green sweater.

"Oh, look!" cried a young African-American girl in pigtails as she pointed at Wendy. "There's Miss Alice!" Another child scampered to Garst's desk and stretched out her arms to hug Wendy, who bent down and eagerly reciprocated. Only then did I learn that, behind our backs, Wendy volunteered most every second Saturday of the month for a literacy program at the Martin Luther King Jr. Memorial Library. Clad in a pink little-girl dress, a wide black "Alice band" in her hair, she would read *Alice's Adventures in Wonderland* and other classics to students bused in from the slums.

I watched her talk to the children as if she had been tutoring them all year long—never missing a name.

"Okay, Leila," Wendy asked the pigtailed girl, "who said, 'I'm late, I'm late for a very important date'?"

"George McWilliams," I wanted to say—a time-fixated Mad Hatter, except that *others* had to worry about being late. Or was Mac instead the Queen of Hearts, yelling, "Off with their heads"? Or neither? As phenomena to invent, both McWilliams and Wendy would have defied the imagination even of Lewis Carroll.

The whole scene with the slum children was so typical of Wendy. I can also remember her feature story about a twelve-year-old heroin addict—a real addict, as verified by a colleague who accompanied her: not the fabrication that had sullied the pages of our competition. Best of all, "our" addict, thanks to Wendy, ended up at a treatment center.

Never had I known a more street-smart heiress. Wendy could put on jeans and walk down the meanest alleys in D.C., sassing the hookers and pimps in ways that made them want to know her, not maim or kill her.

೫ᏓᎶᏰ

At last the children sashayed off toward the press room and a pile of free copies of the *Telegram*—the Children's Page of which Miss Alice, in a soft, fetching voice, had recommended on orders from the Queen. If the students didn't know the answers to the page's current events quiz by Saturday, they might lose their heads.

Once again Wendy had shown how she could transcend race and class and every preconceived notion of likability.

I'll forever recall the aftermath of her chicken-and-rice dinner with friends in a decaying Anacostia neighborhood with lackadaisical garbage collection. They were authentic friends, not get-to-know-for-a-cause friends, and as a strategist Wendy gave them her best. A giant pile of pet droppings, laced with the carcasses of dead rats, ended up on the lawn of a sanitation bureaucrat in Kalorama Heights.

Wendy was the only Vassar-educated debutante I knew who had learned community organizing under Saul Alinsky. As reported by the *DC Gazette*, she had helped Alinsky flesh out at least two of the thirteen *Rules for Radicals*. The first was, "Ridicule is man's most potent weapon," while the other was, "A good tactic is one your people enjoy."

I, in fact, wondered if Wendy's pink Mercedes and Watergate co-op served as camouflage to hide quiet, heartfelt subversion, albeit without the least trace of dogmatism. One day Wendy could mock a 350,000-dollar wedding or a Bible-thumping businesswoman with a fondness for rotting slum properties in Baltimore and insurance schemes aimed at bilking the poor. The next she might write of a rich Kennedy-era society hostess, dying of breast cancer, and make readers feel the sting of the chemo and pray for a remission.

She herself was from a family that looked down upon the Bachelors and Spinsters Ball—indeed, most of the standard black-tie affairs—the way middle-class people sneered at disco dances in the ghetto. The Blevins had decided that if you worried about status, you lacked it altogether, and they were right, for all of Georgetown parroted and ignored such wit from above.

Wendy thumbed her long, aristocratic nose at the showier of the rich, covering their parties as if she were a police reporter specializing in Mafia funerals. Off the canapé circuit, she often wore the most plebeian clothes. But her hair, if never in an elaborate coiffure, was always perfectly combed, and she valued her complexion enough never to use makeup. A profile in the *London Times* said she looked like the heroine of a gothic novel dressed in Levi's. She could even get away with addressing colleagues as "dear," a dangerous word because it had been appropriated in Washington by female social climbers and the gossip column of the rival paper.

൦൦ൽ

"Jon, dear," Wendy said out of nowhere, "I hear you're going to grind Sy Solomon into little specks of dust." She didn't smile, she didn't frown, she just said it.

"Where'd you hear that?"

"Please, dear," she responded, "who *doesn't* know?"

Garst reddened ever so slightly.

"Jesus, Rexwood," I said, "don't you have better things to do than eavesdrop on E.J. and me?"

"I was only trying to stay informed—in case E.J. wants me to help you," Garst said.

"I hope he likes me too much for that."

"Too bad you feel that way," Wendy said, with a realistic-sounding air of regret, "because I could write half your story for you."

"How?" I asked.

Wendy was enticingly silent.

"Listen," I said, "this is one for Pierre."

I was speaking *Telegram* parlance for a retreat to the lunchroom, known as the Pierre L'Enfant Room. "Lunchroom" had done quite nicely until the U.S. Bicentennial and the arrival of a zealous promotion man. No matter what the name, it was still a great place to go in moods of paranoia. When *Telegram* reporters said, "This is one for Pierre," they meant business.

"All right, dear. Apologies accepted in advance."

I nodded.

"I keep up with Sy's people," Wendy said in the lunchroom, between sips of mineral water, an obscure brand from Maine. "The parties, dear. Everyone goes to Sy's parties."

"Who's 'everyone'—besides Mac?"

"Yes, he goes. And the gray hairs from the networks. And other papers. And—oh, the Prez has been known to drop by from time to time."

"Planning a Sy party piece?" I asked.

"Are you kidding? There are party-parties, and there are name-in-the-paper parties. Sy gives party-parties."

"But haven't you built yourself up by turning party-parties into name-in-the-paper parties?"

"I can't help it," Wendy protested. "Sy brings out the lady in me. He's a dear, that man."

"How's his old Maverick getting along?" I asked.

"It's in the shop now"—she winked—"but that's no problem."

"Got a few spares, huh?"

"What's today? Friday? It must be his Caddy day."

"The way Mac speaks, Sy's a Maverick man, pure and simple." So was that what Mac *thought*, or just what he *said*? I suspected the latter.

"Maybe he thinks the Cadillac belongs to the maid."

"But," I asked, curious about the discrepancy, "aren't he and Sy good friends?"

"They are, dear. Sy's good friends with everyone."

"What do Sy and the Prez talk about?" I asked.

"Oh, things. Like art. Sy used to be a Dali man, but he's going back to van Gogh."

"What about politics? The Prez doesn't mind a little shop talk with Sy, does he?"

"The Prez is definitely going to dump Pratt."

Huey Pratt was vice president of the United States—a Mississippi Baptist who favored *The Sound of Music* over baroque music.

"You told Mac yet?" I asked.

"He already knows."

"Jesus—when are we breaking the story?"

"When the Prez says to."

"When the Prez says? I was just thinking Mac might have a little say in the matter."

"Oh, he does, dear. But right now that's party-party stuff. I really shouldn't be talking like this."

"I'll send you your peanuts in the morning."

As a gossip you had to give as well as get. No one could accuse Wendy of hoarding.

"The Prez adores The Elephant."

"I suppose he sends in all the Chuckles Couple stories." CC was shorthand for Mac and his improbable girlfriend, Luci Elkins—as far apart in IQ points as in years.

"He could if he wanted," Wendy said. "He probably knows more about the *Telegram* than you do."

"Like what?"

"The usual. Who's hired. Who's fired. At a party-party, that's where I got the word on my last raise."

"Am I getting a raise?"

"I don't know. Ask the Prez."

⇣☍⇢

A "party-party" was as good a place as any for Wendy to learn she'd be making more money; certainly she didn't press the issue at the office. I can't conceive of a Blevin worrying about mundane matters like earning an extra few dollars a week. Just two centuries ago, give or take a few years, the Blevins weren't even mixing with the untitled.

Contrary to rumor and sarcasm, the family never claimed lineage back to William the Conqueror. They were quite content that one of them had been knighted for success in dispatching infidels during the Crusades. Wendy's father, Morrison Blevin, had endeared himself to the great unwashed as one of Franklin Roosevelt's cabinet members. He survived, physically if not politically, into the Eisenhower years—a tough antique who at the time of his death was chairman of MTB Industries.

Even two decades after the Hunting Lodge Affair, some Washingtonians still snicker about Morrison Blevin. He calculated he'd win five fighter plane contracts for every thousand ducks the generals bagged at his place on the Eastern Shore. Morrison was a large, strong man with a huge walrus moustache and a penchant for jogging; he went on to outrun and outlive two wives many years younger.

I remembered reading of his mother. Pale, gloomy, and languid, she had "fallen" off the Calvert Street Bridge in D.C., perhaps the city's most attractive jumping point for suicides. Morrison might well have sucked up whatever vitality she had left while still alive, passing it on in time to Wendy.

The third Mrs. Blevin, Wendy's mother, came from a nouveau-riche family of mere *Mayflower* vintage. Morrison married Melissa a few years after World War II, when he was seventy-three, she twenty-seven, and Wendy, as it turned out, five months in Mrs. Blevin's womb. Tongues clucked; Morrison rejoiced. The higher his sperm count, the greater would be Wall Street's faith in his longevity and the value of MTB stock.

Wendy grew up on the Blevin estate in Potomac when it was still WASPy and horsey. Every once in a while a neighbor, Drew Pearson, made unflattering mention of Morrison Blevin in newspaper columns. And young Wendy horrified Potomac and pleased Morrison when she encountered Pearson at a community supper and summarily spat on him. Wendy—at least according to what she told me in the Pierre L'Enfant Room—was once "precociously malicious."

I don't know how she ended up at Sidwell Friends. It was said that the headmaster valued "curiosity and good decorum"; I suppose Wendy was curious.

Old Morrison had died while she was still in the first grade; and under the influence of the Quakers, she put aside her malice and concentrated on wildness. Years later, she liked to brag how, at seventeen, she'd flown furtively to Europe in an MTB jet for an abortion. Then there was her Lady Godiva ride through Montgomery County's staidest horse show. One of the judges—perhaps kindred in spirit with Morrison—unsuccessfully tried to have Wendy's Arabian awarded the fifth-place ribbon.

Wendy spent a good part of her time at Vassar fucking the leader of the Dartmouth Students for a Democratic Society. When a recruiter from MTB Industries visited Dartmouth, Wendy and her lover helped hold him hostage in the administration building. As a political organizer, though, Wendy is best remembered for her

Parisian blue jeans and her participation in a movement called "Flush with Indignation." She crisscrossed New York, imploring students to keep their toilets going so water pressures would drop enough to register strong opposition to the grafters in Saigon. The CIA allegedly tampered with the meters of the Poughkeepsie Water Department.

She celebrated her graduation with a six-month odyssey through Europe; and then, having nothing better to do, she returned home to look for work. To her amazement, she discovered that many employers were put off by her grades, politics, even decorum, so she settled for a lowly job in a public-relations firm whose major client was MTB Industries.

A few causes and firings later, Wendy took up with one of the *Telegram's* national editors long enough to insinuate herself into a job at the newspaper. He defected eventually to the *New York Times*, but Wendy stayed in Washington—writing learned articles on trends in hem lengths.

She was spared a career of it, however, when McWilliams heard of her past and asked if she was still as outrageous as she had been in her "Flush with Indignation" days. Wendy said, "No." McWilliams said, "That's too bad. I was planning to offer you a column."

Wendy raced out of the Shark's Cage into the middle of the newsroom, jumped on a copy desk, and stripped to her waist.

Some dismissed this as just another sign of her wildness. Yet I wondered if she hadn't also intended to deliver the ultimate parody of Mac's aspirations for the People Page. Mightn't the Alinskian side of Wendy have prompted her to persist in her old outrageousness as another form of subversion?

The next day, whatever the reasons for the nudity, Wendy began writing up Georgetown for the People Page.

Chapter 5

Back inside the eyesore at Eighteenth and F, I handed my letter to Zumweltnar with the *Telegram's* two-thousand-dollar check stapled to it. He held the note close to his sullen face as if searching for a tiny flaw. Zumweltnar gave me a date to see the first of the leases, adding, bosslike, "Nine o'clock *sharp*. Incidentally, Stone. Why are you interested in Solomon?"

Then he smiled, breaking for just a few seconds out of his dourness, and I wondered how much he knew.

ଛଠୟ

My next stop, Room 4022, where Margo Danialson worked, looked like a duplicate of Zumweltnar's office, the same blend of Howard Johnson's and Amtrak. Old clips started crossing my mind. Richard Nixon's men had saddled GSA with the relatives and friends of good Republicans, from a Supreme Court justice on down. I wondered how many of the people in the room had stolen in during Tricky's time.

A man not much older than I was sporting a crew cut and three-piece suit. Nearby sat a gray-haired crone who could have been a leftover from the Truman administration, or even before. For all I knew, she'd leased a wigwam from Pocahontas's grandfather.[1]

Only toward the far end of the room did I find Margo Danialson's nameplate, at a desk into which a towering bank of file cabinets threatened to crash. Someone had haphazardly piled real estate journals on her desk, and Margo or one of her colleagues had let coffee stain the covers of a leasing manual.

"Hi," I said to the possible coffee-spiller.

Squeakily, she swiveled toward me; one of the wheels of her chair dropped off.

"Jesus, this place is falling apart."

"You must be—"

"Jonathan Stone."

She appeared to be in her early twenties, with freckles, a nose ever so slightly too large, brown eyes, and chestnut hair—long but a little ragged at the ends, as if she wanted to be attractive without looking like a mannequin.

In fact she was wearing pants that looked suspiciously close to jeans, and I wondered if she'd be vulnerable to the more realistic of the folk songs from the '60s. Maybe some of Joni Mitchell's? Then I saw Ms. Danialson giving me a frown that would have done Zumweltnar proud.

"Remember me?" I said.

"Unfortunately. I'm supposed to have you go through channels. So, get your rear end out of here."

"I thought we were going to have lunch together."

"Only if you use arsenic seasoning."

"Hey, listen, I'm sorry I caused trouble for you. So I'll apologize—with lunch."

Ms. Danialson mulled that over,

"There's a real nice little Italian spot near Dupont Circle, and I doubt the GSA crowd hangs out around there."

"My God, you're a pest." But a small smile betrayed her.

"The most persistent in Washington."

"Anyway, I don't take my lunch break for another ten minutes."

"No problem." I reached for my wallet and pulled out $3.00. "Look, take a cab, and I'll meet you there in twenty-five minutes." I gave her the address and name of the restaurant—too obscure to be expensive.

But Ms. Danialson was shunning the $3.00. "You have your nerve—investigating us, then bribing us."

"All the more reason I'd like to talk to you," I said. "If you're principled enough to worry about cab money, you might have a few things on your mind about what's happening at GSA."

"Quick! Behind you!"

I saw the gray-haired crone shuffling toward us.

"Oh my God, here comes Mrs. Fogart."

"Your boss?"

"She never lets me forget it."

"Who's your visitor, Ms. Danialson?" Mrs. Fogart spoke like one of the sterner chaperons at an elementary-school picnic.

"That reporter."

"Ms. Danialson! I told you! Public Information's handling this."

"Which is what I'm telling this Stone character."

Mrs. Fogart summoned up her best frown for me. "Leave! And step on it, before I call the security guards."

"I'm leaving," I said. "But I'll be back."

"That's for Mr. Zumweltnar to decide," Mrs. Fogart said.

"I'll be back. And when I return, I don't want to have any more dealings with that Danialson woman."

"Oh, don't you worry about that!" Margo snapped. "It's been a long time since I've run into someone as creepy as you."

I retreated to a phone booth on the other side of the fourth floor and dialed Margo's number. Ever so lightly I placed one hand on the hook—ready to hang up if anyone else came on the line.

The connection clicked.

"Leases." Margo had answered.

"Jon Stone. It's still on."

"But she's—"

"Then you can't argue. Make up your mind. Yes or no? Twenty-five minutes from now at Angelo's?"

"Okay."

Chapter 6

Angelo's was two blocks off Connecticut Avenue in an old town house, an ornate, turreted affair that the restorers had somehow overlooked. Maybe the preservationists could make it historic-safe before Solomon razed the building for another high-rise.

I bought the evening newspaper at a nearby rack, digested a treatise on Bullard and the economy, then turned to The Elephant column:

> Big Mac's gotten the D.C. government
> to put up extra streetlights in front
> of Luci's place on P Street. Elephant's
> relieved it won't get mugged next time
> it leaves off some peanuts.

"I won't tell." Margo was beside me on the bench, giggling. "Shame on you—reading the other paper."

"Jesus, if it isn't the goody-goody bureaucrat."

"I'm not just a bureaucrat," Margo said. "I'm Margo Danialson, B.A. in Medieval Studies, Oberlin College."

"I'm Sir Lancelot," I said in keeping with her major.

"No, you're not, you're just a pushy reporter."

"You Oberlin people, you're always full of shit."

"How do you know?"

"Because I served time in Marseilles." It was a steel town near the college—as large a city as could exist without anyone having heard of it.

Everybody in the area looked down on Marseilles; the Cleveland papers said Marseilleans wed in bowling shirts. Oberlin students condescended toward Marseilleans the way some missionaries from the school must have sneered during the nineteenth century at the Chinese.

"On the paper there?" Margo asked.

I nodded. "Not the *Telegram* but okay for what it was. I just prefer a white-collar factory town to a blue-collar factory town."

Angelo's actually mixed elements of both. It was my kind of Italian restaurant, with red-checkered tablecloths and a Sicilian-born waiter who still cursed the old Senators baseball team for becoming the Minnesota Twins.

"I remember something else about Marseilles," Margo said, as we stepped inside.

"What? That steel workers don't go around calling each other 'My dear fellow'?" I'd gone there fed up with the urbanity of the University of Virginia English Department.

"Didn't one of the Kent State victims come from Marseilles?"

"I wrote up his funeral." The hearse and the mourners had waited twenty minutes while a coal train rumbled past on the way to the mills.

I copped an imaginary glance at the legs under Margo's pants. They were long, and I suspected they were skier's legs—slender but strong enough for cycling and the slopes. Did she backpack, too?

ଈଔଓ

No, I was not yet feeling Stackelbaum-level chemistry, but I wanted to know Margo better, *much* better.

Donna had suspended our "love buddy" sessions once again, a new man having shown up without my bothersome scruples. Instantly and passionately, he'd demanded an exclusive, and she had acceded. My suspension might even be a gentle termination.

She was light on facts about him, except to say he was lanky and bearded, owned a red Lamborghini, but never drove it at more than five or ten miles an hour above the speed limit.

Not a single traffic citation tainted his driving record, Donna marveled. So Washington-like of him. Let any lawlessness be minor and sustainable.

With Donna silent on this righteous citizen's name, I wondered if she was simply keeping her promise to spare me the details of her work. Just which special-interest group might he have come from? The nuclear industry? Or oil, gas, or coal? A solar or geothermal man was out of character for her—too distant a payoff. Then I recalled Donna's feelings against sugar daddies. Had she changed her mind?

I remembered the stares we had drawn, when we'd dined two weeks earlier at Chez François, from a fortyish mesomorph in a thousand-dollar suit. Might he have been gauging the worth of my Garfinckel's attire and his chances of outbidding me? Women, real estate, and legislation—the holy trinity of the Washington market-place.

∞♥∞

Inside Angelo's I ordered salad, garlic bread, and Chicken Parmesan, but Margo contented herself with just a small bowl of pork-trotter soup.

"Relax, I'm paying for this."

"What about Jiminy Cricket?" Margo asked. I remembered him as a Walt Disney character with profundities like, "Let your conscience be your guide." He'd better stay away from Washington; the politicians would step on him.

"You know, of course, we're talking just for background," she said. "Nothing for quotation."

"Jeez, you know the lingo."

"I was arts editor of the *Review*," Margo said. "So! What do you want to know about leases?"

"Why does Solomon have so many?"

"I couldn't tell you."

"But you work there," I said.

"Not long enough to know. But if you're looking for some technical stuff… The difference between a good lease and a bad lease. The average annual rent as of the present fiscal year. And how many rolls of toilet paper the janitors ought to put in the average ladies' room."

"Look, where do you think I should start?"

"Come to my place, and I'll tell you," Margo said.

∞♥∞

The biggest leakaholic on Capitol Hill called me that week about Solomon. His name was Fred Green, and I'd met him years ago while interning with one of the more devious of the oil-state liberals. Green was short, fat, and red-complected. A vein protruded unnervingly from his forehead. He always seemed on the verge of a stroke. He was given to twenty-five-hundred-calorie lunches and sessions with sources in obscure Little Taverns, the very hamburger chain co-owned by the late J. Edgar Hoover.

As a result of Green's labors, his boss, a dim-witted womanizer from Georgia, was one of the more exalted people on the Hill. Columnists were more loyal to Green than to their readers and the truth, so they called Congressman Hinson able and well informed. With Green around, Hinson might have been the latter.

Green flaunted documents from all the big bureaucracies, including the Central Intelligence Agency. Some of Hinson's enemies implied that Green had CIA connections, that his leaks advanced certain factions at the Agency, but I discounted the gossip. Green simply couldn't decide whether to be a newsman or a politico.

"How come you're calling? Who told you I was investigating Sy—"

"Just keep digging," Green said.

"Where's the shovel go?"

"I can't say, except the campaign donations are just the start."

"So what's next? The line that you'll deny having spoken to me? So can't I at least tell my editors?"

"No. *Nobody* at the *Telegram* right now."

"Why not?"

Silence.

Chapter 7

I walked over to Wendy Blevin's desk, the only one with a bouquet of white roses and a "Virginia is for Lovers" sign in French.

"Would you believe," I said, "someone's telling half the town about my Solomon story." I was doing my best to avoid a prosecutorial tone.

"Don't look at me, dear."

"Sorry. It's just the way you were talking about him. 'He's a dear, that man,'" I mimicked as humorously as I could.

"You're a dear, everyone's a dear." Wendy laughed. "You think I'm talking to Solomon? Is that it, dear?"

"No, no, of course not," I momentarily retreated.

"Well, actually, we're having an affair. The three of us. Sy and me and his wife. A trio. Sy and Ida and Wendy. They're going to film it for all the theaters. All the porno flicks on Fourteenth Street."

"Thanks for the scoop—I'll give it to The Elephant."

"No, thanks; peanuts make me fat."

"Just so you haven't talked to anyone," I said.

Emphatically, Wendy shook her head.

Whether she was spoiling my investigation or not, I liked her, and it seemed useless just then to press further.

"You investigative types"—she laughed—"you're career paranoids."

Career paranoids? Such an interesting choice of words. Mightn't paranoia and prudence at times overlap?

ଚଠଔଔ

My worries about Wendy paled in import compared to the most notable event of the day—yet another profile of her in *Redbook*. Let me skip the formulaic gush, take you past the horseless nudity in the newsroom, and recall Wendy as she more routinely existed on the job during her years with the *Telegram*.

Wendy dressed for name-in-the-paper parties as though modeling in Paris. Anthropologists wore loincloths when studying the natives of New Guinea; Wendy carefully blended in at the right moments with the pretentious victims of her High Society stories. After hours, however, Wendy favored shabby jeans, and not the high-fashion kind, for she was beginning to think of herself as above stylishness. She mercilessly ridiculed rich matrons' preoccupation with clothes—endearing herself to the young secretaries and clerks among her readers, some of whom, in turn, consciously imitated her own indifference to style.

The department stores and the *Telegram*'s advertising staff complained. But a readership survey showed Wendy was the main draw of the People Page, and the circulation people prevailed. Vicky Simpson, our publisher, gave Wendy free rein as long as she didn't ridicule the party-parties. The name-in-the-paper kind tended to be fair game.

Most People Page reporters worked more than fifty feet from the Shark's Cage. But Mac soon moved Wendy to a desk near him—all the better to gloat over his new star and benefit from her gossip about the unfortunates on his shit list.

In two months *The Saturday Review* was calling Wendy "one of the most literate of America's gossip columnists. Clerks and secretaries can chuckle over her accounts of the misdoings of the Washington elite. Yet she is perfectly capable of preceding her irreverence with an apt quote from Eliot or Thackeray."

A news magazine swooned over her in its press section. The *Telegram* started syndicating her three times a week on the national wire it grudgingly shared with the *New York Times*.

The smart social climbers barred her from their parties, except for the ones who were intelligent enough to know that a Blevin hatchet job enhanced their standing as much as a positive piece by a less glamorous columnist.

Whether Wendy was writing up people or their parties, her subjects never knew where they stood with her. I'll forever recall her profile of General Jesus Sanchez, a member of the Papudoian junta that was at the time in the middle of a love-hate relationship with the United States. In my eyes he looked like a dried-up little shrimp in the accompanying photo, and, in fact, Wendy did not lie in her story. She just passed over the unflattering facts to depict him as a Latin-American Clark Gable. What is remarkable is that Wendy's left-wing politics were the antithesis of Sanchez's. I can remember Mac at the time posting a memo on the newsroom bulletin board, complimenting Wendy on her "objectivity and total professionalism."

The most amazing fact about Wendy was that she deserved every syllable of praise, every dollar of the $75,000 a year that The Elephant said she earned from the *Telegram* and her syndicated column. She *was* good. She did know the classics. Party girl though she'd been, all along she was a closet reader. And most importantly, she worked.

Occasionally, on my way home from a late date, I'd drop by the *Telegram* to tidy up a feature story and find Wendy still at her newfangled video display terminal. She'd write and rewrite a piece about a politician from Boise, Idaho, as if she were George Eliot toiling over *Middlemarch*. She bought a pair of hideous horn-rims, which she donned only at the VDT, "to show how I'm martyring my eyes."

Above all, I liked her voice, which was so soft, so charming, so melodious, that more than one profile compared her during a *Great Gatsby* craze to Daisy Buchanan. I myself disagreed somewhat; Wendy's voice, if often indiscreet, was never "full of money." Had she been born to a waitress, had she grown up behind a pizza parlor in Prince George's County, I suspect she would have sounded just as enchanting.

Every now and then I tried to lure her to my apartment, but she always pleaded Other Plans—a vagueness evident, too, when The Elephant queried her about her whereabouts on certain weekends. Rumors abounded, and twice a year a New York gossip columnist mated her with Teddy Kennedy. Yet somehow no one could really pin down the identity of Wendy's mysterious lover, if any.

The most the world knew was that she regularly "flew out of the cuckoo's nest" and headed north. I never could remember whether the phrasing was Wendy's or The Elephant's. What can be said with certainty is that, lover or not, somebody saw fit to send Wendy each week a bouquet of three dozen giant white roses, the flowers I mentioned earlier. Each arrived in a Waterford crystal vase, and no one could ever discover the giver. Wendy fended us off with jokes when we asked.

Deepening the mystery, the rose couriers were not little women in floral dresses or ponytailed delivery boys but swarthy and muscular men in foreign-looking brown suits. Politely, carefully, Wendy kept her distance from any male reporter at the *Telegram* who showed signs of wanting to become something more than a newspaper buddy. Her silk-screened cards never said, "Merry Christmas," or "I wish you a very Merry Christmas!" It was always a cautious, "You are wished a Merry Christmas," as if she were giving people the equivalent of an air kiss from across the street.

One winter evening, Wendy cajoled several of us into riding with her to the National Christmas Tree at the White House. Snow was swirling as we crowded into her Mercedes, and I suspect she drove us there as much as anything for the sheer fun of seeing if she could do it.

I recalled the seventy-foot Colorado spruce, all the red, green, and blue twinkles, the white flakes in Wendy's long blond hair, her little shivers in a thin azure coat, the Handel music on the car radio, her well-controlled soprano, and the eagerness of a surly cop not to give her a parking ticket—after he belatedly recognized her from the photograph that ran with her columns. I'm not one for festivities, and if nothing else, my very presence was proof of her sway over men.

And yet, no matter how powerful an admirer might be protecting Wendy, I worried about her. Most journalists in Washington had rubber skins capable of springing back after the most vicious abuses from lovers, spouses, or editors. But Wendy's skin seemed made of a magic glass—elegant, tough, unyielding, except when given the hardest blows, any one of which might shatter it into shards that could never be glued together.

Chapter 8

Not quite certain whether I was seeing a friend or a news source, I took the Metro to Margo's. I was headed toward a nineteenth-century row house in a section of Washington several miles northeast of the Capitol. The neighborhood was too seedy to be coveted by the greedier real estate people. Margo and some Oberlin chums, it turned out, rented from a senile alumna who had fled to one of the Golden Age ghettos along Wisconsin Avenue.

"May I be scurrilous?" she asked, as we clopped down some rotting stairs into the basement. Her jeans were real, not just the quasi jeans she wore to placate the likes of Elsie Fogart.

"You'll never really be successful at it if you have to ask permission," I said.

"My friend upstairs heard it when he was researching his Ph.D. About the landlady. That she caught syphilis from a senator during the New Deal."

"I hope it was some Kluxer from down South."

"While she was an assistant to a lobbyist. Maybe she retired on disability."

We reached Margo's place downstairs, a dim, musty warren with one wall of stone—I felt as if I were in the dungeon of a medieval castle. She owned a scarred dresser and a bookshelf, of cinder blocks and wood, in which I saw mostly books by European writers. The room contained no chairs, just a mattress and pillows—Margo struck me as austere enough to be very rich or poor.

Playfully, I frowned at a poster of a frowning, wide-eyed face that looked as if its owner were trying to stare away a firing squad.

"Don't you like Franz?" Margo asked. "I've been rereading him ever since I started at GSA. Just call me Ms. K."

"I like 'Guinevere' better," I said.

"You're sweet, but I'm only a GS-7." Margo smiled. "Now Queen—that's too high even for an eighteen. If I'm medieval, I'm probably somewhere between a serf and one of your lower-ranking nuns."

I was warming up more and more toward Margo, jeans and all. She seemed to dress, think, and live for herself, the antithesis of Donna, who forever worried about her standing with abbots and mothers superior—such comparisons, of course, being hierarchical rather than moral.

"You won't break your vows, will you, if we talk about leasing now?"

"Only the ones to the public information office," Margo said. Whereupon she delved into GSA esoterica.

"So remember," she finally said, "Standard Form 2-A says leases must list all partners in partnerships. GSA's very sloppy about it. And right now I'm very bored with it. Hey, Lancelot, I've got some great Acapulco Gold."

"I'm allergic to it," I said.

"Look, there's a man in our office who just might talk. Would you trust a dirty old man? He's always reaching for my tits, which annoys the hell out of me since I like dirty *young* men."

"What's his name?"

"Lucky O'Brien." She looked him up in the Virginia phone book, and I jotted his number down.

"But why do you think he'll talk?"

"Because he's been around GSA forever, and he's only a GS-11."

"And he thinks he ought to be administrator?"

"That's the idea," Margo said. "The resentful sort."

"May I use your name with him?"

"If he ever found out we were talking, he'd traduce me unless I let him seduce me," Ms. K. said.

☙◅

At 9:05 on the Zumweltnar's designated day, I reported to Room 6038. Inside was a long mahogany table and a carpet that seemed almost thick enough to be grass. The ceiling was of spongy material, and I wondered what secrets had disappeared into the pores above me.

"You're five minutes late," Zumweltnar said.

"Big deal."

"When I said nine, I meant nine."

"I was up late last night."

"Just don't let it happen again, okay?" Zumweltnar said, and took another stab at asking why I was interested in Solomon.

He looked well ensconced as a bureaucrat; a large lapel button indicated he was one of GSA's chief bullies for the Amalgamated Givers Fund. All over Washington, bosses squeezed workers in the name of charity. Sy Solomon headed Amalgamated's Construction Division, and I recalled a file photo that showed him eating filet mignon at a "War Against Want" dinner. To his right had been the former chairwoman of the Communications Division, Mrs. Victoria Simpson, publisher of the *Telegram*.

Zumweltnar reached for a briefcase, from which he produced a manila folder with the first of the leases, then silently left the room.

On the Xeroxes, GSA had whited out "proprietary information" not included under the Freedom of Information Act. I wondered if the hidden facts were proprietary in the normal commercial way. Maybe they were proprietary instead in the sense that Solomon and the other landlords owned GSA.

Later, when I wandered into the hall for a snack from a sandwich machine, it gypped me out of seventy-five cents. A label told me where my money would go—to a businessman I recognized as a White House guest and friend of Sy Solomon.

I'd just settled down again in Room 6038 when a female visitor arrived, wearing heavy makeup and a uniform like an airline stewardess's.

"Excuse me, sir," she said in a throaty voice. "We're taking a survey." An eyelash fluttered. "Are you satisfied with the maintenance services in this building?"

I gave her my opinion of that crooked sandwich machine.

"Very good, sir," the woman said, like a butler in a Wodehouse novel, and strolled from the room.

I suspected something foul. It didn't seem right—making such a ceremony out of keeping a building in shape. Maybe the woman had come to entrap or spy on me. Then my fear vanished, and I laughed. The stewardess must simply be GSA's way of glamorizing its role as the government's main janitor.

Wearily and warily, I kept picking away at the leases, some Solomon-related, some not. I felt less like a reporter than a misfit of a file clerk—banished to a back room and his agency's most boring job—and I almost dozed off. Suddenly a thought roused me. The leases listed just the names of partnerships, not the actual partners.

Elated, I marched into Zumweltnar's office. He was in the middle of a news release, a paean to a new federal building in Skokie, Illinois.

"Wouldn't you be interested in knowing all the people you're doing business with?" I asked. "Jesus, what if the Mafia's investing?"

"Screw you, Stone. We don't care who we're doing business with as long as they're not in jail or under indictment."

"Yet," I said.

ಬಂಛ

A few hours later, my eyes more blurry than the ink on the most smudgy lease, I left GSA and returned to the *Telegram* to interrogate Garst about the Solomon story. Rexwood was reading a book with Oriental and English characters. "What's that?" I asked.

"I want to thank you," he said. "Foreign Desk says they might open a bureau in Seoul."

I laughed.

"What's so funny?"

"I was just joking—about Korean and the future."

"You were?"

"Yes."

"Well, I'm still keeping up with my Serbo-Croatian."

"Serbo-Croatian," I said, "that's the key."

Garst nodded.

"Listen, no offense, but are you *sure* you're not talking about the Solomon story? Everyone in town seems to know I'm on it."

"What the hell?" he said. "Of course not."

I might as well have accused him of deserving twenty years on the Prince George's County beat.

Chapter 9

When I called Margo's dirty old man that evening, a gruff and goofy voice came on the line.

"Yeah, I know," said Lucky O'Brien. "You're the one who's been fucking up Space Management. I didn't like it one bit, the way you just marched in and thought everyone should stop work immediately to answer all of your questions."

"Did I bother you—you yourself?"

O'Brien meditated. "Well, not directly. But this broad I work with—she's complained about you."

"It wasn't that college snot, was it? You know—the hippie."

"Yeah, that's the one," said O'Brien, sounding like a slightly drunk cartoon character.

"These college broads, they think they have it made," I said.

"You ain't kidding."

"Nice stuff," I said, "but I bet she's a bitch to work with. And a pig, too—I saw that desk."

"Isn't it something? But—hey, why are you calling me?"

"Because I've heard some good things about you."

"Is that so?" The tone was between sarcasm and hope.

"No two ways about it," I said. "They say you're the most conscientious guy in the place. Just the man to set me straight on what's happening at GSA."

"So who do I send the flowers to?" O'Brien asked skeptically.

"What the hell?" I said, trying to put him on the defensive. "Here I approach you in confidence, and you want me to give away someone else."

"Well, tell me this. Is it male or female?"

"Who cares?"

"I'm no queer, you know. I mean, the place is full of them. Fags."

"Who?"

"Let's just say I have my contacts, Stone. You don't think you can hang around this place for fifteen years without meeting people, do you?"

"Yeah," I said, "but who are they?"

I was less interested in GSA's sexual practices than leasing ones. About people's private lives I had always been of the "just don't frighten the horses" school. But maybe the flow of semen would in some way correlate with the flow of money.

"Why don't we talk this out face-to-face?"

"Maybe," I said, suppressing my eagerness.

"Hey, I'm not sure I should waste this story on you. I mean, I was saving it for retirement. Why, *The National Enquirer* would pay me a mint."

I interrupted for directions to his home, and a time, and he gave them. "You're an insurance salesman. I don't want the wife to know. Now—about this matter of money."

"Ugh, which left did you say it was after Route 95?"

"The third—Hill View Road. Now—about the money."

"We'll kick it around after I get there," I said to keep his hopes up.

"It could be bigger than Watergate," O'Brien said.

I tried to see if I could somehow manage an audible yawn over the phone. "I've heard that line before."

"I'm not screwing around, Stone. This is worth a good hundred grand."

ℬ℃ℬ

Lucky O'Brien's neighborhood teemed with boxy Colonials priced in the seventy-thousand-dollar range, and outside every third one I could see a car with a full-sized citizens band whip. I was in GS-11 territory for sure.

O'Brien lived in a purple-shuttered house with a camper in the driveway. I wondered if he was the man wearing white bucks whom I'd seen in Room 4022.

A short, obese woman came to the door, which bore Boy Scout and American flag decals. "Are you the salesman Lucky was telling me about?"

"Salesman? No, ma'am. I don't sell anyone. I just give folks the facts."

"You salesmen." Mrs. O'Brien laughed. "Always coming up with a new pitch."

She looked through the window at the Winnebago in the drive-way. "I don't know how much insurance we can afford. We're still paying for the camper."

I heard a baby squall. "Upstairs in the den to your right," Mrs. O'Brien said, and waddled out of sight. I glanced around. The living room was classic Sears & Roebuck. A twenty-one-inch color TV crowded one corner of the room near a fatly cushioned chair, a recliner. Right next to the chair was a little refrigerator on top of which lay beer cans and the sports section of the *Telegram.* An electronic football game occupied most of the coffee table beside the refrigerator. No doubt who bossed that household.

O'Brien reeked of beer when he greeted me upstairs, and a gigantic paunch pressed against a Redskins T-shirt. Sure enough, he was wearing white bucks. O'Brien shut the door, and we sat down on a large couch upholstered with imitation leather. He hardly impressed me. Any moment, I expected him to say he'd personally skinned a pseudocow for the couch.

"I want a certified check," he said.

"*If* there's a check."

"I'm watching myself, Stone. You reporters, you lie worse than the politicians."

"Shall we talk about insurance now?" I asked.

O'Brien struggled for the right comeback.

"Look," I said, "before you 'win' your hundred grand, maybe—can you tell me a few things about Sy Solo—"

"Sy? Sure. Me and the boys, we've had some pretty good lunches off him. Sy, he's not stuck-up like them other big shots. You gonna expose Sy Solomon for taking us out to lunch?"

"Anything you can eat in one sitting is legitimate graft," I said. "I mean, it wasn't a hundred-dollar deal, was it?"

"A hundred and ten once." O'Brien said it proudly, as if happy someone thought him worth a one-hundred-and-ten-dollar lunch. He seemed too drunk to be discreet.

"You mean each guy's?" I double-checked.

"Hey, he flew us in his jet to this fancy-pants seafood joint in New York."

"When?"

O'Brien fumbled for the date. It was around the time the real estate page had said that the GSA leased Vulture's Point.

"You think Sy gives good deals?" I asked.

"Would you bitch about a hundred-and-ten-dollar lunch? Oh, Sy, he's a good one. Just one hell of a great guy. You know he started out as a bricklayer?"

I knew that—from the puffery on the Real Estate page. But O'Brien wouldn't stop: "A bricklayer, I said! And he built a house. And rented it. And another house. And apartments. Can you imagine—right during the Depression? And—Get it? That Sy, he's just an ordinary fellow made good. Hey, he even got my oldest a ticket to the Redskins when they were all sold out. Not bad for a Jew."

"I'm Jewish," I said. "And you know, O'Brien, you're not bad for a bigot."

"Jews! Always covering up for each other. You got a scandal, cherchez le Jew." The last syllable of "cherchez" came out like the ending of "Perez." O'Brien burped, and slurred on. "Hey, you know about Sy's son, don't you?"

"Just that he has one," I said, the articles fuzzy in my mind.

"The poor kid, he's been mixed up for years. He just went crazy when he was seventeen. He stole a car and drove it into a hospital. The poor kid, he must have been stoned."

"Oh, I'm sorry," I said, as if O'Brien were the boy's father.

"They didn't lock him up, of course. Old Sy knows enough judges to take care of that. But the kid, he's at a crazy farm in Maine. And a damned expensive one, too. Three thou a month."

Solomon has enough money to send us all there, I thought.

"Hey, Sy's a pretty good poker player, too," O'Brien said. "But a good loser. A friend and me, we won a hundred and fifty dollars from him. Hey, can you beat that—me beating a millionaire?"

"You play often?" I casually asked.

"Oh, no, just that one time, but Sy, he visited my pal's house. Why, he even brought some Milk Bone along, 'cause my buddy had been talking about his German shepherd at lunch. Sy, he's just one of the boys. Hey, he drives a—"

"A Maverick?"

I waited for O'Brien to ask me how I knew the make of the car, or to react in some other meaningful way. Here was a Talker, not a Thinker interested in sorting out facts—bad for his credibility, great in terms of my eliciting noises from him in the first place.

"Down-to-earth, wouldn't you say?" O'Brien piped up again. "And conscientious as all get-out. Why, Sy, he'll call you at home to make sure his papers are in order. Now, about the hundred thou."

"But how can we pay when we don't even know what's for sale?"

"The goods on Mr. Big."

"Who's Mr. Big." I joked. "Bullard?"

"God," O'Brien said. "I got the goods on God." He leaned back on the couch and chuckled crazily.

"All right," I said. "I'll pass it on to the Religion editor." I decided I was enjoying myself and hadn't a thing to lose.

"Well, it ain't God but it's someone's guardian angel."

"Who?" I asked.

"I'm not saying," O'Brien replied between guzzles.

Of course not, I thought. All the angels flew out of Washington a long time ago.

For a moment there was silence between us; and then in his beery voice, O'Brien said: "All right, I'll tell you one name. Harold Jones." GSA's administrator.

Again O'Brien laughed like a drunk. "I was just thinking—an angel watching over a fairy. Hey, that's pretty good." O'Brien grinned idiotically. "Hey, you know what they say at GSA? 'When we "blow" a deal, we make it.' So you'll pay?"

"Call me in a day or so," I said to put him off.

"Hey," he asked, "you won't squeal on me, will you?"

"I'll keep it all to myself." Drunk or not, eager for a deal or not, O'Brien had exposed much more of himself than I'd counted on; it was as if he expected his confessions to exonerate him.

Then again, he might be conscienceless to the point where he didn't even grasp the full importance of what he'd spilled about the hundred-and-ten-dollar lunches.

Of course there were minor difficulties, such as whether most of what he'd said was true.

"You won't think I'm one of these hippie protesters," O'Brien asked, "will you? I'm doing this because I'm a red-blooded American.

It's simple. I hate queers, and I want a hundred thousand dollars."

ଡ଼ଔଔ

The phone jangled through my door the next day when I was returning from a lease-gawking session, and I nearly bent the key out of shape.

More than I'd suspected, I worried I would miss Margo's call—we'd made iffy plans to take in one of the sillier Woody Allen films. I broke into my apartment and grabbed the receiver as if I were Solomon reaching for another lease.

"Pretty good, tracking you down like this, huh?" said Lucky O'Brien in his beer slur.

"I'm in the book, O'Brien. You got any bombs, you just send them my way."

"Hey, it's Golden Lease now. A code name, you gotta have a name in this business, right?"

"We'll call you Money Bags," I responded.

"Hey, I'm being reasonable about this," O'Brien said. "I'll let you have the story for forty thousand dollars."

O'Brien had finally worn me out. "Look," I said with all the indignation I could scrounge from journalism seminars, "I'm not buying any news. That's called checkbook journalism."

"No, it ain't," O'Brien said. "It's called supporting my family. My wife ... my kids ... my bucktoothed son and his dentist ... my daughter and her allergy shots ... the little baby. It's all for my family, see?"

I wanted to say, "Of course. Most everything's 'for my family'—most of the corruption, most of the shadiness around this town. If more people lived in sin, there'd be less of it."

I actually said, "I'm awfully sorry, Golden Lease, but it's just not going to work out."

"But what if I lowered the price?" O'Brien asked.

"Still no deal," I said.

"Even if it's only five grand?"

"Why five?" I inquired.

"Because," O'Brien said, "that's how much the wife and me have to go on our camper."

Chapter 10

"Oh no," Margo said, as we left the theater. In front of us on the sidewalk lay a wizened old man with his head bashed in. Two policemen were processing the body—muttering obscenities about having to work the night shift.

"Must have been a mugging," I said.

"Those cops," Margo said, "you'd think they'd—"

"We'll take a cab to your place," I said, holding her hand. The fingers were long and thin, and I wondered if she had tried any piano courses at Oberlin Conservatory. On the other hand she was tanned and walked with an outdoorswoman's strides, as if to suggest another side of her.

"I'd rather get mugged on the subway. Those arches in the stations, they're just like a cathedral I studied." Margo looked down at a bloody ticket stub near the corpse. "Has anyone ever threatened your life?"

"Not that I know of," I said, "unless you include Mac when he's in a foul mood."

"I thought you were an investigative reporter," Margo said.

"I'm a housing reporter more or less. The villains I write about—they'd pull a real estate ad before they pulled a gun."

In her room Margo lit some long candles atop her bookshelf and tuned an old radio to a classical station. The flames flickered alongside the stone wall.

"I feel terribly Arthurian tonight," Margo said. "You don't mind the radio, do you?"

"I like some canticles," I said.

Margo peered up at me. "How tall are you, anyway?"

"Six-foot-three."

"You never played basketball, did you?"

"No," I said, as we sat down on the mattress.

"Well, you look like a pole, a walking pole." She lit up a marijuana cigarette, and I started coughing.

"Please—my allergy. Oh for the days when that stuff didn't get to me. I even got busted."

"Where?"

"In Charlottesville," I said. "They couldn't find room for me in the regular jail, so they put me in the Juvenile Detention Room."

"You went to UVA?"

I nodded.

"I dated someone from there once. My roomie's brother."

My arm was around Margo, and her flesh felt firm through the faded shirt she was wearing.

"Always went around in ties," she said. "A real ass."

"Am I?"

"You're not wearing a tie, but as for being an ass…"

"That's why I became a reporter," I said, "so I wouldn't have to strangle in a tie."

"You work on the paper, there?"

"I wrote the most obnoxious columns in favor of the Vietnam War."

"In favor?"

"Yes, I toed the *Telegram* line."

"*They* were for the war?"

"When I was reading them in college. It was the sixties, remember, but I learned my lesson."

"That's good," Margo said.

"After Johnson conferred an ambassadorship on the chief of the editorial page."

"Then why'd you go to work for them?"

"Because I'm from here, and it was supposed to be among the least corrupt of the big-city papers," I said. "Why'd you go to work for GSA?"

"Because I need the money for grad school. I'm actually threatening to write a master's thesis on Kafka." She broke loose and kissed me on the lips. "Listen, Lancelot, if I let you seduce me, you won't traduce me, will you?"

"Not at all," I said. "I'll even give you a good reference."

Margo unbuttoned her shirt, and I felt her breasts, which were not large, but firm, and as nice as the telephone voice had somehow suggested.

"Jonathan?" It was the first time she'd addressed me by that non-Arthurian name. "I *might* be falling in love with you."

"That's against the rules," I said.

"You mean, the *Telegram's*?" she asked.

"You're not allowed to be prematurely sentimental if you went to Oberlin."

"Relax, Jonathan," Margo said. "I'm applying for a dispensation."

Chapter 11

I grew up near the Huntsley Cutoff. That's what McLean people called the road that the State Highway Department hacked out when a county supervisor by that name objected to the street's being widened in front of his mansion.

My family lived in a glassy wooden house designed by an oddball architect. We had a good view of the Potomac, plenty of woods in front, and a winding driveway along which my father had staked CHILDREN PLAYING signs.

If we'd been run over, chances are it would have been by family friends. He'd also thrown up a NO TRESPASSING sign for good measure.

We had moved into McLean back in the fifties, when you could buy a river overlook without being an heir or a war profiteer—we sneered at the pseudo–Mount Vernons built for rich, dull people.

My favorite house, though, was a Marine general's fortress, several miles to our south. It was a gigantic brick Colonial with a circular driveway and a masonry wall topped by a series of blue lanterns. An American eagle perched on each. Fiercely, the birds stared down at intruders. They seemed enough to frighten and peck to death the most communistic burglar.

When I went to my parents' home for dinner one evening during the Solomon investigation, I felt as if my own family were pecking me. I was just glad that Catherine, my college-age sister, couldn't make it that evening. She was visiting a friend, Debby Brown, the daughter of an unrepentant Watergater. My sister couldn't fathom Woodstein and the like; at the depth of the scandal, she'd asked, "Why are they always picking on Debby's father?"

My father and I went into the dining room, and he loosened his tie.

"You know," he said, "how hard I've been bucking for that raise. Well, the boys at the office are talking about you."

"What's that got to do with the raise?"

"They say you're going after Sy Solomon," he said, as if kinship with me could ruin his career. "I don't know him myself, but I understand he's done a lot of good for the community. Elton's known him fifteen years."

Elton was my father's boss, the man to whom he dutifully lost on the tennis court. My father was over six feet tall, long-armed, and muscular. Coronary problems notwithstanding, he could still whack a tennis ball at 85 mph against nonbosses and nonclients.

I remembered The P Word, as we called it in our family—a euphemistic adjective for the snakes my father counseled.

"Well, what else do you expect?" he would say after a client dissimulated and lied his way to safety at a congressional hearing. "He's *political*." It was how my father lived with himself and avoided cirrhosis of the liver.

Few clients prevaricated in my father's world; they were just "political."

The word could have simply meant, "Attuned to the nuances of the kowtow." But my father had expanded the definition to cover essential sleaze, the unspoken part of job descriptions on K Street and the Hill.

"Elton tells me Solomon's the best guy the Amalgamated Fund ever had," my father said. "They're on the board together."

"So," I asked, "what are you trying to say?"

"Well, put it this way. Solomon gave them six hundred thousand dollars last year."

I charitably avoided guessing what percentage that was of Solomon's income.

"See what I mean?" my father said. "He's a community man."

"Maybe. But he could be ripping off the taxpayers big-time."

"Not if he's dealing with your father," said my mother, just a few inches shorter than Dad and herself no slouch on the tennis court.

Tennis, in fact, was how they had first met, and they still could not agree on the winner of the first match.

I recalled a snapshot of them honeymooning in California in the 1940s. My square-jawed father sat at the wheel of their portholed Buick, and my blue-eyed mother was smiling next to him. She wore a Katharine-Hepburn-style hairdo of *Philadelphia Story* length even if she lacked the accompanying eccentricity.

Both had light, almost blondish hair, while mine was pitch-black and my eyes dark brown like my maternal grandfather's, as if I'd reverted in those respects to the ancestral Semitic looks.

I was not square-jawed, either, just average in the chin department and the same way at tennis.

৩০০৪

"Oh," I said, picking up on my mother's statement, as my father loosened his collar, "so you *do* know him?"

"Just the firm," he said. "Now we don't deal with him ourselves, but some of our clients do. Like Lincoln National Bank."

"And?"

"They and a bunch of other banks around town have made loans for some of his government projects."

"But that's their problem, not ours," I said.

"Mine, though. I work for their PR firm, and they've loaned twenty-five million dollars to Solomon."

"So?"

"You're my son."

"Makes no difference," I said. "I'm over twenty-one."

My father gulped down a martini. "Look, I didn't mean to tell you this until I knew for sure, but there's going to be a new opening in our firm. And you've got a great background in housing now. And you know a few things about banking, too. Why, you'd be a natural to handle accounts like Lincoln."

"Question. Who the hell told your outfit I was on this story?"

"Oh come on," he said. "I wouldn't ask you to reveal your sources, would I?"

৩০০৪

"Jesus, you're grim," I said, entering Margo's dungeon of a room the next day. "Sex is still 'in,' isn't it?"

"I thought you'd be interested in something else," she said.

"Of course I love your personality, too."

"I'm talking about GSA."

"I thought you wanted to mess around tonight," I said.

"Even if a building's going to fall down? Maybe." Hmm. The building or the sex?

We sat on her mattress. Right next to the picture of Franz I'd seen a dartboard—with the secretary of state's visage in the bull's-eye area. Margo must be somewhat passionate on the Papudoian question.

For the first time I noticed *The Danialson Dynasty* on a lower shelf, half-hidden amid some cookbooks. So Margo belonged to the cereal family? A cornflake-fed heiress? The reason for her spare surroundings? A woman strict enough with herself enough to be old-money-rich?

Then I remembered the facts. I'd actually read the book, in college, and the story was not so happy, with the whole family going broke during the Depression, the Kelloggs having almost literally eaten the Danialsons' breakfast.

"So what's the lowdown?" I asked.

"That's the word, all right," Margo said. "The northeastern corner of the building is lower than the others. It's sinking and tilting, nice and slow."

"Along with your respect for building inspectors?"

"Sy built into a hill. Scraped off part of it and used the fill dirt on the rest."

I recalled Vulture's riverside location near muddy marshes. Suppose the whole schmear, all fourteen floors, got sucked down into the ooze. A perfect Washington metaphor.

"And then," Margo said, confidently enough to suggest she understood the trade journals on her desk at GSA, "he actually had the nerve to use spread footing to support the columns."

"Spread" seemed appropriate enough, given Solomon's fondness for empire building.

"Big squares of concrete, maybe twenty feet per side and four feet thick," she said. "Nice, but what if the fill on the northeast end has organic matter still in it? Not the most stable deal here."

"Kinda like the interest rates," I couldn't resist.

"He'd have been better off with a raft," Margo said.

A raft? I could just envision Solomon's creation floating down the Potomac into the Chesapeake Bay. What next? The Atlantic, then a global voyage? Less colorfully, I recalled construction jargon from my public housing beat. Margo probably meant a large stretch of concrete on which all the columns of the building could have sat.

"But if Solomon had done it *really* right, he'd have driven pilings down to the rock," Margo said. "And then the columns could have rested on them, no sweat. But he used the spread footing instead. Must have saved him a pile of money."

So the missing rebars and the rest, the delights Fenton had mentioned, were just the start.

"Any cracks visible?" I asked.

"Just the storage area, that's all," Margo said. "It's going to be an office soon. With dandy carpeting wall to wall."

"Sounds like Solomon's given you a special briefing," I said

"Only accidentally. I was in the room when they talked it over with Elsie."

"The gods are on our side."

"It wasn't just 'they,'" Margo said. "Solomon himself came. And guess who's moving into the storage area?"

"The Northern Virginia leasing operation?"

Margo nodded.

I remembered what happened years ago in Marseilles when skeptics said Lake Erie was never safe for swimming. The mayor dived in during one of the "clean" periods and caught typhoid.

"I'm just glad you're not in that building. I wouldn't go there without an ejection seat and a special shield with steel girders."

"I should have told you. They're reorganizing the leasing operation, and I asked for a transfer there." The way Margo spoke, she might as well have been announcing a trip to the drugstore.

"But why would you want to be a Kamikaze pilot for GSA?"

"You."

"Me?"

"Well, *partly*. So I can find out what's going on."

"And get yourself killed?"

"Don't be so egotistical," Margo said, toying with one of her darts, "I'm also getting a promotion."

"What the hell," I said. "All that means is a more expensive funeral."

"I've calculated it to the day," she said. "How much time I need to work here before I can do grad school. The more money I get, the faster the escape."

"I feel duly humble."

"Maybe I'll like you enough in time for you to be the main reason.

"But the building," I protested.

"It's gradual," Margo said. "They're pretty sure they'll be able to predict when it's about to come down. If it does."

"The way Solomon predicted interest rates?" I asked. "How much time do they give it?"

"Oh, maybe a decade or so, with tip-offs. Like if the elevators stop working, or the windows won't open. It's like heart problems, normally. You get sick before you kick the bucket. I mean, the cracks still aren't *that* large."

I told Margo of my friend the marathon runner with the perfect cholesterol count and blood pressure who'd dropped dead at twenty-five of a massive coronary. Just what was "normally"?

My mind raced ahead a decade. Jones, the GSA administrator, would long since have retired, and Solomon would have died or sold the building. At least I assumed that Solomon would have flipped Vulture's and profited if still alive. Which counted more for the man—prudence or sheer vanity?

"Does the IRS know exactly what's happening?"

"Well, they're sort of in denial. Like they keep thinking that GSA just wants to use that storage space for offices. A little easier than wondering when the building will crumble. Just how would you feel if you worked for IRS and signed off on the deal?"

"So what's prompted all this—the cover-up operation right now? They've known about that building a long time."

"Isn't that obvious?" she asked. "Solomon's heard about you."

"But I haven't been on the story that long."

"They'd have had to do something sooner or later," Margo said. "You just speeded things up a little. Okay, wanna play darts?"

Chapter 12

I'd tired of gawking at Solomon's leases, so the following morning, on a whim, I phoned in absent at GSA and descended on a nearby courthouse to puzzle out some records.

Vulture's Point was my obsession of the day. Maybe Solomon's crowd had distrusted each other enough to leave me with some useful hints on real estate papers.

The Roxland County Courthouse was a redbrick building with a big white cupola, a Mount Vernon for bureaucrats. Metro Desk had assigned me the territory just after I began at the *Telegram*, and I recalled the talent of the courthouse regulars for gossiping and crafting baroquely crooked land deals.

Roxland County was where Southern wiliness mixed with Northern greed.

Once a zoning lawyer had jabbered about his work to an impractical prosecutor, who hadn't been bribed well enough to keep up with inflation. The result was that a quorum of the county board served time rather than serving the taxpayers.

Until the last appeal, the *Telegram's* real estate editor wrote columns bemoaning "harassment of future-minded officials." Finally, the furor faded, and Roxland County elected a new board and settled down to unheralded scandals.

Roxland was still pastoral in many places, but in the size of the bribes, it might as well have been New York City—well, at least the suburbs.

In the courthouse basement near the land records, I ran into a jovial lawyer named Stonewall Lee, perhaps the most accomplished fixer on the northern Virginia zoning scene. He was a chain smoker with yellowed fingers and teeth and incipient emphysema, but memories of his better days sustained him.

Back when I was raking Roxland's muck, he'd invite friends to lunch and—supplying ingenious rationales along the way—brag about payoffs made past the statute of limitations.

I suppose he hoped they'd gossip and drum up more business for him.

Stonewall reminisced nostalgically about the days when a county supervisor could become his forever for the price of a Jersey and half a year's worth of fertilizer.

ഇൻ⊗ങ

"How ya doing, you ole smear artist you?" Stonewall slapped me on the back and grinned as if he'd just consummated a twenty-five-thousand-dollar payoff.

"Fine, you ole bagman."

"You aren't bothering one of my clients, are you?" Whenever he saw me near the records, he rightly suspected the worst.

"Not this time, Stonewall," I said. "At least I don't think, 'cause this man's too crooked for you."

"Hey, you're hurting my feelings," Stonewall said, and shuffled on—perhaps headed toward another fix.

Over the years we'd been at odds in the best good-ole-boy way. I wished Stonewall would drop by GSA to teach Zumweltnar how to be agreeably crooked.

I dillydallied long enough to flirt with a title searcher. Then I ventured into the county records. Through this bureaucratic mish-mash, Stonewall and friends weaved like alligators slithering around a familiar swamp.

At length I found the right documents for Vulture's Point Limited Partnership. Scanning down the papers, I felt as if I'd crashed one of Solomon's party-parties.

Enough Solomons showed up to make the partnership records look somewhat like a family reunion in legalese.

Judge Philips contributed $67,000 and perhaps the goodwill of his robed friends if Solomon ever rankled an intractable prosecutor. I saw the names of Philipses from as far away as Honolulu.

The legislative branch had a fitting representative in Congressman John Boynton through his real estate firm. On the Ways and Means Committee, Boynton wheedled like a lobbyist for the National Association of Realtors. He poked loopholes in tax laws as if he were Jack the Ripper turned loose with an ice pick.

Medicine was represented by $127,000 from Dr. Fishwell Burnes,
a pillar of the AMA. Wendy Blevin later told me Dr. Burnes had
treated the wife of the chairman of the House Public Works Committee for palpitations in the ass.

None other than Harry Lyonsdale pitched in for labor. He was
president of a truck drivers' union from whose pension fund he'd invested $250,000. I assumed that Solomon's building supplies always
arrived on time.

Hilton Kahn, Esq., the eager young predator who'd drawn up
the partnership documents, plunked down thirty grand. One of my
friends at a leftish think tank suspected Kahn of working for the
CIA—I suspected him of nothing more menacing than lobbying for
the Continental Cigarette Company. Kahn seemed too greedy to be
a good spook. I'd met him several years earlier when he was one of
the phonies at Citizens Voice—prepping for a sellout to the other
side.

Kahn knew he was liberal because he wore a beard and occasionally appeared before federal judges without wearing a tie. Nowadays
he worked for Apple and Foster, the most worthless of the good-
willy law firms. Well into the 1960s, its only black was a doorman
who dressed like a jockey statue on a redneck's lawn.

Luci Elkins, Mac's spectacularly mismatched girlfriend, better
known as the First Hairdresser to Mrs. Bullard, had styled enough
heads to pay for a twenty-five-thousand-dollar investment in Vulture's Point. And I even saw a journalist's name—that of Roswell
Albertson, the perpetrator of one of the duller columns on our
competitor's Op Ed page. He occasionally played second base in
White House softball games.

Duke Odysseus put in $87,500. He was the parking and vending
mogul whose machine had rooked me out of seventy-five cents at
GSA.

Christopher Marns, chairman of Lincoln National Bank, entered
the partnership through its Seventh Amendment. Presumably Solomon no longer fretted quite so much about interest rates. Marns was
a robber baron's great-grandson, and back in '72 he'd bought one of
the more expensive ambassadorships from the Committee to Re-
elect the President. He was a scowling, hawk-nosed man with that

blend of viciousness and dignity peculiar to bankers.

In one way or another nearly every investor could give "Sy" his money's worth.

A few names mystified me, though, including an original partner's. Just who the hell had invested $90,000 through "Marvin Forester, Trustee," but tip-toed out of the partnership in the Ninth Amendment? Then I noticed the Chicago address and grew a trifle more suspicious of Eddy Bullard.

ಬಂಗ

Roxland County charged a dollar a page for Xeroxes, and that day I gave the thieves there enough business to build a new courthouse wing. Or so it seemed to me. In the name of accuracy, I went on a hundred-and-fifteen-dollar spending spree; I'd rather look foolish to the *Telegram's* auditors than its readers.

Deadline time loomed when I returned to the paper, yet E.J. seemed oblivious to it all—a cipher in pinstripes. He was mechanically doodling little A-frames shaped like the retirement home he was building; I hesitated to end his reverie. If he'd been a criminal defendant, the *Telegram's* court reporter would have pronounced him Pale and Gaunt.

Before I could finish my meditation, however, E.J. looked up, alert and back in the world of Creative Tension.

"I've just bled one hundred and fifteen dollars of Vicky's money," I said. "For a very good cause. Look—the partnership papers for Vulture's Point." I shuffled the pages. "Here's the Ninth Amendment."

With a finger I stabbed at "Marvin Forester, Trustee."

"What about it?"

"A trustee? With a Chicago address? Now, excuse the cynicism, but you don't suppose that Bullard—"

"A few people have been known to live in Chicago besides Eddy Bullard."

"But you know what Bullard was at the time, don't you? Chairman of the Governmental Affairs Committee."

E.J. cracked a slight smile, but I also saw enough of a frown to suggest he still needed more convincing.

"That's only a committee overseeing GSA, that's all."

"But Jon, that's not even Bullard's address. Nor his law firm's."

"You don't think he'd make things that easy for us, do you?"

"But don't you remember what you wrote in your own memo?" E.J. asked. "About congressmen and senators in partnerships with federal leases? How it would be too risky. Flatly illegal. Why should they screw around with a federal lease when Solomon has other investments?"

"I've changed my mind since that memo."

"I think you were right the first time."

"Sometimes politicians are dumber than we give them credit for," I said.

"Ditto for reporters."

E.J. kept gazing at the documents.

"For crying out loud," he said, "it's not even within the statute of limitations anymore. Assuming it's Bullard."

"There's more." Triumphantly I flipped the pages to one with the name of Congressman Boynton's real estate firm.

"Is he on a committee overseeing GSA?" E.J. asked.

"No."

"And he's not a personal investor in the partnership?"

"Just through the firm," I said.

"Your memo mentioned just partnerships and individuals. The law doesn't include congressmen in corporations, does it?"

"No," I said, "but it's an odd couple. Here's Solomon, the supposedly liberal Democrat, in cahoots with a conservative Republican."

"What the hell do you mean by 'cahoots'? So far all you have are some names together."

E.J. handed me a telephone directory. "Here—try this conspiracy on for size."

Chapter 13

"Hello," said O'Brien on the phone. "Golden Lease reporting!" He sounded as if he'd guzzled a six-pack from the refrigerator by his recliner.

"I'm sorry, Goldy, I'm just not buying any news."

"Maybe you don't have to," he said.

"Then what the hell have you been holding out?"

"Of course I ain't doing something for nothing," O'Brien said. "You know any good broads at the *Telegram?*"

"Look, O'Brien, I'm a reporter, not a pimp." At least so far I'd never written for the PR-like Real Estate section.

"What about Hollywood? The movie rights."

"So you can work for GSA and get money for exposing it in a movie?"

"Hey," O'Brien said, "it's more than my pension."

"The movie rights, they're all yours."

"Whoopee!"

I might as well have passed on the name of a busty nymphomaniac.

"You'll still let me have the byline on the story, won't you?" I asked.

"Yeah, I suppose."

"I guess you're greedy, and I'm vain," I said. "Now what the hell's the story?"

"It's about Eddy Bullard."

"But you said it wasn't."

"I just said it was someone's guardian angel."

"And," I asked, "you have proof he's not an angel of any kind?"

"Hell yeah!" said O'Brien. "Hey, Bullard got Jones his job."

"So?"

"And Jones, he's a fag."

"And," I asked, "that's how Bullard controls him? Bullard's not one, is he?"

"But he knows Jones is," O'Brien said. "Blackmail."

"But why?"

"Don't know, Stone. But this broad said—" Not another word came, and I suspected he'd drunkenly dropped the phone.

"So what's the rest of it, O'Brien?"

"Hey, you got your story now, right?" I supposed he would next ask me to recommend a good movie agent.

"Jesus, O'Brien, you haven't even told me her name."

"There's a hitch," he said between burps.

"What?"

"She's married, and I was screwin' her."

I recalled the paunch and the beer smell. Sex with O'Brien didn't sound like the most plausible of events with anyone short of his wife. But Washington was, is, and will be full of women and men with oddities.

"I'll sell insurance again," I said.

"Huh?"

"I'll keep it from her husband."

"It's Carol Collingwood," O'Brien said.

I checked the spelling and asked if I could invoke O'Brien's name with her.

"If you help me write the book—"

"And she works for GSA?"

"Used to. For Ed Gurnsley." The deputy administrator. "Hey, that Gurnsley, he's one, too. A fag. If it wasn't for those two queers, I'd be a GS-16 for sure. They both started in leasing, see."

"What's her phone number?"

"I don't know, except she's living someplace in New York with a Greek name."

"Does she drive?"

"Like the Indy 500," O'Brien said. "Fast on the road, fast in bed. Hey, why you wanna know?"

"Her license," I said. "It'll tell me her address."

"Hey, that's pretty good. I'll use it in the movie."

"Who's starring?"

"Paul Newman and Robert Redford," he said. "Dustin Hoffman, we'll fit him in somehow."

"And Paul Newman's you?"

"That's right," O'Brien said. "You're Hoffman, of course."

"But he's too short, and besides, that was about another newspaper."

"It doesn't matter, just so I'm Newman."

∞∞

Carol Collingwood's was a brisk, husky voice that hinted of too much snobbery and cigarette smoking, and I envisioned a tall woman addicted to the phoniest of boutiques. If she'd screwed O'Brien, it must have been because she enjoyed occasional flings with inferiors.

"You're calling from a newspaper?" she asked. Her tone implied that I might as well have been with a supermarket tabloid.

"The *Washington Telegram*. When you were at GSA, you knew a man named Lucky O'Brien who—"

"Who?"

"Lucky O'Brien in Space Management."

"Who?"

"Don't kid around with me, Mrs. Collingwood. He says you drive like—"

"Are you a reporter or a traffic cop?"

"Just a reporter who knows you knew O'Brien."

After a minute or so of silence: "So what if I did?"

"Mrs. Collingwood, there's nothing to worry about," I said. "I just want to ask you a few questions."

"Are you trying to blackmail me?"

"You have something you could be blackmailed for?"

"Why, of course not."

"Mrs. Collingwood, I couldn't care less about your sex life," I said. "I just want to ask you a few questions."

After another long silence: "Mr. Stone, this is Troy, New York, not Washington, D.C., and my husband is—Are you going to print my name?"

"Relax, Mrs. Collingwood."

"I have your word?"

"Just tell me about Jones and Bullard and Vulture's Point." The last two words were my bluff of the day—big enough, in fact, to be a Dover-sized cliff.

"What can I say? I was Mr. Gurnsley's special assistant, and they were both nice enough men. But GSA ... such a tacky place, if you know what I mean. Why, someone even scratched a swastika in the elevator."

"Why'd you work there, then?" Mrs. Collingwood hardly struck me as just another workingwoman who had grappled her way up the GS scale. "Politics?"

"My husband was with Interior."

"And he just happened to hear that GSA had an opening?"

"He raised money for Eddy Bullard," she said matter-of-factly.

"Oh my goodness, are you going to write about him?"

"Not your husband, just the president. Now, about that special arrangement that Eddy Bullard had with Harold Jones—"

A phone call later: "It was just a few snatches over the intercom. Harold, he had so many things on his mind, and he just happened to leave the set on at the wrong time."

"While he was talking to Bullard," I prodded.

"And don't ask me exactly what they were saying, because I've forgotten," Mrs. Collingwood said. "All I remember is that the president was in there reminding Harold that he and Mr. Gurnsley were homo..." She left the word primly unfinished.

"The president came to GSA?"

"It must have been terribly sensitive."

"And yet you don't remember their exact words?"

"Believe me, please, I don't!" She sounded panicky enough to be convincing.

"Mrs. Collingwood," I said in a voice suggesting I was loosening the screws slightly, "could you please tell me when it happened? The conversation between Harold Jones and the president?"

She gave me a pre–Vulture's Point date, timed just right to reinforce my cynicism.

"You're going to be fair to Harold and Mr. Gurnsley, aren't you? You're going to destroy that man—both, I mean. They're family men, you know. Harold, he has three children, and Mr. Gurnsley and his wife have a new grandson."

"You know Harold well?" I couldn't help noticing that, rank aside, it was "Harold" Jones and "Mr." Gurnsley.

"My husband and I had them over for dinner."

"The Joneses?"

"Such a nice couple," she said. "And he deserved all the breaks. Harold *worked* his way up to the top of the pyramid."

"And Eddy Bullard noticed what a fine job he was doing by way of the Governmental Affairs Committee?"

"Now Eddy, he's cut from the same cloth." Mrs. Collingwood cleared her throat. "President Bullard respects hard work, and Harold's so eager to please. You know, I don't think blackmail's the word, Mr. Stone. Harold and the president must have been having a heart-to-heart talk and ... Well, what I mean to say is that President Bullard wants top talent in his government, and he'll do anything to make his people feel comfortable in their jobs."

考考

I glanced at E.J.'s VDT. He was substituting for another editor and reviewing some copy for the People Page, Wendy Blevin's interview with the author of a dress-for-success book. E.J. himself might as well have written it. He polished his shoes well enough to be a banking magnate, and he'd always believed in Hart, Schaffner & Marx and the ability of pinstripes to impart authority.

"What would you say if I told you I'd caught the president of the United States blackmailing the administrator of GSA? Would you believe, a source says Bullard put the screws on Jones for being gay?"

"A Republican source, I take it."

"Someone from Bullard's own administration," I said.

"Who, Huey Pratt?"

"I'm not saying at the moment." Nor would I ever, at least in O'Brien's case, not until E.J. drew his last paycheck from the *Telegram*.

"What's Solomon's role in all this?"

"So far none, but—"

"So far Sy Solomon looks as clean as a hound's tooth."

"Just sit back and let the dentist finish the X-rays."

"Well, my butt's getting damned sore in the waiting room," E.J. said.

Chapter 14

"Hey, Lancelot," Margo had asked, "how'd you like to play tourist?"

"Jesus, that doesn't sound very Arthurian to me," I'd said. "Can you imagine Guinevere paying a dollar twenty-five for a hot dog?"

"I'm infatuated with the idea of pedal-boating ... past the cherry trees ... the Jefferson Memorial."

"But I thought we could meet my friends at—"

"Sh! I'm your Secret Source."

"Okay, but knowing my luck, Zumweltnar will be trailing in the next boat."

"I'll pass myself off as the little old lady from Dubuque."

So we found ourselves aboard what looked like lawn furniture mounted atop two torpedoes. To our left we saw a fellow pedalist moving briskly backward. "We'll try it," I said.

We found we could go faster backward than forward, and I wondered if somebody had installed a speed control that worked only when we moved ahead.

"Jesus," I said, "this boat reminds me of Bullard's Papudoian policy."

"Oh, there's got to be a meaning in that somewhere," Margo allowed.

From the PA system on the dock a stern warning boomed: "Most people think a pedal boat cannot tip over, but that is not true. Last year alone there were seven pedal boat accidents here at the Tidal Basin."

Gravely the lecture went on; it was a bit like listening to emergency lunar-landing instructions. The pomposity of it all amused me, and I knew that the lecturer would have done well in public relations at GSA.

I wondered if Zumweltnar's lying was contagious. Recently, Margo had given me some less-than-convincing stories as to her whereabouts on certain nights.

But for the time being I took it in stride. Washington was The City of the Great Dump, a town of Dumpers and Dumpees, an eternal junkyard for politicians, friends, and lovers.

It was the place where the Constitution allowed a Dump every two years and a greater one every four.

Margo smiled at me, credibly, I thought, and I felt content to risk being a Dumpee.

Everyone has a flaw, and that was mine—too much trust to cast a problematic friend onto the garbage heap.

Perhaps it was one reason, beyond chemistry and common memories, that I had kept the flame burning so long with Donna Stackelbaum.

All too often I was a pushover for friends and family when it wouldn't interfere with my job, no small condition. Margo in too short a time had moved from source to friend, but there was nothing I could do about it.

I wanted to believe in her—I could summon up only so much skepticism, lest it divert me from more deserving and essential targets.

Such was my nature, as much a part of me as my height or aversion to liver, pork, sauerkraut, or Eddy Bullard.

However frequently I argued with my family, it was intimate, intramural, the antithesis of genuine alienation. I rejoiced that my father wasn't partnered up with Solomon and that my job and values prevented the slightest connection with Sy.

Otherwise, I could well have poured my entire life savings into Vulture's Point. But I had my work, my firewall, my built-in skepticism—I was safe.

"How's your building?" I asked.

"Still up there, I guess." Margo shrugged. "We're moving in next month."

"And the cracks? Growing?"

"Who's to say? But I'll tell you this. Some of the windows are cracked, and one of the lower-level freight elevators is kaput. And a few doors won't open. *Not* good news."

"So the marathon runner might yet have his heart attack?

Margo nodded.

"Just don't take any family heirlooms to the office," I said.

"Nothing other than Franz." Margo laughed. "I got a little photograph of him in a desk frame. Elsie thought he was my grandfather." Margo smiled weakly. "But what's this problem you said you were having? On the way over here—"

"Zumweltnar's going to grab me by the throat," I said, "while Solomon thrusts a knife deep into my heart."

"I'll cheer them on."

"Ever have one of these periods when you feel paranoid about everybody?"

"Every day."

"Would you believe, my editor's girlfriend is one of the investors in Vulture's Point?"

"Maybe you're more perceptive than paranoid," Margo said.

"More paranoid, for the moment. But guess who keeps advertising his condominiums every week on the back page of the real estate section?"

"You mean they're afraid Solomon would cancel an ad?"

"If Solomon wanted, he and his friends could cancel half the section."

"And your job, too?"

"It's Jon Stone versus several million a year in advertising."

"But they can't just fire you," Margo protested with a fierce push on a pedal. "Doesn't the *Telegram* have a union?"

"And also a labor-relations department," I said. "They've done their job so well, there's hardly any union left to relate to. The circulation people, they're the only ones with a real union. Those drivers act as if they own the—Jesus! If you see my boss, please be nice enough not to remind him that the Drivers' Union owns part of Vulture's Point."

Chapter 15

Vulture's Point juts into the Potomac near one of the smellier sewage-treatment plants in Roxland County. George Washington himself named the land—normally he was more sensitive to property values. I remembered Vulture's Point from my days on the Roxland County beat. Some real estate speculators had bribed the county board into rezoning the Point for pseudo–Mount Vernons. But builders held not only their noses but also their money, and they did so even after an imaginative crook tried to peddle the land as "Potomac Gardens." Solomon swooped in at a foreclosure sale. I don't know whether the additional zoning changes had come as cheap as the land.

Without the largesse of GSA, I could never have envisioned an office building amid the marshes. Stores and restaurants were miles away, and the homes in the area were outrageously priced—a clerk could afford one about as easily as I could afford Solomon's mansion. Other than a solitary bus line and the offerings of a bike rental shop up the river toward Alexandria, no public transportation existed.

In the shadow of Vulture's Point, I felt like an insect under a steamroller—the building hulked fourteen stories above me. Solomon's architects had inflicted on it a face of plate glass and cheap metal panels, and already some panels were buckling. Vulture's Point looked less like an office building than a huge pile of oversized gas stations.

For a second I imagined the building as a human; I saw a pimply high-school dropout in a tight motorcycle jacket. He weighed three hundred pounds, a misfit whose ugly bulk seemed to destine him to pump gas by day and burgle Colonials by night.

I suspected he'd be the meanest brawler in the seediest bars, and he wouldn't slurp soup at a French restaurant—he'd mug its customers outside. Vulture's Point was Solomon's blue-collar crime against white-collar suburbia.

The lobby of Vulture's was an institutional yellow that clashed with the cheap red carpeting. Just looking at the combination, I could have upchucked.

My fist lightly hit the wall, and the resulting thud hinted of the thinnest plasterboard. Solomon might as well have built a Quonset hut. Almost half the fluorescents in the corridors were off; apparently someone esteemed energy over eyesight.

Even more, however, the halls' narrowness affected me. They were just wide enough for four or five of Fenton's fat-assed bureaucrats—I felt like a claustrophobic ant inside its hill's narrowest tunnel.

I lingered at a bulletin board. It bore the normal federal hodge-podge of carpool notices and Equal Employment Opportunity promises, except I also saw an antibribery warning. One of the items in an ethics code posting, it gave the building some character. Presumably Internal Revenue looked askance at hundred-and-ten-dollar lunches with the wrong people.

As I turned from the board I saw a bearded man wearing wire-rims and dressed in cords—he resembled a fortyish graduate student.

I walked up to Wire Rims and flashed my press card. In a neutral way, I asked what he thought of the ant-narrow halls and cramped stairwells—the despair of the county fire marshals, he said. A few tax people on the fourth floor had even bought rope ladders.

Oh, the joys of working at Vulture's. It often took ten minutes to catch an elevator at quitting time unless you were on the top floor, the lair of the most senior 'crats, who enjoyed priority over the peons below.

"And then there's this Research Assistance Section up there," Wire Rims said. "Which is fine, except no one's ever said what they're researching."

"Ways to make income-tax forms more complicated?"

"The rumor is, it's CIA," he said. "Those guards, that's the weird thing—the submachine guns. Someone saw them hiding 'em inside the guard booth."

"Do you know anything about cracks in the floor here?"

"Oh, that." Wire Rims laughed. "We used to joke about the building falling down."

"Is it?"

"Don't you think if it was going to fall down, it would have done so already? Why, this building's a good five or six years old."

I wished his building a happy seventh birthday, then headed toward the enigma on the top floor.

Up there someone had kicked in the wallboard next to the elevator. I could just see some white-haired taxman seething because his express elevator service had failed him.

Wandering through the upper tunnel, I finally came across glass doors emblazoned with gold letters: RESEARCH ASSISTANCE SECTION.

Outside the doors stood a booth, inside which guards gazed from left to right, up and down like motorized TV cameras. The men were huge, crew-cut, and sullen; they seemed handsomer, neater, slightly tamer versions of the imaginary gas jockey.

As dogs they would have been crosses between Great Danes and Doberman pinschers, and I'd have named them all "Fang."

How to approach this human K-9 corps? I couldn't sneak into Research Assistance as a bureaucrat—even with a borrowed ID—since the *Telegram* forbade reporters from masquerading as civilians. If I ever wanted to expose an insane asylum from the inside, I'd have to go crazy first.

I retreated to a men's room to comb my hair, unpatriotically long. Then, wondering if the K-9 corps would gun me down, I strolled toward the glass doors.

A guard instantly descended on me from the booth, as if a spring had propelled him. "Sir! Your identification!"

"You mean I can't come in?" I asked with competent surprise.

"What is the stated nature of your presence at this location?" the guard gobbledygooked.

He had a pointy Russian-looking nose, and I wondered, unfairly, if his ancestors and the Eastern European side of my mother's family had met at pogrom time. Did some of his relatives *still* live over there? Might he have not just a security clearance to preserve, but also faded old photos of a great-grandfather wearing a saber and cavalry boots?

I showed my *Telegram* card. "Maybe you can help. I'm studying working conditions inside certain buildings—how are yours?"

"I'm ordering you to move on!" The guard stepped inside the booth and picked up a phone. How to respond? Take a Civil Service examination so I could honestly say I worked at Vulture's?

Half-expecting a spook in a trench coat to be trailing me, I went down to the seventh floor and hunted up the storage area Margo had mentioned.

Inside the area, workmen were furiously hammering up panels and installing partitions and fluorescents. Some other men were laying a blue carpet. Already it covered most of the floor, and it looked intimidatingly expensive.

A grizzled, elderly man, perhaps a supervisor, gazed up from the carpetwork he'd been inspecting.

"You from GSA?"

"GSA's been my life these days," I said, and inquired about the cracks.

"Well, someone around here, they thought they saw another one opening up. Funny, they just tell us to keep on filling and carpeting. But you know these government types."

I frowned convincingly, asked a few more questions, then wandered off to see if GSA had done anything about the stuck doors, the broken windows, and the defective freight elevator.

All were fine again for the moment, at least the doors and windows I checked.

Then I visited a building manager, a gap-toothed man wearing a polka-dot bow tie, askew. I asked about the little trifles and the chances of the building seeing its seventh birthday.

"You expect *everything* to work, *all* the time?" Bow Tie protested. "Hundreds of doors and windows? We're not talking about a cozy little bungalow."

"No early warnings? No symptoms here?"

"It's safe, I tell you," he said. "Why, the Drivers' Union even owns part of it. Their pension fund."

"Which also invests in gambling casinos."

"They even represent some of the clerical help here," Bow Tie scolded me. "Do you think they'd invest in a building that was going to fall down on their own people?"

ഇൗ

Bow Tie's line echoed in my head as I drove back to the *Telegram* in the moist swelter of the Washington summer. The heat made me wonder about the air-conditioning system at Vulture's Point. If it failed, might that be another harbinger of worse troubles to come? Maybe bad enough to rile even the tolerant rank and file of the Drivers' Union?

At the *Telegram*, I resumed work on a rogues' row of bad buildings, a jumble of notes I'd jotted, based on old clips and a trip to the Library of Congress.

The lore among engineers was that the Tower of Babel was history's first and worst failure, except that its demise had happened with help from Jehovah, who inflicted a multiplicity of tongues on the builders. A little like the division between engineers and English majors? Or, worse, between them and architects?

Mankind's record was hardly spotless over the millennia. Of the Seven Wonders of the World, only Khufu's Pyramid had survived. Pyramids. I remembered GSA's symbol, the pyramid on Zumweltnar's door. Some hope?

Then again, GSA had at least overseen the creation of Vulture's Point, and if it couldn't even fill out all the names on the leases, as plainly required by law, could we really trust it to oversee Solomon?

I remembered where his building permits had come from—the Roxland County Courthouse, a thriving marketplace for corrupt bureaucrats and their valued customers. The Roxland Fire Marshal's office, mentioned by Wire Rims as objecting to the narrow halls, was freakish in its honesty. Looking over the papers for Vulture's Point, I had been struck by the *lack* of stop orders and other pesky little blemishes in the records for Vulture's Point.

Maybe Roxland and the feds should resurrect the Code of Hammurabi, among the better cuneiform inscriptions from the First Dynasty of Babylon.

"If a builder builds a house for a man and does not make its construction firm and the house collapses and causes the death of the owner of the house," it read in part, "that builder shall be put to death.

"If it causes the death of a son of the owner, a son of that builder shall be put to death.

"If it causes the death of a slave of the owner, the builder shall give the owner a slave of equal value."

So did IRS and CIA minions qualify under the slave clause? Oh, the subtleties of Life and Property and the conflicts between the two. Not to mention the possibility of the death of a *daughter*. Or *wife*? Property, all of them?

Then I resumed my tour of the more modern sections of my rogues' row. Over in England, the Ronan Point housing project had fallen in 1968 after Ivy Hodge, a cake decorator, had lit a match to get her stove going. She was looking forward to her morning tea. Instead, an explosion in her corner flat, on the eighteenth floor of the twenty-two-story complex, had blown out her walls.

Miraculously, just four people had died after Ronan collapsed, floor by floor, amid a fog of gray dust. Rescuers had found Ivy gazing up at the sky that had replaced her ceiling. How about the cooks in the Vulture's Point cafeteria? Sufficiently respectful and watchful around gas stoves? Might Vulture's Point be Ronan redux?

In Boston in the early seventies, two-thirds of an apartment building had tumbled down, starting with the roof, where the concrete hadn't been up to the cold weather. Regardless of the summer heat of the moment, could the Washington winter have softened up Vulture's for the same fate?

And then, of course, in Fairfax County, Virginia, on March 2, 1973, part of Skyline Plaza had fallen, with a rumble heard for miles. I remembered writing of Doug Wilkins, a mechanic's helper trapped in a pile of lumber and concrete, a fragment from which stayed in his lung for nine months. For nine days he had lingered in a coma before waking up to the agony from the chip and a battered skull.

Luke Sellers, working for the concrete subcontractor, had died the day before he was to be married.

Then there was young Phil Riccardi, just twenty-one, who could not hear even frantic shouts over the noise of his grinding machine. Warned futilely, he had just waved and smiled and ground away. His family had collected less than $4,000, total, as workers' compensation.

So just how would Phil have fit in under the Code of Hammurabi? As a son or slave?

Chapter 16

Margo and I splashed in my tub.

The hot water came and went in great bursts, the bathroom was windowless, and we almost suffocated from the steam mixed with the smell of marijuana. It was like boiling ourselves to death inside a pothead's sauna parlor. My eyes were red from the pot. But Margo was having too much fun for me to ask her to stop.

Somehow the ring of my phone penetrated her fumes and mind. "Oh, I'll get it." She laughed. "I'm clearest. Tadpole committee says so."

Margo stumbled her way out of the bathroom, and seconds later I heard the phone crashing on the floor, then: "Parsonage ... No, ma'am ... the Reverend Stone, he's invisible indisposed ... Affirmative, ma'am. The Reverend Stone's in the bath."

Belatedly I left the tub to wrestle the phone away.

"Ma'am." Margo giggled. "Of course he's there. The water ... it's very wet ... Yes, ma'am. Full of tadpoles."

I was in the bedroom by then, and about to grab the receiver, when Margo carefully dropped it on the cradle.

"Old bitch, Southern accent," she told me. "Says she's your mother."

ജിയ

"Jonathan," came the inevitable grilling over the phone the next day, "just *who* was that drunk?"

"Huh?"

"In your apartment," my mother said.

"She wasn't drunk," I said honestly.

"Lord help her if she was sober. I just hope you're not running around with some trampish secretary."

"She's not a secretary," I said of Margo. "She's a professional."

"That's good."

"On Fourteenth Street."

"What?"

"A hooker."

"Jonathan."

"She's a bureaucrat, actually."

"She keeps the whorehouse records?"

"Definitely. Works at GSA."

"Is she from a good family?"

"I don't know if she's eligible for the DAR."

"What does her father do?"

"He's a priest. Episcopalian."

"I don't care if her father's the Pope," my mother said, "the way she was carrying on. Incidentally, Donna Stackelbaum's mother asked about you the other day. You know about Donna, don't you? She just made GS-17."

Over the years, I'd memorized the entire pro-Donna spiel: vale-dictorian at Langley High School, bachelor's in business administration from the University of Virginia, JD and MBA from Duke—our friendship aside, an entirely insufferable set of credentials.

"Why," demanded my mother, exasperated, "wasn't *Donna* the one who answered?"

Donna and I had hidden our love buddydom from our parents as well as she'd concealed her breast size from any pervs and Puritans lurking within the Nuclear Regulatory Commission.

"That woman is going places," my mother marveled.

"Jeeze, I'm a reporter, not a recruiter." What was I going to do—hire Donna for kitchen duty at the nearest federal correctional institution?

My father came on the line just then. "Who was that drunken woman?" I loved my parents, but sometimes wondered if our family didn't argue for sport the way the Kennedys played touch football.

"Your father had some chest pains last night," my mother said as if Margo had precipitated them.

"I'm sorry," I told him. "How are you feeling—"

"At least we don't go picking on another Jew," he said. "Now that drunken woman business I can stomach alone," he said, "and your antibusiness attitudes, too. But together—"

"Let's talk about those pains," I tried.

"Better to talk about the cause of them," my father said. "Elton King and I had a good talk, and he makes a lot of sense. About

Solomon. You're not going after some pawnshop operator. You're taking on a pillar of the Jewish community."

"Isn't it better to replace the pillar before the whole building falls down?" I asked. "Besides, who says this is the 1940s? Are we really answerable for each other's sins? Look, it isn't as if I'm a raving Nazi."

I had to grant my father a few points, however—I recalled the O'Brien, as well as the bristle-haired bigots at an automobile-supply store near the Appalachian Trail.

Al Bergmann, my old hiking partner, whose face looked far more Jewish than mine, had been bargaining over a new tire to replace a blowout. We'd left the store to grab some lunch. Returned early, we could hear a few snatches of laughter through the closed door of the salesmen's lounge, then Anglo-Saxonisms, along with talk of "Jewing us down."

The crew cuts were in their thirties, no older, and most likely a long way from either tolerance or the grave.

None other than Elton King, in fact, my father's well of wisdom on ethnic relations, had belonged for years to a restricted golf club.

The truth is that I'd fallen in love with Margo in spite of her being gentile, not because of it—a natural enough feeling from someone whose German relatives on his father's side had most likely died in a concentration camp. Propagating well was the best revenge.

I recalled the original family name, "Faberstein." Given the prejudices against Jews in the upper reaches of the public-relations industry in the early fifties, the change to "Stone" was hardly happenstance.

Decades earlier "Faberstein" had actually been one of the stellar names of Bowlington, Alabama, where my parents had grown up. Jacob Faberstein had even served in the Civil War, killing eighteen Yankees at Fort Blakeley and narrowly missing death from an unexploded cannonball that fell just short of his butt.

"Faberstein," in big, balloon-style lettering, had gone on to adorn a hardware store in the town square. Jews back then had been enough of a novelty for most of the local bigots to overlook them.

That was before my parents, fresh from coed softball games and ZBT fraternity mixers at the University of Alabama, went up North to the land of hiring quotas and "gentleman's agreements" in real estate title offices. I could all too easily understand why my father felt the way he did.

Still, I was not about to live down to bigots' expectations and cover up the Solomon story. Let "Zionist conspiracies" begin elsewhere.

I remembered my readings about the World War II era, when Jews were trying in vain to persuade major newspapers to promote the Holocaust to regular front-page status. That was a time to think protectively Jewish, as opposed to covering up the crimes of a goniff, if Solomon indeed were a thief.

What Judaism I had was of the Spinozan variety, a faith of facts and syllogisms. I'd pledged a far more demanding fraternity than ZBT, the brotherhood of Aristotelians and Spinozans. I was no philosopher, but *The Ethics* fit, and not just the logic of it all. "Good and evil fortunes," I remembered from my college days, "fall to the lot of pious and impious alike."

Just what syllogisms applied here? Major premise: Reporters like me report on significant misdoings. Minor premise: If Solomon has cheated to win millions in government leasing businesses, "significant misdoings" applies. Conclusion: Assuming he's a crook, put the bastard on page A-1 as part of the natural order of things.

No man was pure devil; Solomon might well be stealing to give more to charity, but multimillion thefts defied relativism. So did illogical cover-ups, whether of the Holocaust, corruption, or cracks under the carpet.

"Anyway," I told my father, "who the hell is Elton King to speak for the Jews? He's not even Jewish."

"Which means he can be more objective," my father said. "As an expert."

"As an expert lobbyist for Lincoln Bank?"

Some old memories stirred in my brain later, after I hung up and started reflecting on Seymour Solomon and the Jewish community and how Sy was so piously philanthropic.

In the late sixties, returned from Charlottesville and some putdowns by WASPy bigots there, I'd shaken my pelvis at a few dances given by the Washington Jewish Association. WJA occupied a sprawling, modernistic structure, a loose adaptation, I suspected, of a museum designed by Frank Lloyd Wright.

But it was not the architecture that I remembered. Nor the Simon and Garfunkel music, nor the women wearing clinky jewelry, nor the young female bureaucrats and GS-9s who courted them in sports cars with quadraphonic tape players.

I was thinking instead of a large panel of polished mahogany on the wall just outside the art gallery, across the hall from the gym and sauna.

It was an honor roll of sorts, a place for neat rows of metal strips with the names of the Association's largest contributors, and I'd scanned down the rows to see if any friends or clients of my father were among them.

Particularly I remembered the way the Association had laid out the strips.

You began at the bottom with the copper-surfaced ones. There I had dimly recognized a few names—those of the smaller merchants, maybe a lobbyist or two whom I'd read about in the society pages, or a best-selling novelist ridiculed by the critics for making too much money and vacationing in the Borsch Belt.

Then you moved up to the silver people, for instance the larger used-car dealers, the vice president of a small bank, the assistant publisher of the evening newspaper, the people who, in the hierarchy of the charitable, would have been bucking hard for their GS-16s.

In the very top row, finally, you saw the golden people, the Association's big angels, but even they weren't secure in the hearts of the fund-raisers; for each June, after pledge time, the strips of those who couldn't keep up were unscrewed. You'd lose your golden reputation if you didn't give $20,000 once more.

Other, older Associations—say, those in Philadelphia or Boston—perhaps affixed their name strips permanently or glorified the generous with plaques that stayed hung. But Washington was different, a place of mobility, geographical and financial.

Throughout the years, however, I knew of a strip whose screws nobody disturbed. It was the long one that gleamed above all the others, the one honoring the biggest giver. An irony came to mind—trivial, perfectly irrelevant, but unavoidable to me even a month after Passover. No one resented Seymour Solomon for having enriched himself through an agency whose official symbol included an Egyptian pyramid.

Chapter 17

In his best Mafia-enforcer tone, Zumweltnar snarled, "Nothing for you today. Legal's too busy."

"At what?" I demanded. "Censoring the agency phone book?"

"That wouldn't be such a bad idea," Zumweltnar said. "Not if it stopped you from bothering people."

Feeling a tad violent toward bureaucrats and lawyers alike, I left for the GSA library. A legal directory there might list the enigmatic Marvin Forester—the trustee for Vulture's invisible investor. I chided myself for not acting earlier on the premise that a lawyer is the best accomplice in a white-collar crime.

On the way downstairs I gambled with another of Duke Odysseus's vending machines. This one looked extralarcenous; all around the bottom I saw dents—presumably from kicks of cheated customers.

But I plunked in three quarters anyway, closed my eyes for luck as if playing the slots in Vegas, and jabbed at the button for baloney sandwiches. To my astonishment, the machine spilled out not only a sandwich but also my money, and I pondered whether my cynicism had gone too far.

In the legal directory, however, I turned unhesitatingly to the listings for the president's old law firm. Everyone knew that Pensler and Magnusson was one of the larger and more redoubtable of the legal mills in the Midwest. And P & M was profitably bipartisan, too. It was said that the firm recruited Republicans and Democrats, conservatives and liberals, like an investor diversifying his portfolio.

The directory included Marvin Forester right after a Johnsonian secretary of agriculture and a Nixonian commissioner of the Federal Communications Commission. I read on. Forester held his B.A. and J.D. from the University of Chicago, Bullard's school, and, by way of a Rhodes scholarship, had been at Oxford when the president and Mac were.

He'd worked for Justice, and I supposed he got along just swim-
mingly with the present attorney general—himself an alumnus of
U.C., Oxford, and the law firm.

ଚ୦ଓଷ

Over the phone, Marvin Forester, a native son of Baxter, Montana, came across as a parody of a BBC announcer.

"Anyway," I was telling Forester, "we're doing this story on real
estate trends and—"

"But I'm not even a real estate lawyer," Forester protested in a
rumbling voice.

"Of course," I said, my skepticism rising. "I'm just trying to find out
how you heard of a certain investment opportunity in our area."

"I don't follow you at all, sir. I don't own any real estate outside
Illinois."

"Not even as a trustee?"

"You must have the wrong gentleman, sir. I'm not real estate—I'm
corporate."

"Except in Roxland County, Virginia," I said.

"Mr. Stone, do you know the fee here is two hundred fifty dollars
an hour? What I'm saying, sir, is that you're wasting my time."

I remembered the photos in the newsroom library—the beret
covering the bald spot, the stone house on Lake Michigan, the English sports car. The voice matched up well.

"Just tell me about the potential you saw in Vulture's Point Limited Partnership," I said.

"Vulture's what? Never heard of it."

"The documents, they're right in front of me," I said. "All the details." I inflicted on Forester the dates of the supposedly nonexistent
investment. "I'm just thinking our readers might be pleased to know
that Eddy Bullard believed in the future of Washington real estate."

Over the line came a loud sigh.

"Nice to know our president's been a good businessman," I said. "I
just don't understand why he'd hide it."

"What are you talking about, sir?"

"The trust arrangement," I kept bluffing. "It's all in the documents."

"You're not writing one of those muckraking articles, are you?"

"Never for the Real Estate section," I said truthfully. "The readers there like the positive approach."

"I'm glad to hear you say that."

"On the other hand," I said, "if you're ashamed of free enter-prise—"

"See here! I'm not hiding a thing!"

"Then why the trustee arrangement?"

"To protect his privacy," Forester snapped. "How'd you like it if you were a United States senator and someone called you up to complain of a leaky toilet? Really, Mr. Stone! I think I've given you enough time."

"Too busy fixing the toilet, eh?"

"You've already taken up a good twenty dollars' worth." Forester was lapsing into a plebeian growl.

"Hold on," I said. "What about this being a government lease?"

"Mr. Stone, aren't you stretching it? It was six years ago. The stat-ute of limitations has... What you should know is that the whole bloody thing was an accident."

"An accident?"

"Why, certainly," he said. "This man Solomon has a number of partnerships, and he simply forgot that Eddy Bullard was an investor in the building."

"I see."

"Mr. Bullard, of course, left the partnership just as soon as he found out who the tenant was."

Of course. It was one of the biggest Washingtonisms of them all—among the better dullers of journalistic curiosity among the lemmings. I put up my best fight against the Novocain. "You mean to say he invested ninety thousand dollars in a building without knowing who'd rent it?" I asked.

"Eddy Bullard trusts Mr. Solomon's judgment completely—much more than I trust yours. Which is why, Mr. Stone, I'm terminating this conversation."

"I'll get my facts elsewhere."

"I'm sure John Quinton would be delighted to help you," Forester paltered.

Johnny Quinton drew $71,000 a year lying as Bullard's press sec-
retary. He was a dangerously lovable old fart—famous for his cigars and his talent for smoking up the clearest issues. Quinton had
worked at the *New York Daily News* with McWilliams, and Wendy
said he and Mac occasionally exchanged rumors as well as Coronas.

"Good-bye, Mr. Stone," Forester said, and hung up.

So Bullard had dabbled in white-collar crime! I strutted over to
E.J.'s desk—feeling as smug as Garst after a fitting at Brooks Broth-
ers.

In front of E.J. a video display terminal glowed with a summary of
a poll. Only 30 percent of the American people could stomach the
way Bullard ran the country, and I wondered how the administration would react. Either the United States would invade Papudo, or
Johnny Quinton would pass out cigars to more editors.

E.J. fidgeted as I crowed over my triumph.

"I thought I told you the trustee angle was a waste of time," he
said finally. "You keep forgetting about politicians in partnerships.
Don't you think Solomon would have been damned foolish to include Bullard in one leasing to the government? Wouldn't it be more
logical for Solomon to have Bullard in a private building?"

"Screw logic," I said. "I'm just telling you what happened."

"An accident, apparently," E.J. said. "Solomon's too smart for that
kind of crap."

"Even if the lease expressly banned congressmen? Jesus Christ,
wouldn't Solomon pick that up? What the fuck? You think he
moves his lips when he reads?"

Suddenly we heard McWilliams yelling across newsroom. "Stone!
Rawson! Into my office!"

The mitt was lying in the usual place on the shelf there, and I
suspected that the Shark's Cage would soon resound with smacks.

"Sit down!" McWilliams commanded us. "I'm not sure whether
you can stand and think at the same time." McWilliams's voice
crackled and rasped, and I decided that if a shark could speak, it
would sound like Mac.

He glared at E.J.: "What sort of shit are you two trying to pile on
Forester?"

"I didn't authorize that call," E.J. said, shaking.

"I'm happy to say it was my own idea," I spoke up.

"Not after I'm done with you!" McWilliams roared. "Now according to Forester, you called up saying you were from our Real Estate section."

"Bullshit!" I said. "He asked me whether I was doing an exposé and I just said we'd never do one in the Real Estate section. He wouldn't have talked if—"

"That was fucking stupid of you—we'd do anything in the Real Estate section," McWilliams lied. "We might even publish your stories there. All of them. You'd better shape up fast, pal." I sneaked a glance at the mitt on the shelf. "Stone! When I talk to you, pal, you look me in the eye!" I had been, just about the entire time. But McWilliams delighted in making his adversaries of the moment feel as if they were wimping out.

I tried to outstare him; his eyes were small and shone threateningly, like a shark's. But it was the teeth, crowded and jagged, that most reminded me of a picture of Little Mac.

"You're blinking, pal. Is that why you harass people over the phone?"

"You authorize it, I'll fly to Chicago."

"You've done enough damage here." McWilliams glowered. "I think Forester made it clear to you the whole thing's an accident. Use what brains you have—would a man of Forester's caliber jeopardize his career over some fly-shit lease?"

"Fly-shit? It must be a good four million a year. Anyway, why's Forester so virtuous?"

"What kind of dolt are you, pal? He's just on the board of Citizens Voice, the Ford Foundation, the—"

"He could be on Mount Sinai, for all I care. I'm just trying to find out why—"

"I don't like the way you're speaking to me, pal. You apologize fast!"

"All right, I'm sorry."

"I'll say you are! Because, pal, I'm giving you only one more week on this story."

"Sorry," I repeated. "I just thought you admired reporters with balls."

"But not if they screw my friends."

"You know Forester, you say?"

"Well enough to murder you when I heard how you treated him."

"Then why didn't he tell me he knew you?"

"Because, pal, he knows better than to let himself be accused of bullying a fly-shit reporter."

Someone else from the P & M crowd came to mind just then—the attorney general, who'd once represented Tele-Circuits, Inc. He believed so strongly in wiretapping and hidden microphones that I suspected that the electronics outfit was still among his legal clients.

"I suppose you know Simon Ellsman, too."

"From Oxford," McWilliams said. "What difference does it make?"

"I'm just curious," I said. "It's one of the qualifications of the job."

"Along with discretion, pal." McWilliams shifted his frown to E.J. and started gazing at the famous MacRolex, our exit signal.

"How you ever recommended this clown as your successor is beyond me," Mac said. "Don't forget: a story one week from now, or he's out on his ass."

Chapter 18

I felt a flash of pain in my chest that night, my back ached, and I wondered how fit I was to breathe, much less ski.

Wrinkles thickening, hair thinning, I was far from prime heart attack age but ever closer. I had canceled the evening with Margo and resolved to finish up my brooding and moping as soon as I could.

I remembered a January day in 1955—replete with howling, frigid winds, blown in from the northern hinterlands, a rude trespass on the Washington elite.

My father had shuffled through the door and said he had just lost his major public-relations account and probably his job.

Then my mother hugged and kissed him, poured our best Scotch, and drove to Safeway for several pounds of steak, as if to remind us we still lived in a neighborhood of Mercurys and Cadillacs.

After dinner, we asked my father to show movies of our vacation in the tropics of Mexico. He was threading the film through the projector on the oak table in our living room when I heard the Kodak smash into the floor.

I turned around from a newscast reviling a former client, the very account that not so coincidentally had just drifted away. My father was slumped against the table, his face as white as the movie screen. The rescue squad came and—

⋙⋘

The phone was ringing, but I almost didn't pick it up, I was so afraid my voice would crack.

"Finally!" my father exulted. "Old Elton's coming through!"

Subject to anointment by the executive committee, he was about to become a vice president of his public-affairs company, at $97,000 a year, having been sufficiently "political" in his dealings with his bosses and lost enough tennis games to Elton King.

"But," my father said on my congratulations, "you can never tell about something coming up at the last minute. Not that Elton's pressuring me or anything. But he was hoping you'd change your mind about Solomon."

"So Elton's my new editor now? The guy who'll tell me whom and what to investigate?"

"Why, Jon, just why are you doing it?"

"You mean why *not*? Just tell me. Why are all those leases going to Eddy's friend?"

"Can't you be more constructive?"

"In other words, I should rhapsodize about high-rises. Especially, of course, those financed by Lincoln Bank."

"I think you're being quite selfish. You're assassinating that man for the sake of your career."

"You want me to succeed in my job, don't you?"

"Would I want you to succeed if you were working as a burglar?"

"What's the parallel?"

"Antisocial behavior."

"Jesus Christ," I said, "I'm exposing it, not committing it."

One of us would prevail over the other; either the *Telegram* somehow would publish my exposé, or his crowd would squelch it. No one would fire a gun, stab with a knife, or pound with fists. But our disagreement still seemed almost physical, a matter of my heart versus his.

I fell asleep wondering if I should risk violating both the Fifth and Sixth Commandments at once so I could catch Seymour Solomon breaking the Eighth.

Chapter 19

A gargantuan black man towered over my desk the next morning after I'd schlepped myself back to the office. He was bald, jut-jawed, and wore a turtleneck; he looked like a bar bouncer on his day off.

"You Stone?" The baritone voice was vaguely familiar.

The visitor shook my hand gently, as if afraid he'd crush it, and announced he was Lew Fenton.

"Do you mind if we take a little walk outside?" I said.

"I didn't give my real name to the guard," Fenton said.

"Wanna breathe some fresh carbon monoxide outside?"

In the elevator, Fenton shook my hand again. "Congratulations. Your name's mud in the Public Buildings Service." He grinned. "You must be doing a hell of a good job. Enjoy the sights at Vulture's Point?"

"Jesus—you do have your sources there."

"Show you something when we're outside." It was a Xerox of some gobbledygook commanding GSA people to report all sightings of me. "Look"—Fenton chuckled—"it says you're 'unreliable.'"

"I never did have much talent for rewriting their press releases."

As we sauntered up Connecticut Avenue, I could hear Solomon's bulldozers growling in the next block.

His crews were wrecking the Wilson Hotel, a bay-windowed jewel of a building where several generations of congressmen had whored and plotted. With shocking irreverence toward the scoundrels of the past, he'd grabbed the land for another high-rise.

"Got a tip," Fenton said. "Check out a guy who approved Vulture's Point for the county."

"Why?"

"His son goes to this fancy school. Midwell Jones?"

"Sidwell Friends?"

"Solomon, he got the kid a scholarship there around the time he put up Vulture's."

"On the board there, isn't he?"

"Don't know," Fenton said. "All I know, mister, is that you'd better write your story fast. That building's not going to stay up forever."

ജଔ

In a still-rural part of Roxland County, I caught up with the scholarship boy's father. Mike Cox lived on five acres, but his house was a shack by Roxland standards: a weathered bungalow hidden by trees at the end of a dirt driveway.

When the door opened, I saw a pitted face and gray hair that bristled belligerently. Cox appeared fit for the cover of a rifle magazine.

Summoning up a slight Southern accent, I talked my way into the living room: "Crazy deadline, sir. These editors—always pushy about things."

Cox nodded approvingly, as if aware of the *Telegram*'s campaign for gun control.

"Trying to check out this crazy rumor," I said. "About Vulture's Point. Some crazy agitator's saying it's going to fall down."

Mike Cox motioned toward a chair by his fireplace, and I plopped down, after gazing at a picture on the mantel. In ancient color, nearly faded to black and white, Cox appeared alongside a rangy blond woman and an alert-looking boy whom I took to be his son.

"Care for a beer?"

"Care for a pencil, if you don't mind."

"What?"

"A pencil," I said. "Forgot mine."

Having established myself as a friendly incompetent, I pumped away.

"This agitator keeps saying you're the guy who approved the plans for the place."

"My boss and I, we sure did," Cox said proudly. "Hey, you mean Lew Fenton, right?"

I nodded.

"That Negrah?" Cox said it as if Fenton's race detracted from his reliability.

"Mentioned something about some slabs and rebarbs. Plus, there's the issue of the land. Kinda watery and all that. You don't think he could've driven down pilings?"

"Pilings? You think he's got money to throw away?"

I somehow resisted a comeback.

"Of course not," I said. "Just tell me—who did the soil analysis?"

"Don't remember," Cox said. "Wish I could help you. Honest, I'm not trying to hide a thing." Belatedly, he scratched his head.

As ineptly as I could, I elicited some more technical details about Vulture's, only to hear Cox lie through his teeth or plead forgetfulness. I made a mental note to recheck certain county documents.

"All those details," I said. "Bet that job's a killer."

"You got that right—I put in seventy hours last week. I'm doing a college man's job. I mean, they've been supposed to hire one for the last eight years."

"You don't say?"

"But, hey—the salary, it's not that much. And my boss, he likes me. You realize I was the one that put in all the recommendations on Vulture's Point? The engineering end. He trusts me, see?"

"Very impressive."

"I was in the Army Corps of Engineers a dozen years."

"Plenty of good experience, huh?"

"You put me against a college man, I'll come out on top anytime."

"Another thing," I said. "A little touchy, but you know those agitators—how they'll bug you forever if you don't have the answers."

Cox rocked back in his old chair. "You just relax, son—we have all the answers."

"About your boy. Was he ever a student at this Sidwell Friends School?"

Faintly, Cox wrinkled his brow. "Graduated top of his class. Sure you won't have a beer?"

"This agitator, he said Sy Solomon helped your boy get a scholarship there."

Cox nodded. "Fact of the matter is, Sy wanted to help out. Happened around the time they were cutting up my wife. Stomach cancer. Medical bills from the floor to the ceiling, and the insurance company messed up the paperwork."

"Sy paid 'em?"

"Let's just say Sy likes to do good works in private. Well, assuming it happened."

"And Fenton's carping in public," I said. "We don't want him bitching without the right side coming out, do we?"

"I'll think about it."

"Relax. Sy's not bragging. You're just saying what happened."

Cox sighed. "You see, I wanted the boy to go to a good school. Where he'd be meeting the right folks. You know about my boy?"

"Tell me anything you'd like."

"Sy and me, we'd known each other for years—you know he started building here back in the forties? So we go out for drinks—nothing wrong with that, is there?—and you know how it is, we started talking about our folks.

"And Sy asks, 'How's the wife?' And—well, what could I say? Told him the truth. That she was dying. And then Sy, he starts talking about his folks. About his wife. How she's always buying out the store. About his boy. Only child, just like mine. About how the kid's in a mental institution.

"So I tell him about Jeff; and Sy, he wants more, so I tell him more. How Jeff wants to be a senator. Hey, corny, isn't it? But don't you knock Jeff. He'll make it, 'cause he's a genius, that kid. But these schools, hey that's another thing. I mean, the rich people here, they send their kids to private schools.

"But the rest of us—different story. You ever been inside an English class here?

"Hey, Jeff was telling me about this game of musical chairs they play in high school. How you move from chair to chair according to how well you know your Shakespeare. In the ninth grade, for Chrissake. Musical chairs in the ninth grade? I might not be an English teacher, but by God, I want my kid to know his Shakespeare!

"Of course Sy leveled with me. Said Sidwell's sorta liberal. That I might not like everything. But hey, the rich kids go there, right? And I think—hey, it can't be too pink if there's rich ones. So Sy spends half a day talking some big shots into letting Jeff in. Even got 'em to pay for the buses and whatnot so Jeff could make it out there without me driving. Used to get up at five o'clock. Every school day."

"Sounds like a wonderful kid," I said.

"Know you'd like meeting him, except he's up at Harvard. Won himself a scholarship there. Sy, he's a saint. I just can't say enough good things. Hey, I told Jeff, 'You turn out like Sy Solomon, you'll make your daddy proud.'"

Chapter 20

Before Mac banished me to the Real Estate section, perhaps I should beg ahead of time for Obituaries instead. I felt infinitely more charitable toward stiffs than toward real estate men—at least I'd never heard of a corpse bribing a politician.

I was deep in my nightmares when the phone jarred me. "I figured you'd be calling anyway," a friendly voice said in a slight Yiddish accent, "so I'm calling to see if I can be of any help. Sy Solomon, Jon."

"Oh, hello, Sy, delighted you called," I recovered.

"You're not going to write about me without talking to me, are you?"

"The pleasure's mine."

"Jon," Solomon said, as if he'd been first-naming me for the past decade, "we have ourselves a problem here. You talked to Mike Cox this week, didn't you? Well, he's a little upset about things, and I was just thinking you and I could get together."

"Why, sure, Sy."

"Mac and I, we're good friends, and I want to help you."

&OCB

The Abraham Solomon Building dominated a block on a greeny hill in northwest Washington.

It loomed over its neighbors as a castle might over peasant huts.

The windows were heavily tinted, somewhat oval, and bordered by silvery metal—the building seemed to be wearing row after row of sunglasses. In privacy its occupants could peer down at the commoners below.

Seymour Solomon Companies shared the building with a nest of lobbyists. Gazing at the luminous directory, I saw the names of everything from phony citizens groups to a gang of cigarette companies. A mélange of furriers, travel agencies, stereo stores, and stockbrokers filled the first floor. If a politician accepted a bribe upstairs, he could dispose of it before he even left the building.

I stepped off the elevator into Solomon's outer offices and surveyed his tastes or his decorator's. The room looked as if someone couldn't decide whether to imitate a society doctor or the hero of a Dewar's "Doers" whiskey ad. I saw a Renoir, art in the Warhol vein, a glass coffee table heavy with *New Yorkers*, a leather couch I recalled from an ad in the magazine, Selig chairs, and ungainly lamps that seemed to be straining their goosenecks.

Nowhere did I see a picture of any of Solomon's buildings; perhaps his decorator had pronounced them insufficiently aesthetic.

I announced myself, and presently Solomon strolled into sight, even more massive than the file photographs had suggested. His neck resembled a wrestler's, and I suspected that biceps bulged under the well-cut suit.

Although Solomon had been a bricklayer once, his body seemed less the result of happenstance than of contrivance. His skin was deeply and evenly tanned, not in the least burned, as if he had consulted with a dermatologist before flying off to Bermuda.

Solomon's hair was black, flecked with gray, and trimmed to the last strand,. His teeth gleamed; his blue eyes shone as brightly as those of people years younger. I recalled some baritone-voiced politicians on the staider Sunday talk shows, the Alpha males whose fans confused vibrancy with competence. But Solomon had outdone them all—I might as well have been watching him on color television with the hue control turned up.

He first-named me again, and I admired his friendliness, worthy of a soft-sell commercial for one of the greedier oil companies.

"Jon, you just come right into my office."

"Sure, Sy."

"I give you my solemn promise, Jon. This building is not going to fall down while we're talking."

I smiled enough to keep him happy.

We shook hands, and I saw why the *Telegram* had photographed him at times with a partly closed fist—the tips of two fingers were missing from his right hand. I wondered how deft a bricklayer he'd been.

But when I looked again at his face, he once more seemed fit for the greens at the most exclusive country club. If his nose were prominent, it somehow begged for the WASPish description of "aquiline." Despite thick eyebrows and heavy jaw and cheekbones, everything intimated strength, not coarseness. I remembered the Maverick automobile and Mac's assurance that Sy was a Regular Guy. Perhaps Solomon changed clothes and miens along with cars.

As though I were one of Solomon's junior colleagues, he put his heavy hand on my shoulder and guided me toward his personal office. He sat down at a small mahogany table near the window there, and I sank into a low, cushioned chair facing the light.

Nothing disturbed his tabletop but a small pad and a push-button phone—I saw just one drawer in the table, and nary a file cabinet in the room. Solomon might be a Regular Guy with his Maverick acquaintances, but he had furnished his office in Great Man Simple. There he could rise above the trappings of paperwork, like an auto executive unsullied by factory grease.

On the wall smiled a woman with an Elkins hairdo—the creation of the First Hairdresser—and a somewhat misshapen face. Solomon obviously had married before he became successful. No wrinkles marred the face, though, as if a plastic surgeon had concentrated on the correctable.

Beside a window were pictures of Solomon grinning away with the last three presidents; each photograph bore a notation in the vein of, "To my good friend Sy." I supposed that the White House souvenirs were as good a way as any of reducing Solomon's paperwork.

"Mac thought the world of your FHA stories," Solomon said. "Terrible, the scandals. FHA I deal with as little as I can. It's just a crying shame that the rest of the government isn't as honest as GSA."

I withdrew a little tape recorder from my coat pocket.

With a frown and a wave of a hand Solomon showed his displeasure. "You're a reporter, I trust a reporter."

"But you'd trust me more, wouldn't you, if we had this on tape," I said.

"Jon, this is personal. You tape all you want later. Not now. Please. Mac will understand. Please. This is not a broadcasting session."

Grudgingly I replaced the recorder in my pocket. If Solomon lost his temper, I might lose my interview.

"Now, Jon, I'm not telling you what to write. I just want to say that Mike Cox is quite worried about his boy. Now, Mike told you the boy's interested in politics, eh?"

I nodded.

"I'd hate to see Jeff ruined before he even finished school."

"Ruined?"

"By an irresponsible newspaper article."

"I'm not writing about Jeff. I'm writing about his father."

"Have you talked to Mac?"

"None of the editors yet," I said honestly.

"Please, Jon. Don't ruin the boy. Please. I help lots of young people. Rich ones. Poor ones. Jews. Christians. I've always believed in education. I swear to God, Jon, that's the only reason I helped Jeff get into Sidwell Friends. And the father? You want Mike Cox to lose his job? Him, a workingman? A little guy? Is that who you pick on? You want to pick on someone, then you pick on Sy Solomon. Not someone like Mike. Mike I've known twenty-five years. A man of integrity, I promise you, Jon."

"How about the building?"

"Just as solid as Mike. A man like Mike, he's not going to let it fall down."

"What about Sy Solomon?"

"Fifty years I've been a builder. You ask anyone in the trade about me. They'll tell you."

"Have you and GSA figured out how to break the news to IRS? For real?"

"I don't understand, Jon."

"The cracks. The carpeting. I know all about it. The stuck doors, too. And the lower-level freight elevator. And the broken windows. Omens, maybe?"

"What is this, Jon, a horror movie? I trust the architects and engineers. For Seymour Solomon, only the best! You think I just chose the lowest bidders? Contractors or employees—I hire only the best! And let me ask you this. Are the windows *still* broken? And the other things? You tell me the problems, I'll get my people on the job."

"They're fixed," I admitted.

"There you go, Jon. We hire only the best."

"Look," I said, "we're talking *symptoms* here."

Besides which a little detail remained. However stellar the architects and engineers—and I still didn't know, one way or other—had Solomon followed their instructions?

With the shadier builders, how much difference existed between plans and execution? Might Solomon have actually used some reputable engineers and architects as a cover? I remembered the stories a friend had told me, a brilliant Langley classmate pulling down more than half a million dollars a year as a scriptwriter in Hollywood. He owned a Jag and a mansion now. But some of the finished products bore only accidental resemblances to the visions inside his head. The worst producers could start out with *Citizen Kane* and end up with *Bikini Newscasters from Mars*. An exaggeration here? Of course. But I still wondered about a parallel with Solomon.

"So who reconciled the execution with the plans?" I asked.

"Only the best."

"You mean your own people?"

"Almost entirely, I'm proud to say. But enough of the windows and the rest. Distractions, Jon, nothing more."

"Not for Lew Fenton."

Solomon shrugged and frowned like a pacifist accused of the My Lai massacre. "Of course it's falling down. All buildings fall down someday. All people die someday."

"The way Fenton tells it, a lot of people are going to die with that building."

"Lew Fenton, what does he know? A poor misguided shvartze. Now I don't wish to speak ill of Lew Fenton, but you've heard of the raise, perhaps? The man's so dumb he fights me after I give his people a raise."

"Ten cents an hour?"

"The best I could do, Jon. I promise you, Seymour Solomon Companies pays its people tops."

"But the building—"

"The building I don't want to discuss. Enough of it! You want to discuss GSA now?"

"What about GSA?"

"Don't fool yourself, Jon. I know you're asking about me there, and I don't just mean the way you picked on Mike. People tell me—"

"Like Larry Zumweltnar or Marvin Forester?"

"What are you getting at, Jon?"

"The trustee for Eddy Bullard in Vulture's Point," I said.

"Jon, I did not want to bring this up. Yes, Mr. Forester talked to me, and he said you were very rude. But what's the point of all this? Mr. Forester has explained. Eddy Bullard just happened to be in the wrong partnership. What more can I say? A very stupid mistake. A mistake, that's all. I accept the blame. Just a very stupid accident. Do you think I'd violate the law? Do you think President Bullard would violate the law? Jon, if you speak like that, I must ask you to leave."

"Tell me about the accident," I said—careful not to let sarcasm put quotes around the word.

"Accidents, schmacksidents. Who cares? That's all it was. Do you want to hear my story? How I am what I am today? Then you'll understand. A man like me, I respect the law. You take out your tape recorder, and I'll tell you my story, eh? You play it in RFK Stadium if you want. About Sy Solomon there are no secrets."

I set up my recorder on his table, and Solomon squinted eagerly at the plastic window showing the tape.

"It's on?"

I nodded.

"Good," he said, "I'll tell you my story." His eyes flashed, his smile widened; I would hear, I would believe.

Chapter 21

"I was born in Washington, but my parents came from Europe, the village of Kankov, two-hundred miles west of Moscow, a *Fiddler on the Roof* kind of place."

Solomon had thickened his accent slightly, as if, in telling the story, he felt it sacrilegious to speak like a native-born American. But I kept noticing the pseudo–Ivy League tie, the manicured nails, the absence of anything, other than the accent and two missing fingertips, that would suggest his origins.

"Now in northern Russia it gets very, very cold in the winter," Solomon said, "and the tax collector, he threw water on the bedding of the people if they didn't pay. And the tax collector, you know who he was? My father. Now he did not want to be one, but the czar said to each village, 'You must have a tax collector. For a Jewish village, a Jewish tax collector.'

"And so my father kept dumping water on the bedding of the family of the village butcher. So the butcher and his family left for America, and the next year half the families in the village followed. The pogroms."

Oh, to speak up! But this was Seymour Solomon's story, and who was I to intrude?

"My father," Solomon said, "he came here, too, and he said to the butcher, 'For what I've done I'm very sorry, but this is America, and I hope we'll be friends.' And the butcher gave him a job in his new shop. While my father studied English."

Studied English? I wondered if Solomon had made a career of *un*studying it. His locution and accent, though subtle, made it seem as if he had grown up in Kankov. An act to disarm investors? Or just the sounds of an immigrant's son who had loved his father and could only melt just so much into the American pot, the necktie notwithstanding? His edifice, after all, was not the Seymour Solomon Building but rather named after Abraham. Might filial fidelity have reigned over ego?

"The butcher had a young girl," Solomon went on in his Kankovian way, "and my father said, 'I wish to marry your daughter.' And so they were married. The tax collector and the butcher's daughter. Now a friend of my father's came to Washington to be a cantor. And my father thought, 'This is America—here I won't be ashamed to work for the government.'

"So he goes to Washington, and everywhere people thumb their noses. A funny foreigner with this accent—him a clerk? Him a tax collector? Not even a citizen yet, and he wants to work for the government?

"Now the agencies, they all turn him down. So he starts back to Union Station, and just before his train leaves, a friend of my father's friend runs up. He's a butcher himself, and he tells my father, 'Abe, you stay in Washington. My best man just quit.' And my father asks, 'How much?'

"And the other man tells him. And my father says, 'For five dollars more a week, I work in Washington.' So my father brought my mother back from New York, and he worked very hard as a butcher until a stroke killed him.

"Now a year after my father comes to Washington, a son is born. Me. I grow up four miles from here, and I become good friends with the son of my father's boss. Herschel Peretz. Herschel and I, we go to school together and he's just a small boy and I protect him from the goyim. The gangs. Not like New York, but they had them.

"Herschel helps me with my homework. I play football. The only Jew on the team. For Herschel, the debate squad. He goes off to college. My father dies, and my sister and I work in the store of my father's friend, until the A&P moves in across the street, and the neighborhood's changing, so there's less people wanting kosher.

"So then I work as a bricklayer. The only Jew most of the time. I do well. And I start my own little bricklaying company. And do well again. Even in the Depression. So I start a construction company, and I build a house and sell it. And then another house. And more.

"And soon I start to think. Why am I building houses for other people? My father—what if he'd owned his friend's butcher shop? He might not have died so early if he'd had something to show for his trouble.

"Now a construction company—what's a construction company? Some men and machines for hire. Nothing permanent. The buildings it builds, they're for other people. At least with most companies. Why, it's like children. You have a son, you want to watch him grow up. Same with a building. Good or bad, it's yours. So I build a house to rent. And another. And more. And apartments.

"By now I'm married. To my old girlfriend from high school. We live cheaply. Right above the boiler room of one of our apartments. Ida and me, we live so cheaply we don't even own a good radio. All our money, it goes for more apartments. I borrow a lot and the banks trust me because I work hard and I'm an honest man. So they keep lending, and I keep building.

"Now the war comes, and I volunteer for the army, but the government says, 'No, no, we need you to put up barracks for our soldiers.' They like my barracks and after the war I get a call from someone I knew when he was an army officer. He says, 'Sy, I'm with the leasing program now. Have you ever built an office building?'

"I tell him, 'For you I'll build the best.' 'But you must bid against others,' he says. 'No problem,' I say. 'The best man, he builds the building, eh?'

"But an office building's tricky. Lots of rules and regulations. Zoning, taxes, you name it, you need a good lawyer. Now Ida says, 'What about our good friend Shelly Peretz? Isn't he a lawyer now?' And I tell Ida, 'Shelly we must forget.' Ida says, 'Why?' I tell her, 'Shelly's with Apple and Foster now.

"Ida says, 'Sounds like vaudeville act.' I tell her, 'You don't know about Apple and Foster? The best lawyers in town? FDR they worked for. The New Deal, they helped set it up. Apple and Foster we cannot afford.'

"And Ida says, 'If you want the best building, you get the best lawyer.'

"I go downtown to Shelly's office, and I'm scared. A thick carpet. A blond secretary. And the name on the door—it isn't even Herschel anymore. It's Shelton. Shelton Philips. But he slaps me on the back, and says, 'For you, Sy, it's always Shelly. Sure I'll be your lawyer. You just leave everything to us. Apple and Foster, they're old government hands. They know how it's done.'"

"I tell Shelly, 'I'm an honest man. We must not bribe.' Shelly says, 'Remember your homework? How I always insisted you work out your own problems? How we both agreed we should never cheat? I'm still your same Shelly.' So we bid and we win, and I run home and smother Ida with kisses. I tell her, 'Imagine me the government's landlord.' My own father they wouldn't make a clerk, and now I'm their landlord.

"And Jon, that isn't even all the story. You know who moves into the building? Internal Revenue. The tax collectors. Just like Vulture's Point. My first office building, it's just as good as Vulture's, too. A fine building. I put it up forty cents per square foot cheaper than the competition. Back in the 1940s, Jon! The walls are so strong you could make it a bomb shelter. You've seen it? Less than two blocks from the White House. President Bullard—if he wants to admire my building, he just walks down the street.

"Now Shelly and I, we do very well together, and one day he says an old friend would like to see me. I come to Shelly's office, and there's Duke Odysseus. I say, 'Duke, what are you doing here?' Duke I used to beat up when he picked on Shelly at school.

"You know his original name? Diogenes. Maybe I'm why he changed it—I used to tease him about it. So anyway, Duke tells me he just quit the *Telegram*. You know he worked there, Jon? He used to be one of the drivers delivering the paper to the boys. Now please don't quote me—Duke sometimes gets touchy about his past. Why I don't know. He's just like me. A hard worker.

"So Duke and Shelly and I go to lunch, and Duke says he's been saving his money for a new business. Buying up land for parking lots. Duke says, 'Driving a truck you can't park everywhere. I want to help people so they won't get tickets.' And Shelly says, 'Sy, Duke's bitten off a little more than he can chew. Didn't you say you were looking for land … for that building we talked about?' I nod. And from then on, Duke and me make money together. Him buying land. Me building on it. Duke I trust. A man of honor.

"Now Shelly, he works hard at the law firm, and he meets many, many important people. And they invite him to their houses and he invites them to his, and he invites me, too. He tells me, 'Sy, I'm not ashamed of my old friends.' I feel nervous anyway. All the congressmen and famous people. But Shelly tells me, 'Sy, you've changed. You can quote Isaac Singer. You know art. You help run the Amalgamated Appeal. You dress like a gentleman. You go to concerts. So what if you're not nobility? Neither am I. Just remember: Cream rises to the top.' I go along with that—my good friend Shelly has just been nominated a federal judge.

"Time passes. I read more books. Ida and I go to more concerts. We meet more famous people at Shelly's. And then one day Shelly says he wants to recommend me for Burning Tree. Think about it—Burning Tree, the country club for presidents. But Shelly says, 'Just act yourself, and you'll get in.' And I do. Everyone thinks the others are going to blackball me, but nobody does. You trust people, they'll trust you.

"Now out on the golf course I meet a very nice gentleman. His caddy doesn't show up, and I say, 'Sir, would you like to use mine a while?' We talk, and he learns I'm in real estate. Humbly he asks me for advice. On investments. I ask what he does for a living. A senator, he says. I remember my father again. How even the clerks looked down on him. And now a senator's asking Abe Solomon's son for advice!"

"And that's how Eddy Bullard ended up in Vulture's Point?"

"Please, Jon. I thought we agreed. No dirt about Eddy Bullard. Yes, Eddy Bullard came to me for advice. Because, Jon, he's very careful about his money. He wanted a safe place for it. For his children. The president, he's a man of character. Just like Shelly. Just like Duke. The first thing Eddy tells me when I go to his house, he says, 'Sy, I'm a senator. I must not put my money in anything crooked.'"

"Then why the trustee?"

"Jon, please! You talk more about this nonsense, you must go."

"So how'd Congressman Boynton's company end up in Vulture's?"

"A friend, Jon. Shelly and I, we have many friends."

"But Boynton's a Republican," I prodded. "Partisan as they come."

"Republican, Democrat, Republicrat, it doesn't matter. He's a friend, Jon." I remembered how Eddy Bullard's old law firm had brought everybody together in blissful, profitable harmony.

"Sy," I asked, "are you liberal or conservative?"

"A liberal, I am proud to say. I believe in human dignity."

"And in supporting conservative congressmen, too?"

"I don't understand your question, Jon."

"The campaign records show you've given at least eight thousand dollars to Boynton. A conservative Republican?"

"I wouldn't be surprised, Jon. Congressman Boynton is a man of honor. Just like Shelly. Just like Duke. Just like Eddy Bullard. Men of honor I like no matter who they are. Jews. Christians. Arabs. It makes no difference to me, Jon. Decency—it's the first thing I look for in a politician. Please, try to understand. Do you want another Watergate? Please, Jon. I am very concerned about our country. That is why we need more men of character."

"There was also Charles Rutland, Frank Dowlinger, Tom Hinelly."

"What's your question?"

"They're all on committees overseeing GSA."

"All fine men, Jon. All decent."

"And all on GSA-related committees."

"Please, Jon. I give to many people. On GSA committees. Off GSA committees. It makes no difference. Character, Jon. That's what they all have in common."

"But didn't Hinelly almost go to jail for—"

"A mistake. Hinelly I trusted because Congressman Boynton said he was a fine man."

"Boynton's on the Republican congressional campaign committee, isn't he?"

"What's your point?"

"He's also on a committee making tax laws affecting real estate, and yet—"

"Jon, please. If you talk this way—"

"Isn't there a law saying you can't contribute if you're a government contractor? At least some kinds."

"I don't understand, Jon."

"Section 611 of Title 18 of the United States Code?"

"What can I say? I haven't read it."

"I have a present, Sy." I handed him a Xerox. "Here. Your own personal copy."

"Oh—that law. Yes, yes, I remember it now, Jon. Old stuff. Nothing to worry about at all, Jon. All it says is, you can't sell a lot of things to the government and give. Not that you can't *lease* a building and give."

"But some lawyers think that—"

"Please, Jon. Very carefully I studied it. Hilton Kahn—you know him? A very fine young man. Used to be with Citizens Voice. A very very fine young man. With Apple and Foster now. Hilton and I, we went over the law very carefully, Jon, and I promise you, it does not include us. You want to know about Section 611, I'll tell you who you ask. Victoria Simpson. A landlord, too."

I almost dropped my notebook. "Who?"

"Mrs. Simpson. Your publisher. A very fine lady. I serve on her concert board. Which is why I know, Jon. You see, Mrs. Simpson didn't give all the land to the National Park Service. I have to tell you—some of it she leases. Twenty acres and a house, she leases it to the Park Service. Through GSA, just like me. Another landlord just like me. Another contributor just like me. All the politicians she helps. Section 611—Mrs. Simpson can tell you all about it. Would she break the law?"

I reached for my recorder on the table, but Solomon waved me away.

"Oh, keep it going." He laughed enthusiastically. "Mrs. Simpson's very proud of her gifts. And me? I'm proud to know Vicky. And I met her the best possible way, Jon. Doing good deeds. At Amalgamated Appeal. I run the Construction Division—she's with Communications. I walk up to her, and say, 'Mrs. Simpson, what a fine job you're doing.' And Mrs. Simpson laughs, and I say, 'No, no, please. I like the way you always meet your quotas.'

"Mrs. Simpson and I see each other at many many meetings, and she invites me to her house. Ida, too. And Ida tells Vicky what fine concerts she has. Vicky laughs. I say, 'No, no, we like your musicians very much.' Ida says, 'We always buy season tickets.' Vicky says, 'Sy, you're a very good organizer. A gentleman, too. Someone with fine manners. Would you like to serve on our board?' And through Vicky, I meet many many fine people.

"Mac I meet at a concert. A very fine man. A mensch. An old Brooklyn boy. Lived in the same neighborhood where my father-in-law had his first shop. Mac and I talk about Isaac Singer and all the famous composers. His friend I like, too. You know Luci? Luci Elkins?"

"One of your investors, isn't she?" Luci, of course, was also the First Hairdresser.

Solomon nodded. "Ida she helps look more pretty. I'm grateful. I tell Luci, 'I'd like to help you make more money.' Luci says, 'Your wife always pays me fairly.' I say, 'No, no. What I'm trying to say is, I'd like to invite you to become one of my investors.' Luci says, 'I'm just a poor girl from South Carolina.' I say, 'Please, Ida's very grateful. If you don't have the money, I'll lend it to you.' Luci says, 'Oh no, I couldn't.' I tell her, 'Please, I'd be honored. If you lose money, Sy Solomon forgets about the loan.'

"Of course I risk nothing, I'm a good businessman, and Luci makes money and is very very happy. Now Jon, think about it. Would Vicky be friends with a crook? Would Mac? Would Luci honor me with her investment if she didn't trust me?"

"So you're a generous, honest man," I pumped.

"I have this saying, Jon. Solomon's Golden Rule. Do unto your friends as you would have them do unto you. You help your friends, that's really just helping yourself. Because someday, Jon, they'll try to help you back."

"Sy, forgive me. I'm just wondering if you were ever kind enough to lend money to Eddy Bullard."

"Please. I thought we weren't going to talk about Eddy."

"Excuse me," I said politely enough to have been sipping tea with Vicky. "I'm just trying to find out the facts. About the president."

Solomon scowled at my recorder. "You're very rude. Leave!"

"But what about your charities? Don't you want to talk about them? Mac was telling me about the Methodist Home and—"

"Jon, please." With a huge hand Solomon gestured toward the door. "Please. Go. Be a mensch."

"But your charities, don't you want people to know about your charities?"

"Please, Jon. I'd rather do my good deeds without an audience."

Chapter 22

The red light on my answering machine was blinking when I returned to my apartment, directly from the Solomon interview. Had Sy already complained to Mac?

Instead, however, I heard my mother's voice:

"Jonathan! Come quickly! You've killed your father. Metropolitan Hospital—Intensive Care Unit."

That was all. I ran out to my car and drove into the dusk, toward the towering white hospital complex built in no small part with Seymour Solomon's millions.

"Intensive Care Unit," at least, was better than "morgue," and so I held out hope and pondered how Spinoza would have handled this.

The original syllogism was that I was a reporter, that in the natural order of things it was my job to expose crooks, that if Solomon qualified, then my response was inevitable: Do whatever I can to write up the sleaze for Page A-1. There was nothing Oedipal here, just a clash of values and goals—mine versus my father's.

And yet I couldn't help remembering his wan face, the beads of sweat on it, the labored breathing, when his heart had almost failed him the last time around. I had watched him nearly die then and there.

So, Stone, I thought, here's another syllogism for you—maybe even more in the natural order of things: one reflecting a son's love of his father.

Major premise: My father works in a high-stress job, hardly a cardiac nirvana, where his boss wants him to be good to clients. Minor premise: My investigating Seymour Solomon was not good for Lincoln National Bank, a backer of his construction projects as well as a major client of my father's company. Conclusion: I should get off the story. Granted, I was skipping over nuances; I wasn't Herbert Stone, just his son. But under the circumstances, I cared not a whit.

When I reached the ICU, I could find neither parent and wondered if my destination would be the morgue. For twenty minutes the hospital bureaucracy was at a loss as to their whereabouts.

At length, however, a jowly clerk informed me that I should go to Room 617, where, amid a tangle of tubes and wires and the blips and beeps of the monitoring apparatuses, I found my father resting, apparently asleep.

"How is he?" I asked my mother.

"I'm surprised you'd be concerned," she said. "You didn't seem to be three weeks ago."

"How is he?" I repeated.

"I warned you," she said.

"Dad?" I drew closer to my father.

"Psst! He's asleep."

Or was he? Had his head stirred slightly?

"What if I told you I'd stop?" I said to my mother in a lowered voice.

"What's the catch here, Jonathan?"

"Nothing. Just four words. 'I'm off the story.'"

"Do you mean it?" my mother asked.

I nodded, and she hugged me, and I knew I preferred the second syllogism.

No, I wasn't Jack Burden investigating the Judge for Willie Stark in *All the King's Men*. Mac, if anything, would be happier to see me end, in a quiet way, my threat to both Solomon and the *Telegram's* advertising revenue.

Far more importantly, I'd add to my father's job security. I remembered the Great Twitch that had caused Jack to drive the Judge, his own father, to suicide. I hadn't any Twitch to boss me, and in fact, by the end of the book, Jack himself was refusing to live by the Twitch. Why should I?

"We're lucky, Jonathan. The medicine—they think it was his blood-pressure pills. Just another few days for observation, then he's out. Just promise. You're really off the story?"

"No more Solomoning," I said. "Let someone else expose the bastard. Someone with a father with a stronger heart."

Just then, my father's head moved.

"Lydia, stop it!"

"Dad!"

"I've heard every word," he said.

"Herbert!" my mother said. "Just calm down and rest. Cathy's due in tonight."

"I've figured it out," my father said.

"Shh."

"The formula," he said. "What's going to get me to ninety-nine. Elton King, he can go to hell!"

A nurse had entered the room, and my mother's pallor was matching my father's.

"What did you say?" I asked.

"One more time. *Elton King can go to hell!*"

"Your hero?"

"I mean, I did a little sorting when I was on that stretcher. Priorities. You can call up Elton and tell him I'm out. I don't ever want to say The P Word again. A liar's a liar. No more 'he's political' crap. From now on, someone else'll have to help them do their lying. Not Herb Stone."

"Why don't you go back to sleep, Herbert?" my mother said.

"Mr. Stone, time for your sedative," the nurse said as she reached over to feel his pulse.

"No, damn it," my father said, "I want to talk."

"You'd better take that sedative," the nurse persisted.

"But Herbert," my mother said, "what are we going to live on?"

"What are we going to live on?" repeated my father, incredulous. "My God, Lydia, we're worth one and a half million, between the house and the stocks. I'll just find another job. Hopefully one where I don't have to use The P Word."

"Take your sedative," my mother said.

"Go to sleep," I said. "I'm off the story."

"The hell you are," my father said as if to encourage me.

"But you've said it's a crock."

"Still think that way," he said.

"So I'll get off the story."

"Hell no. If *you* believe it, then go after it, and if McWilliams fires you—so what? It just might keep you out of the cardiac ICU."

"But Dad."

"Maybe this is your ticket to a better newspaper."

"There'll always be Macs," I said.

"There'll always be Eltons. That's the point. If you run into one, you just move on."

"If that's what you *really* think."

"I do, Jon. All right, nurse, give me that pill."

Chapter 23

Again and again McWilliams smacked his mitt like a drunken boxer trying to murder a punching bag. Never, I suspected, had McWilliams hit his glove so hard for anyone.

If he'd restrained himself just slightly, I wouldn't have laughed. But at that moment, he was unwittingly in self-parody mode. It was as if he were a crazed Muhammad Ali, and the glove a bag with Joe Frazier's face on it.

"What's so funny, pal?"

"Nothing," I lied.

"You think I'm funny?"

Energetically, I shook my head.

"I think you're funny, pal. A clown of a fly-shit reporter. Only a fly-shit reporter goes off half-cocked on an interview."

"Where's E.J.?" I asked, like a criminal suspect demanding to see his lawyer.

"I don't know if the poor man could stand it. What I'm going to do to you, pal. I'm going to bust your ass. As of tomorrow, you're reporting to the Real Estate section."

Once more I tried to outstare the sharklike eyes.

"Fuck you, McWilliams!"

"That's better, pal. I don't like people who let themselves get stepped on,"

"So I'm not going to Real Estate." I took care to make that a statement, not a question.

"Nice try," he said, "but I'm editor, and you're not. So, pal, you just let me do the stepping."

"Fuck you again, then."

"You're improving, Stone."

"So—"

"You're not going to Real Estate after all."

I grinned.

"No, not at all, pal. You're going back to where you started. The Roxland beat."

"I guess it's pretty academic now, but how come you're transferring me? Exactly why? Simply because I had the balls to investigate your buddy Solomon?"

"Because you're a rude, fly-shit reporter. Isn't that enough? You didn't even check with your boss before you went off half-cocked. Maybe if E.J. had seen your questions, you wouldn't have made such a fool of yourself."

"Jesus, you weren't even at the interview."

"Sy told me all about it. Last night. On the phone."

"You trust him over me?"

McWilliams nodded.

"Don't you at least want to hear my version?"

"I don't have time, pal."

"Don't have time? Jesus, I've been on this story for months."

"Another reason I'm busting you. You've wasted enough time already. Just answer me. Are Solomon's prices any higher than the other landlords'? You've looked through enough leases? That's the issue, pal."

"The issue is the fucking president of the United States breaking the law. Plus the prices the government could have gotten if there'd been more competition. A pretty penny's difference. You take the volume of business, and it's gonna matter. Big."

"You don't like my friends, do you, pal?"

"Not if they break the law." In vain, I tried to make that my exit line.

"Just a minute," Mac said. "You stay right where you are. You scared of me?"

"You can take this job and shove it up your rear. I'm a big boy now. I can stand in the unemployment line with the other working stiffs."

"You're stiff, all right. Inflexible."

"Morally," I said.

Already I had a possible scenario in mind for myself if Mac didn't fire me instantly. I'd tough it out at the *Telegram* but quietly save up enough money to let me quit and focus on the search for another job.

"Here's another order for you to ignore. I want that tape." The one from the interview. "Because, pal, we might be able to use some of it for a personality profile."

"Jesus, Real Estate just had a—"

"It's for the People Page, pal," Mac said, not so casually glancing at his Rolex.

"I'll write it, then."

"I don't think you're objective enough, pal. Sy deserves better than a hatchet job by a fly-shit reporter. I'm assigning it to a professional."

"Who?"

"Wendy Blevin."

&OCЗ

"So then," I told Margo, around half a Little Tavern hamburger in my mouth, "I said, 'Fuck you, McWilliams!'"

"To your editor?"

"I don't think Mac's been demoted to copy aide lately."

"What about you?"

"I suppose the Roxland beat's the same thing."

"At least it isn't the Real Estate section."

I nodded thankfully. "If I'm going to be a sellout, I might as well be an honest one. Write advertising copy or something At least nothing disguised as news."

"Jonathan, I'm sh—"

"If there's one thing I can't stand," I said, "it's an underpaid whore. Particularly if it's me. Dad thinks I'd draw fifty-five grand the first year on the job. Working for his firm. PR."

Carefully Margo pursed her lips. Then: "FUCK YOU, JONATHAN!"

All the other customers were watching and murmuring.

"Hey, relax," I told Margo, "I'm still on the side of the angels. Promise me—no more whore talk."

"But you really told him, 'Fuck you!'? Your boss?"

"Fuck you," I said in a discreet, low voice. "Just like that."

Frowning, a hamburger-slinger spun around from his grill. "No more dirty language, mister, or you and the lady leave."

I turned to Margo: "Gotta remember this is a highly moral place. Would you believe, J. Edgar Hoover owned Little Tavern stock."

"Must have croaked after eating his hamburgers."

"I beg your pardon, Guinevere. I'll take Little Tavern over McDonald's any old time. At least they don't order their people to smile forever."

"But this building. It looks like ..." The Little Tavern had a peaked green roof, white tile along the sides, and a portico of wood or pseudowood.

"Agreed," I said. "It looks like the outhouse of a Howard Johnson's."

Delicately, Margo wiped the hamburger grease off her fingers. "What if he'd fired you on the spot?"

"I was so pissed off, I wouldn't have cared one way or the other. Besides, you might say he treats reporters like Little Mac."

Margo wrinkled her brow in bewilderment.

"That shark Mac used to play around with at the Sans Souci," I said. "He was always sticking his fingers into the tank and watching Little Mac snap. Not that Mac wanted his fingers bitten. But it tickled him, seeing a member of an inferior species get mad. Which is more or less how he views reporters."

"What?"

"Likes us to snap every now and then," I said, "just so we never bite off a finger."

I dug into my third hamburger.

"The best metaphor came later on," I said. "After Little Mac grew too big for the Sans Souci, Mac bought himself a tank of Siamese fighting fish. Which he supposedly loves to watch tear each other to shreds. Reminds me of the mayhem at the paper—editors versus reporters, reporters backstabbing reporters. He's a genius, Mac, but reporters mean no more to him than the fish do. Well, I suppose it's more fun seeing humans gore each other."

"How are your wounds?"

"Painful. I feel like I bit shredded glass instead of the finger."

"And then what? After the fuck-you session?"

"Made one last series of crazy calls to GSA hoping a story would somehow come through that he couldn't ignore. I called Jones, I called Gurnsley. Or tried to. Zumweltnar came on instead and gave me some bull about them not talking to me anymore. And I asked why. And he said he'd heard what happened between me and Mac. The same fucking afternoon, for Chrissake."

"Mister," said the hamburger-slinger, "I don't want no more dirty words, or I'm calling the cops."

"And then," I told Margo, "I asked how Zumweltnar knew about Mac and me. All he said was"—I whispered—"'Screw you, Stone.' And then he growls one more time and says, 'Stone, don't you ever call here again. You and your investigations—you count as much as a fart in a windstorm.'"

∝∞ω

On my parents' TV screen, Eddy Bullard looked in focus except for his eyebrows; they seemed as fuzzy as the wrinkles were clear. The camera lens zoomed back, and I saw him hurrying down the ramp of Air Force One—a suitcase democratically in each hand.

"Criticize Bullard all you like," my mother said, "but at least he isn't another Nixon."

"But his Papudoian policy—"

"He even carries his own luggage."

"Of course," I said. "To keep his hands busy and discourage autograph seekers."

"Jonathan! Why are you always so negative?"

"Heredity."

"We didn't invite you over for an argument," my mother said.

"Just to talk me into flacking for Dad's firm."

"If you had a good job, you might get to marry a girl like Donna Stackelbaum. Well, if she was still available."

"*Still* available?"

"Donna's engaged," my mother said in her best I-told-you-so tone.

"To?"

"A lawyer. A very successful young lawyer. They're getting married next month."

"A lawyer lobbying for an energy company?"

"As a matter of fact that's how they did meet," my mother said.

"Not Quad-State Atomic, by any chance?" Although I sought to make the question casual, I might as well have been emitting an angry green glow.

"Look, Jonathan," she said, ignoring the specifics, "if you don't have anything nice to say, don't say it."

"I feel tongue-tied."

"Donna says he's just your type. An activist, a fighter for the underdog."

"The dog taking the low road?"

"Jonathan! He's a liberal."

"Off-hours, maybe."

"Hilton's even worked for Citizens Voice."

"What's the last name?"

"Kahn."

"Who's into real estate deals, too?" I asked. And arranging preemployment deals between Quad and sleazy bureaucrats?

"You know him?"

"By reputation," I said accurately. "Met him once."

"Excellent," said my mother, beaming, "and I'm not surprised. Donna's always had such fine taste in men."

෮෬

"Shame—yes, sir, a real shame McWilliams broke you," Stonewall exulted over T-bone at the Roxland Howard Johnson's.

"I'm gonna expose the hell out of all your clients," I said.

"Hey, do that. I can always use the publicity."

"Bring in more business from crooks, huh?"

"Hey," Stonewall said, "if all my clients were honest, people would think I was lazy."

"You're the most diligent lawyer in northern Virginia."

"How's that cheese sandwich?" I asked.

"I like Little Tavern better."

"How'd you like to eat T-bone like me?"

If I puffed up enough developers, maybe he'd even buy me a hundred-and-ten-dollar lunch someday.

"Jon, how'd you like a real job? Regional Planning's looking for an information man. Twenty-nine k. It's actual policy stuff, not just scribbling."

"Thanks for the story."

"Hey, that's off the record."

"Oh, come on, Stonewall," I joshed, "that's a good story—a zoning, lawyer recruiting a flack for Regional Planning. At twenty-nine thousand."

"Hey, I was only trying to do you a favor."

"Along with the developers."

"Hey, don't be snooty." Stonewall laughed. "That's good money."

Then he returned to the con job of the hour, lobbying me on behalf of one of the greedier developers.

We finished lunch, and Stonewall removed from his pocket what looked like a folded twenty-dollar bill. Carefully he put it under the saltshaker.

"Who's the waitress supposed to slip this to?" I asked. "Which politician?"

"It's for her."

"What are you trying to do?" I asked. "Bribe her into giving you more black-eyed peas?"

"Take a closer look at it," Stonewall said.

Instead of a picture of the White House, I saw one of a church.

"Look at the other half," he said.

I picked up the shaker and unfolded the "bill." The other half said, "Disappointed? You won't be if you're saved at—" Someone had stamped in the name of the Roxland Baptist Church.

"But the Secret Service."

"Hey, we obey the law," Stonewall said. Whereupon he pointed out some fine print near the "Dollars" on the "bill": "Gospel Tract. Copyright 1977. Nonnegotiable."

Stonewall smiled. "Clever, isn't it? I'm very religious."

"You ole rascal, you. You must be tithing one-tenth of your fixer fees."

"Hey, I practice what I preach."

I turned over the "bill" and took in a quotation from Romans 6:23: "For the wages of sin is death."

Chapter 24

Huffing up the bike path along the Potomac, Fred Green resembled a blubbery comic's version of a weekend exerciser. Green's face was contorted like a stroke victim's; his bottom sprawled past the tiny seat of his English racer. His body sweated like a sauna customer's, and his orange sweatshirt and green pants clashed absurdly—making him look still fatter. I expected the bike to crumple beneath him any moment.

I looked around to see if we were safely alone. Every Sunday, bikes clogged the path, as though they were cars on Pennsylvania Avenue during the rush hour, but six thirty in the morning wasn't prime cycling time. The pious cyclists must be just awakening for church, and presumably the others were still sleeping off their sins of the night before.

Clumsily, Green dismounted from his bike and waddled toward a log, where I sat whittling.

"What's that?"

"A kosher marshmallow stick," I said. "About that bike?"

"A present. From my cardiologist."

"Then slow down next time." I yawned. "The way you're panting, you'd think he was your funeral director."

Proud of my craft, I handed the stick to Green, who started playing with it.

"Healthier for me than hamburger joints," he said. "Every time I leak a story to you, I gain two pounds."

"Which might explain why you're looking thinner now," I said. "I'm still on your list, aren't I?"

"Jon, I'm here to be serious."

"At six in the morning you'd better be."

"I mean it, Jon. Extraserious. He's dead. My source." Green fumbled around in the pocket of the absurd jogging outfit. "Here. From your own paper, yesterday's."

A yawner of a story reported "a freak accident." Enigmatically a Volkswagen had plunged off the fifth tier of a parking garage owned by Duke Odysseus, Solomon's friend. Only the clipping didn't mention the garage owner, just the address, which I recognized.

"Careful," Green said. "This could get close to home."

"You know how much I love on-street parking."

"Something else. Notice it says Wentworth worked for Internal Revenue?"

"Meaning?"

"CIA. He was a liaison man. Between the two."

I gazed at the clip, and read aloud, "'It appears that workmen may have misplaced temporary barriers used to keep drivers from going over the side.'"

"So," I asked, "appearances are a little misleading?"

"Like the directions in the garage," Green said. "Someone threw up a temporary pointer to guide Wentworth off the edge. The way the garage slanted, that did the job."

Absentmindedly, he started flexing my kosher marshmallow stick.

"You're lucky, Jon. It could have been you. Plan B."

"Not worthy of Plan A, huh? You've hurt my feelings."

"Well, work hard enough," Green said, "and maybe you'll make the next Plan A."

"There. You've restored my self-esteem." I wondered when the stick would break. "But why me? I've got enough reasons to be paranoid."

"Let's just say you were getting close. To some very sensitive relationships."

"For instance?" I asked.

"Well, the buildings," Green said. "The CIA, it's been subsidizing them since the fifties. Solomon's. To help him be the low bidder."

Suddenly I remembered the partnership papers and my scholarly argument with my think-tank friend over whether Hilton Kahn was a spook. If Hilton could marry Donna Stackelbaum, I supposed he could be patriotically nefarious.

"Hilton Kahn. Name mean anything to you?"

Green snapped the marshmallow stick.

"Apple and Foster," I said. "They're in this somehow."

"Sorry about your stick."

"Come on, Fred. Just tell me about Apple and Foster."

"It's very delicate, Jon."

"Fred, you bastard."

"I'll tell you. Just whatever you do, stay away from Odysseus Parking."

What better proof that bicyclists lived longer, healthier lives? I glanced at my Gitane. "Always chain it to a tree, huh? So what's A&F's tie to the CIA?"

"Just that Chubb Apple was one of the people who started it. I mean, he has been known to advise presidents from time to time."

"Gotcha."

"He's still on their contract board. The CIA's."

"But why Solomon?" I asked. "Why's he king of the leases?"

"Because A&F crowned him."

"Because he grew up with an A&F man named Shelton Philips?"

Green nodded. "And was susceptible to a little patriotism mixed in with free enterprise. He thinks he's making flags with Betsy Ross. Protecting the country. Letting the spooks know what's going on in the rest of the government."

"How?"

"Why burgle a building if the landlord has the keys? Plus, he builds in a few extras. Like hidden microphones."

"With a little encouragement from Eddy Bullard?"

Green trembled just slightly. I set my pad aside, picked up a twig near the log, and started whittling another kosher marshmallow stick.

"I know all about Vulture's Point," I said. "The ninety thou, the investment."

"What's wrong with a little old-fashioned corruption? Especially if Bullard was on a Senate committee overseeing GSA. While also working on some matters relating to the CIA."

"But I thought Apple and Foster cleared the way for—"

"Those contract board meetings." Green laughed. "They almost have to call the police. Everybody squabbling over the spoils. All the different factions."

"I thought spooks had better manners."

"In public," he said. "The final irony is that the people on the contract board cancel each other out half the time. Which leaves poor Solomon on his own. Forced to bribe congressmen directly like any other contractor."

"Just out of curiosity," I said. "How come Bullard's no longer an investor in Vulture's?"

"Because he thought one of the factions was about to expose him next time he was up for reelection."

"Who?"

"I'm not saying."

"And that's why he was blackmailing Harold Jones a few years later—fear of exposure?"

"Save your tears," Green said. "They've made up. Harold Jones is going to be a very rich man someday. He's got the building all picked out. The one Solomon's going to build with Jones as an investor."

"And the beneficiary of an interest-free loan?"

"You're almost cynical enough to trade jobs with me."

"This is ridiculous. A murder, and we're talking about some fucking buildings. Can't you give me the details? Like who did it? Exactly who?"

"No."

"Come on, Fred. At least tell me what it involves. That liaison."

"You pay your taxes, don't you?"

"Every five years."

"Then don't worry about your CIA file," Green said. "Plus the proprietaries. Suppose you're a sewing machine company, and your books show you purchased three hundred thousand in bazookas. Internal Revenue might have a few questions."

"Or suppose you're a government landlord secretly subsidized by a faction at the CIA. You might even ask for a little Research Assistance."

"What?"

"The Research Assistance Section at Vulture's Point," I said. "I know all about it."

"Good—then I won't have to tell you more."

"You can if you want."

"No!"

"At least tell me about the building. Vulture's."

"So? They'll just get the people out. It's a long-term thing. You've got months, maybe years, before it goes; well, assuming it does. Just another bet for Solomon. You think he got rich just putting his money into the bank?"

"Well, Lincoln, at least," I said. "But the interest rates. If Solomon's so wired into things, why didn't he even know about that change in the interest rates? The one that caused him to cheapen the construction of the building."

"Factional quarreling and a few broken connections," Green said. "But it's all taken care of."

"With the addition of Christopher Marns to the list of Solomon investors?"

Green smiled.

"How's he making out on the contract board?" I attempted.

"Who says he's on it?"

"I'm asking."

"I'm not saying, What you've got to keep in mind is that Sy Solomon isn't entirely his own man. He's a creation of Apple and Foster. And they've got their own quarrels. Which caused him to lose support just when he needed it. Can't tell you everything. Just that it happened when everything seemed to be clicking into place on the building."

"Then why'd he go ahead?"

"You'd have to ask Solomon."

"Because his father wanted to be a tax—Never mind."

"What?"

"Never mind," I said. "All this bungling, all this quarreling, I still don't believe it."

"Just because they're crooks doesn't mean they're always competent about it."

"You seem to know a lot, Fred."

"Oh, I get around."

"And you're talking now because Wentworth's dead?"

Green nodded. "I'm ambivalent. If it makes the papers, fine. If it doesn't, then fine."

"I suppose you'll next tell me McWilliams is still CIA," I said.

Green just kept playing with the remains of the marshmallow stick.

"Tell me, Fred. Not that I believed them, but those rumors—about you and the CIA?"

"Jon, Jon." Green sighed. "If I was a spook, do you think I'd tell you?"

Chapter 25

McWilliams puffed a fist-sized cloud of smoke, and I started staring into his cold, sharklike eyes.

"You'd better snap out of it fast, pal, or we're going to have to let you go."

"But a murder—"

"Enough of your babble. Just who do you think you are, Stone? Once and for all—you're Metro Desk. Because, pal, you couldn't cut it in the big time."

"But we'll investigate?"

"Pal, we've got better things to do than check out your rumors," McWilliams said.

"If it's such a lowly rumor, how come you're so uptight about it?"

"I don't like that word 'uptight.' You talk English here."

"Yes, Professor Higgins."

"You're sick, pal. CIA this, CIA that. You snot, you think the CIA runs the entire world."

"Only the Northern Hemisphere."

"Out, Stone! And watch your language. I don't like the way you're speaking to me."

"From now on," I said, "I'll get you angry but never uptight."

"Stone! Out!" Mac fixed his eyes on the Rolex.

As I was leaving the Shark's Cage, Wendy Blevin bumped into me; or, perhaps in my daze, I bumped into her.

She wore a billowing peasant dress, which hardly flattered her, but her hair was still light blond, still long, her cheekbones still high, and I decided she was the most aristocratic-looking serf I'd seen in a long time.

Wendy brushed off the part of her dress that had touched me—as if, subconsciously, she were ridding herself of dirt.

"Sorry," I said.

"Oh—it was probably my fault." Her voice wavered; uneasily she studied my face. "Nothing's wrong, is there?"

"Oh, no," I lied.

"That's good."

But she'd paled anyway at the sight of me, as though I were suffering a communicable disease rather than a possibly terminal career.

ഇൻൟ

Sy Solomon will apologize.

Not to me. Just to his good friends Eddy Bullard and George McWilliams.

They're all guffawing around an antique table, with Mac dressed as if at a ratty bar, except that his sneakers rest on two-hundred-year-old oak. He and the others are smoking Cuban cigars, part of a cache from Eddy's summit with Fidel. Maybe the United States won't invade Papudo.

No one else is in the room—certainly not me. I must only imagine; for this is the most exclusive party-party in the free world, the White House Poker Game.

Sy is the dealer, and he will apologize because the $3,000 he has laid out on the table is only Monopoly money.

"What's this shit?" asks the president of the United States.

"Eddy, please. We must be careful. That reporter—"

"Christ, I thought we had that motherfucker off our back two weeks ago."

McWilliams laughs. "Come on, Eddy, where's your sense of humor? The real stuff—do you think Sy'd fuck around with anything but?"

Sy fidgets.

"Well, you have it, don't you?" Mac says, half-jovially, half-accusatorially.

"What?"

"The *real* money, you fucker."

Sy is silent.

"Hey, pal, I like your joke, but let's start."

"All right." Sy begins dealing.

"But you have it, don't you?"

"Forgive me," Sy says.

Mac scowls.

"Because," Sy says, "I respect the law."

"Sy," Eddy says, with affectionate exasperation. "Are you saying you've never broken it?"

"No, no, Eddy, you don't understand. I'm just saying we must be careful."

"Careful?" Mac says. "There's just the three of us."

"Please—appearances. That's all."

"Appearances, my ass! You mean to say I'd compromise my integrity for three thousand bucks? And Eddy—do you mean to say he'd—What the fuck's gotten into you?"

Sy turns up his palms. "Please—I'm sorry. The toy money—you can trade it for the real stuff next time."

ဢOၐ

Even though Luci Elkins was prancing, she looked uncharacteristically scholarly one day on the way to the Shark's Cage. The First Hairdresser was wearing thick-framed glasses and carrying a pile of hardback books.

Then I noticed the titles. They all were astrology books—everything from *The Science of Sun Signs* to *Better Sex under the Zodiac.*

I recalled Mac's contempt for astrology. He'd dropped the daily horoscope column lest it detract from the *Telegram's* journalistic integrity. And yet there was his girlfriend walking through the city room with several pounds of disreputable reading matter.

Just why had Mac made her his lover? The only explanation must be akin to one I'd heard about some macho street dudes who wore high heels and feminine earrings. If they could do that to show they took their masculinity for granted, then Mac could flourish his intellect by way of a dumb girlfriend. Or, I was thinking, his power—because Mac hardly had to flaunt his IQ.

Washington's other editors needed smart wives and lovers. But Mac had risen so high that his status could survive the dimmest woman.

Of course he might cherish Luci not for her striking idiocy but—astrology books notwithstanding—mostly for her obedience. They could well split if he met an equally pliable young woman with a discreet sense of irony.

When Luci walked past me that day, her prance was spirited enough to suggest she jogged regularly with Ms. Bullard. Luci came from South Carolina but seemed an unholy melding of Washington and Los Angeles. Her fingernails were a bright, unnerving orange, the shade of her hair, and they looked acrylic.

Suddenly she turned around: "How come you're staring at me?"

"Oh, not at you," I said. "Just your books."

"My books?"

"I'm terribly interested in astrology," I fibbed. "I'm Aquarian."

"Me, too."

"Congratulations."

"So's Mac. He's so full of peace and love." There was not a decibel of sarcasm in her voice, just pride.

"A very loving person, huh?"

"But working on his chart is so scary," Luci said. "He's on the cusp, you know. People like that, they're capable of absolute greatness."

I wondered how Luci's orange fingernails and astrology books could ever fit within McWilliams's mini-Versailles in millionaire country.

A few years back, when Mac demanded a story for immediate vetting and his facsimile machine was broken, I had actually gone there and beheld the sights myself amid the French baroque on his stereo.

I recalled the floor-to-ceiling bookshelves laden with Greek, Roman, and French literature; Marie-Antoinette vases; a butterfly cabinet worthy of the actual Versailles; and, fittingly for Mac, a replica of an old astronomical clock.

Our self-made Louis XIV had even bought an oil painting by Hyacinthe Rigaud, a favorite of the Sun King.

Like the one and only Luci, MacVersailles existed just to please McWilliams, not impress his pragmatically chosen friends, for whom the right French restaurant or his apartment in town would usually suffice.

Mac did not simply own the books and other objects within his Versailles. He truly knew them. As shared in good faith by The Elephant, he could quote page after page of Proust, dissect and reassemble the clock, and recall battles won and lost by the general in the Rigaud.

I could just see Mac alertly devouring *Remembrance of Things Past* for the eleventh time, taking a moment out to fondle a centuries-old vase, while Luci fell asleep over a copy of *TV Guide*.

He had spent his money and leisure so tastefully that it was distasteful even for his enemies to question the origins of his fortune.

With Luci blabbering so mindlessly away in the newsroom, I felt like steering the conversation to Solomon and his propensity for dispensing gifts to Bullard's friends, including her. But that would be useless. Everyone in town knew she'd remained First Hairdresser by never discussing money or politics with the wrong people. Luci would hardly be likely to tell me how Solomon personified the combination of the two.

"Would you like me to do your chart?" Luci asked.

"Maybe."

"You're not afraid to know yourself, are you?"

"Often."

"A true Aquarian loves everyone, beginning with themselves," Luci said.

We might as well be one huge family with an official creed.

"I just can't get over how well-read you are," I prattled.

"Oh, very," Luci said. "I belong to the Astrological Book Society. It's only a dollar for the first book, and you only have to order three."

"Terrific."

"I joined because I wanted to further my education." Luci smiled at me and held her books more tightly; it was as if, when she hugged them, they could transmit their wisdom.

Chapter 26

Just as Willie Stark was on the verge of being corrupted, the *Late Show* flickered out.

"Can we fix it?" Margo asked, as I snapped off the television.

"*All the King's Men*," I said, "couldn't put this set together again."

"But you said it's your favorite."

"The picture tube's shot." I leaned over in bed and kissed her left ear. "Just remember, kid, man is conceived in sin ... born in corruption ... He passeth from the stink of the didie to the stench of the shroud."

"All right," Margo said, "so you know your Robert Penn Warren."

"'There is always something!'"

Suddenly we heard glass breaking against the floor of the apartment above us.

Then a woman's voice shrilled through my ceiling: "If you have one spark of decency in you." Next came the sound of a body thumping against the floor, and a frantic shriek: "I want to go away! I want to go away!"

"What's going on?" Margo asked,

"Just Stanley and Stella fighting."

"Who?"

"Stanley and Stella Kowalski," I said.

"Jonathan! That's not funny. Someone must be beating the daylights out of that woman."

Margo rolled to the side of the bed and snatched the phone off the floor.

"What are you doing?"

"Calling the police, what else?" she said. "That poor woman."

"But it's just Bob and Sally Blattdorf. Every few weeks they try to get horny by—"

"Killing each other?"

"—by acting out *A Streetcar Named Desire*. This is the scene where Stanley throws the radio out the window. Only, the Blattdorfs use a

Coke bottle on the kitchen floor. They're nice people, actually. He works on the Hill, and she's an attorney with EPA."

"Worried about the disposal of the Coke bottle?"

"It's a fetish, I guess, a literary fetish. Bob, he's no more than a hundred and thirty pounds. And Sally—I've seen better Stellas. A mousy, sexless little thing. But every few weeks, well, I hear these strange sounds."

"And you got up the nerve to ask about it," Margo said.

"After they'd just moved in. When I was still afraid it was murder."

"It sounds like it."

"Oh no," I said, "that's only Scene Three of Act I."

"I've never heard this before," Margo said, "not when I've been up here before."

"Well, they must have forgotten to restock their Coke bottles. Anyway—it's good, cheap psychodrama."

"Bizarre."

"If it were normal," I said, "it wouldn't be psychodrama. Besides, who are they hurting?"

"Well, it makes me feel uncomfortable," Margo said.

There was a silence, a long one, and then I started caressing Margo, though just briefly, for she pulled my hand off her. "What?"

"I'm not in the mood," she said.

"Translate."

"I'm just not."

"Don't tell me you're still down on me for the cathedral." Earlier that weekend I'd somehow overcome my distaste for pomp and accompanied my Episcopalian princess on a tour of Washington National Cathedral. For a rector's daughter, she was reassuringly agnostic.

"All right, yes! I didn't like it at all, Jonathan, the way you looked at the moon rock." The cathedral had a moon rock embedded in a stained-glass window; that was factual—the rest baffled me.

"So," I asked, "what was offensive about the look?"

"Well, the way you were smiling. As if you felt it were campy."

"We're in mind-reading territory."

"Well, you looked like you felt that way. And the guide—she was just a few feet away. Jonathan, Jonathan, haven't you any regard for other people's feelings?"

"I'm flattered. Was I really worth the attention?"

"You have no respect," Margo said.

"How about a little respect for my libido?"

"Not after that shit you gave me on the way back," she said.

"Hey, watch it, we're talking about a church."

"The idea—giving it a price tag as if it were a housing project!"

"So you'll forget it?" I said. "Seventy-five million and still counting."

"I don't care if it's a billion."

"But seventy-five million, think how many housing projects that would be!"

"I don't think that's a fair comparison at all," Margo said. "I mean, anyone can pray there, rich or poor."

"Jesus Christ," I said. "I thought you were an agnostic."

"I am, but ..."

"You're still worried that Daddy will strike you with a thunderbolt?"

"Jonathan, for all I know he's an agnostic."

"Then why the fuss?"

"You won't feel offended, will you?"

"Probably," I said, "but go ahead."

"All right. You have no appreciation. Not unless it's a book. Nothing for art, nothing for architecture. Nothing for—"

"That's a lie. Just because I don't talk about them doesn't mean I don't know about them."

"Just housing projects."

"So I mentioned housing projects. They're ugly, all right?"

"That's not what I mean," Margo said.

"They're like barracks. Army barracks. So we'll just think in terms of how many libraries seventy-five million dollars could have paid for."

"Libraries, books, that's what I mean."

"All right, so we'll think in terms of how many libraries could have been built with gargoyles."

Margo got out of bed and started putting on her underwear. "Just a minute!" I said. "Frankly, I think there's something else."

"What?"

"Something else besides my views on moon rocks."

"What?"

"Somebody else," I said.

"What?"

"You're looking for an excuse to break up. Which is why you insisted we go to the cathedral in the first place."

"Break up?" Margo protested. "Who said you had exclusive rights? You don't own me. You don't even lease me."

"Well, we've been seeing each other often enough. I just assumed."

A muscle in one of Margo's cheeks twitched.

"Oh, I get it," I said.

"Jonathan, don't press me!"

"Why not? What's there to lose?"

"Do you really want to know?"

"Which I suppose means that I've already squeezed out an answer."

"Yes!"

"Who?"

"How do you know it's one?" Margo asked.

"Is it somebody or some bodies?"

"Are we going through that nympho shit again?"

"Okay, so I was only your third."

"Jonathan, did it ever occur to you I might still like Number Two?"

"So it's somebody. Singular."

"I think he is."

"Will the mystery man please step out from behind the screen?" I said.

"You've already seen him, maybe. When you were in my office."

"Who, then? You never would discuss Two."

"Jonathan—credit me with a little tact."

"Who?"

"All right! The man at the desk near Elsie Fogart."

"Wearing the three-piece suit?"

"His name's Tom Newley."

"When did he come to GSA?"

"Why?"

"Just curious, that's all."

"Seven years ago."

"I thought so. A Nixon type if ever I saw one, civil service exam, or not."

"You only saw him once."

"But the look on his face. All business."

"He is business. Which is why I like him."

"What?"

"Do you think I feel comfortable about this?"

"Him, you mean."

"No, you. Your being a reporter."

"Jesus Christ, that's history, medieval and beyond."

"If you've left the *Telegram*, that's news to me."

"Come on! How often do I pump you about what's happening at work? I thought we cleared that up once and for all."

"But that's not the point."

"If I wanted to fuck my way to a story—Jesus Christ, do you think I'd waste so much time screwing around with a GS-7? Besides, I thought you wanted to help me."

"Jonathan, I'm not saying that's your motive." Pause. "It's just weird. You being a reporter."

"But you worked for the *Review*, for Chrissake."

"As arts editor. I don't go barging into people's lives—like that horrid Blevin woman."

I was halfway tempted to tell Margo about Wendy's Anacostia friends, the less-than-so-so garbage collections, and the manure dump on the sanitation bureaucrat's lawn. Wendy was not a gossip monster to me or countless others. From dishwashers to clerks, or uppity *Telegram* reporters, plebes relished the way she put the pompous in their place.

Wendy was part of the natural ecology, not so different from the bears I'd seen along the Appalachian Trail—the ones that, left to themselves, would much rather eat blueberries than me, so long as I was careful with my trash.

"So," I defended Wendy, "no one's supposed to write anything about anyone? Or get 'em photographed? What is this? Have you gone Amish on me or something?"

"Just promise," Margo said. "You won't write about me. Ever."

I shook my head. "Promise. You're neither famous nor infamous. Just comfortably obscure."

"I like my privacy, that's all."

"Look, I'm not Wendy."

"I remember something," Margo said. "A classmate of mine. Her sister, and this wreck—the photograph they published!"

"They?"

"Your paper. Right in the middle of a bridge, her face all cut up, and they put it on the front page."

Oh, the story I could have told! Instead, however, I remained silent, hands shaking.

"Jonathan, is anything wrong?"

"No."

"Well, I might as well get it out. Tom proposed the other day."

"So? I thought you were too liberated for that stuff."

"You really don't know me, do you?"

"Ah! Behold this marvel, this complex woman, this Jamesian heroine!"

"At least he respects me. And cathedrals, I might add. He majored in Greek history. He wants to go to Greece on our honeymoon."

"That's pretty good," I said. "An expert in Greek cathedrals."

"The reporter at work—always stereotyping people. X is a liberal, a lover of the arts. Y is a conservative, a Babbitt."

"A fine future—you and your Nixon man and his Greek cathedrals."

"Do you think they'd have kept him if he wasn't any good. For your information, Jonathan, he's up for a sixteen."

"How long have you dated him?"

"Oh, off and on ever since I started at GSA. But more these past few weeks."

"And you might marry?"

"I didn't say that," Margo said. "I'm just trying to take stock of myself."

"What a couple. You and your blue jeans. Him and his three-piece suits. Jesus Christ, I suppose he can always order one in denim."

"Do you really think you're that different?"

"Don't tell me you're accusing me of wearing three-piece suits," I said.

"No. But the skiing trips you keep talking about. And the stereo. And the bike—even the bike. A three-hundred-dollar bicycle. Do you really think you're ready for a monastery?"

"More so than the owner of a sixteen-thousand-dollar car."

"Tom drives a Chevrolet," Margo said, tucking in her shirt, and heading for the door.

"Wait! The story, is that it? Suppose they liked the Solomon story. Suppose McWilliams was patting my head. Suppose I was getting a promotion."

"And you feel I'm walking out on you because you aren't and Tom is?"

I nodded.

"And you want the truth?"

"I'm not sure you're capable of telling it," I said. "And to think I loved you."

"You never said it before."

"I haven't?" I said. "If nothing else, I just assumed ."

"You assume too many things," Margo said. "No wonder McWilliams won't print your stories."

"I assume," I said, "I assume that when I love someone, she's not going to be seeing some creep behind my back. And not just a creep. A CREEP, capital letters."

"But you want the truth."

"Yes. It's the way the story turned out, isn't it?"

"In a way it is. In a way it isn't."

"Speak, oh complex woman."

"It's not the story," Margo said. "Not at all. I still think they're crooks."

"What, then?"

"Don't you see, Jonathan? You can't do it, you can't do it. Your own paper—they're—Face reality, Jonathan. The advertising. You versus all those millions. Yet you went ahead with it anyway, and now look where it got you. You have no sense of reality, Jonathan, none whatsoever. Why, you're every bit as crazy as those kooks upstairs."

"I thought you liked character."

"Character more than characters. "There's a time when stubbornness becomes craziness," Margo said.

"But I thought you believed in it."

"In craziness?"

"The story," I said. "I mean, moving into that building, telling me to be idealistic."

"And now I'm just saying you should be realistic."

"But don't you remember? The time I said I might go into PR, and you said, 'Fuck you!'"

"Jonathan, I'm terribly upset now. Let's give ourselves a vacation and see what happens."

"I'd rather exercise my curiosity in other ways. Please, I love you."

"Good-bye, Jonathan," Margo said as she twisted the doorknob. "Say hello to the Kowalskis for me."

Chapter 27

She was spunky and pretty, the lady at a zoning hearing the next night. A diamond ring gleamed from her finger, and I wondered who her husband was.

A Bullard man? An unreformed Nixonian? A liberal? A conservative? A corrupter, a corruptee, or someone too indignant to partake? It did look like a big ring. Well, stereotyper or not, I was only reflecting the obsessions of my Washington.

I was deep in my musings, half-asleep on the way back to D.C., when an overgrown tractor-trailer began to pass me: a mobile monument to the tenacity of the trucking lobby. Just in time I slammed down the brakes. The nerve of that man. Had I reacted a quarter of a second later, my Plymouth Valiant would have looked like a scrap-metal sculpture at the Hirshhorn.

Then I scolded myself for driving while a zombie. Jesus, Stone, you mustn't die, I thought—lest one of your fellow paranoids waste time investigating a murder.

What about my friends at that radical think tank? If I wasn't careful, they might worry that Sy's teamster partner had decided to do me in. Then I remembered I'd told no one at the institute about my investigation; maybe I should. Not that I looked forward to becoming a media martyr, but I might as well die with a little fanfare. And then I began to think: Who gives a shit about me anyway? Could the think tank round up a journalistic posse to sniff out my killers? I'd be lucky to rate much more than *The Northern Virginia Sun* and the *Alexandria Gazette*.

I pulled into the parking lot of a McDonald's. It was one of the fast-food joints whose customers' cars cluttered up parts of Route 50 like fatty globules clogging an artery.

As I was sipping my coffee, a girl in her late teens put her tray down on my table, the only occupied one. "Mind if I sit here?"

"Oh, no," I said, even if she was a little too pudgy and pimply to suit me. Her red hair was short and unevenly cut, like a Raggedy Ann doll's; maybe some men would like it, but not most normal ones above GS-9. Raggedy's dress was brief, though far from scandalously so. She reminded me of a teenybopper secretary who'd offered her body and bubble gum to me when I was interning on the Hill. Wendy Blevin would have admonished Raggedy Ann to be more adeptly unstylish.

I looked at Raggedy's tray. She had purchased a Coke, apple pie, and a box of McDonaldland Cookies.

"Want one?"

"What?"

"The cookies—the way you're looking at them."

"Thanks, but I'm about to leave."

"Here—have one," she persisted; and I did, rationalizing that I'd better nourish myself and stay alert for the next tractor-trailer.

Raggedy Ann started munching on what had appeared to be the head of Ronald McDonald, and I studied the ingredients label on the cookie box. Ronald and the Pirate Puppet in my mouth were both made of enriched flour, sugar, beef fat, salt, lecithin, and several other substances with unpronounceable names.

I recalled the days I'd stroll into a McDonald's and find young mothers feeding McDonaldland Cookies to children barely old enough to chew their food. Why couldn't the *Telegram's* food editor magically materialize at the right times to warn Raggedy and the mothers before everyone succumbed to cancer or chronic diabetes?

Then I remembered that I'd go back to Washington by way of Route 66, which set me ruminating further. Some people at the think tank had joined a pollution suit against 66's extension into Roxland County, and that in turn reminded me that the air might kill us all before the food or tractor-trailers did.

"You're yawning," Raggedy said. "You been working tonight?"

"That's what I'll tell the boss."

"What do you do?" she asked.

"Well, I'm a typist of sorts," I said.

Raggedy frowned, a normal enough response in a hierarchical place like the Washington area, and my vanity overcame my humor.

"Well, actually I'm a reporter," I said. "I just type what the boss tells me to."

"You mean you take dictation?"

"Well, in a way," I said wearily.

"Gee, I'm sorry—it sounds like you don't have a fun job at all."

I shook my head.

"I work at a fun place," she said.

"Where? Maybe I ought to apply for a job there."

"The FBI," Raggedy said as proudly as if she were Jimmy Stewart in *The FBI Story.*

"Sounds interesting," I said.

"I work with criminals," Raggedy said.

"You must be very brave."

"I take the rap sheets and put them into the computers."

"So if I robbed a bank you'd handle my record."

"You know," she said, "we're not supposed to talk to strangers."

"Which is why you're talking to me."

Raggedy laughed.

"I could get into big trouble," she said.

Imagine the thrill of it all. A conversation with a stranger was just as wicked to her as a cocaine party would have seemed to a normal schmuck.

"Is it really true," I said lightly, "that the Bureau sends an agent out after you if you're late for work?"

"It happened to a friend of mine, someone really stupid. He'd moved to a place without a phone." She stuffed some more McDonaldland cookies into her mouth. "Are you really a reporter?"

"Theoretically."

"I mean, the kind who writes mean stories."

"When my boss lets me."

"I'd better be careful," Raggedy said. "You might write about me."

I thought of Margo. Not another quasi Amishwoman with reinforcement from her bosses?

"Only if you're bad."

"Let's see your identification," she said, in a curious-little-girl way.

I showed my press pass from the Roxland police.

"Then I bet we have your fingerprints."

"So I won't be free to rob a bank."

"You wouldn't really rob a bank, would you?"

"If I don't get my next raise, maybe."

"I don't know whether we should talk more. They have people everywhere."

"Must keep 'em busy. Now I know why they took so long to find Patty Hearst."

I could just envision a scene. A fifty-three-year-old agent, a balding, humorless sort with three children and a sexless wife, would be eagerly watching us through a TV camera hidden in a trash container. He'd envy Raggedy's youth and tape our every word, lest she betray the Bureau and show the slightest susceptibility to natural urges.

How exciting for both Raggedy and the agent. Most government women nowadays could screw half the town without their bosses' reprimanding them; and yet just one indiscreet wink at me might end Raggedy's career and deny her the pleasures of being further spied on.

Or maybe the FBI simply transferred oversexed women to Butte, Montana.

"My mother's a prison guard," Raggedy said out of nowhere. "Does that scare you?"

"Not if I'm not a prisoner. First you have to catch me after I've robbed that bank."

"What's your name?"

"Sy," I said—grateful she'd forgotten my real one on my ID.

"Mine's Jenny." Raggedy, as I persisted in thinking of her, yawned. "I just got off work."

"Late hours, huh?" A believable story. Even I wasn't paranoid enough to think that an FBI had arranged for a redhead to entrap me that night. At the very least I deserved a prettier one.

"They keep the computers going all the time," Raggedy said.

"Criminals arrested every minute, huh?"

"God I'm tired." Her foot brushed against mine. "Excuse me."

"Sure."

"Hey, what do you do in your spare time? I like to go to movies."

"Oh, rob banks."

"No, really."

"Well, I read, and sometimes I go biking."

"I love to ride. We'll have to get together. My roommate's out of town, and I could use a little fun."

"Thanks, but I've got to get to Washington now. See ya."

"Nice meeting you, Sy. You're sure you don't want to?"

"See ya."

We got up at the same time, and I took one last look at Raggedy: The legs were passable and the figure, if pudgy, was ample in one of the places that obsessed me. Maybe I should follow her to her apartment and help her feel truly wicked. Here was a woman used to obeying orders, at least when the boss was looking, and in bed I'd be the boss. Why not screw the FBI literally?

And think of all the files Raggedy might dutifully fetch for me. Imagine penetrating, so to speak, that Third Reich monstrosity on Pennsylvania Avenue. Besides which, I'd welcome a respite from Complex Women. But I felt too tired for sex, even when I watched Raggedy wiggle her rear as she stepped into the parking lot. And suppose, just suppose, she fell in love with me. How would we spend our time out of bed—prancing around at discos or watching reruns of *Charlie's Angels?*

I remembered Margo's ability to puzzle out the most obscure nuances of Fellini films. About her I cared.

Jesus, Stone, I was thinking, you're not cut out to be a successful cad.

Chapter 28

I was putting on my backpacking clothes the next Sunday when a sudden insight dawned.

With Al Bergmann, my buddy from AP, climbing the Tetons, I hadn't any good friends to go to the Shenandoah Mountains with. Margo and our regular hiking expeditions there were gone.

So was Donna Stackelbaum. Her engagement party and my second encounter with her now-fiancé, the liberal and bearded lawyer-lobbyist, had happened without incident. Hilton Kahn and I knew enough about each other to be politely taciturn.

Wishing the couple my best, I'd pooled in with some Langley friends on a gift of a big, four-poster bed, the one, alas, that Hilton, not I, would be sharing with Donna.

Three commissioners from the Nuclear Regulatory Commission came to the wedding. Within two months, Donna and Hilton moved into a five-hundred-and-fifty-thousand-dollar house near the Washington zoo, in celebration of her new job as a lobbyist for Quad-State Atomic.

Bereft of Stackelbaumian hugs, I stretched out on my Donna-less bed—my hiking boots still on—and just stared at the cracks in the ceiling. I thought of Margo, too. The hugs did not come with the same padding, and at least Donna had given me fair warning and acted as an honorable "love buddy," while Margo hadn't exited as gracefully.

Still, I had offered Margo less reason to stay with me; why had I been so shy about the L Word with *her*? Might it have been, paradoxically, because I felt more comfortable around Margo than around Donna, all the more reason to fear marriage in a city with a California-equivalent divorce rate?

I loved Margo's brains, common sense, and quirkiness, and her defiance of the abbots and mothers superior, while Donna aspired to be one of the latter, a rich one at that, no matter how many cooked bass it would take. The kills in the waters outside Quad's nuclear plant were starting to make the newspapers, inspiring picketers to show up with a giant cartoon of a striped bass with a thermometer protruding from its mouth. I wondered if the feds might actually sniff out Donna's fishiness.

Then, groggily, I arose and stumbled forth for my copy of the Sunday *Telegram*.

ಬಂ

Deep inside the *Telegram* I found my zoning story, the one that had kept me up half the night Thursday.

I glanced at the back of the Metro section. A full-page advertisement boasted of Solomon's newest condominium project, Buckingham Manor, a moated series of town houses that were reached by way of a drawbridge. I supposed it would be raised if too many blacks moved into the area.

Some yellowing papers in the GSA files came to mind. I hadn't quite figured out why the agency had let me see them, except that maybe the censors' eyes had blinked at the wrong times, or the things were considered too old to be dangerous.

The papers revealed a hole in Solomon's character, a nasty nook hidden under his plaque from the Anti-Defamation League. As late as the Kennedy years, his apartments in Virginia had been turning away blacks, even GS-18s, and invoking excuses weak enough to be insulting.

Solomon had reformed only when the Labor Department threatened to pull out of one of his buildings. Why couldn't I have brought that up with E.J. and McWilliams? Mac, if tolerant toward thieves, never condoned bigots.

I turned on my FM radio, hoping to lose myself in Vivaldi, but all that did, somehow, was to depress me. Oh, to get even with the bastard who'd taken me off the investigation! I reflected some more on Solomon and his leases and the gaps in my research, and vowed to ferret out the truth about the dead CIA man and the missteered Volkswagen.

ಬಂ

And so I drove through the mugginess to Prince George's County, where I wouldn't have expected to find myself on a Sunday, or to find CIA widows at any time. On my way to Susan Wentworth's, I passed row after row of grubby garden apartments—the legacy of developers whose ethics made those in Roxland County look like priests.

Prince George's was to the Washington area what West Virginia is to the United States. The people were poorer. Some of the land was rutted and pitted. It was not coal country. It was land-speculation country, and the developers' dozers had gnawed away at many of the natural watersheds.

There were a few nice parts of Prince George's, however, where the inhabitants were sufficiently well-off to wish they were living in McLean.

One such place was Sark-on-the-Potomac—it was across the river from Mount Vernon Plantation, and all the streets bore Scottish names.

The main road was called Loch Ness Boulevard; there were at least half a dozen Loch Nesses in the Washington suburbs; I suppose bureaucrats and military officers felt a secret kinship with deep-water monsters.

Sark's architecture was international in the most offensive way. I saw pagodas with Doric columns, Moorish homes topped by aluminum roofs, and pseudo-Colonials with Air Force insignias painted on the garage doors. Although most of Sark's houses sold in the hundred-fifty-thousand-dollar range, the lots were tiny.

At least a dozen of the better known zoning crooks lived there, lawyers and county officials alike, and I was delighted. I loved the idea of their oversized homes being squeezed onto tiny lots. It was as if they were being punished for having squandered the land in the rest of the county.

But the Wentworth home wasn't like the others. I could see that the family valued privacy over display, for thick bushes and trees hid the house from the road, and the old frame farmhouse, if not a shack, was hardly a showplace either.

The yard was big, almost two acres, and the grass was half a foot high, a contrast to the places across the street, where the lawns looked as if they'd been clipped by a gardener on loan from an estate. In the driveway I saw another Volkswagen, and I decided that the Wentworths probably regarded homes and cars the way Wendy

Blevin did clothes. They felt secure enough not to demand the very best.

I knocked. When she answered the door, Mrs. Wentworth was wearing a faded blue garden dress. Her hair was long and well combed, but her face was tanned and wrinkled enough to upset the calmest dermatologist; I suspect she couldn't make up her mind whether to be outdoorsy or beautiful. I identified myself, and said Fred Green had sent me, something already known to Mrs. Wentworth.

Inside, I sat down in a Victorian love seat. Paintings of marshes and beaches covered most of the walls, and I saw wooden mallards on the floor but no trophies or guns. The bookshelves were full of books on nature and magazines published by the Audubon Society and the Sierra Club, and a grand piano caught my eye, too, as well as the absence of anything electronic—no TV, no stereo, nothing. Presumably Robert Wentworth had been a spook with old-fashioned tastes.

"I like your house," I said—not only to please Mrs. Wentworth but also because I loathed her neighbors'.

"I wish you'd tell the Health Department. The day after the funeral—can you imagine?—this man comes to the door and says someone across the street is put off by the grass. You'd think they'd have waited longer, wouldn't you? When Robert was alive ... Well, I said we'd checked the ordinances, and there was nothing that said we had to cut it all the time."

"You have trees in front, anyway."

"Robert and I—we never liked to cut it. We liked it perfectly well when it was long. The dandelions and all that. But the Health Department man—all he cared about was the mosquitoes. Well, I told that horrible man we don't have any. They wouldn't dare show up—they're not welcome here. And then"—Mrs. Wentworth sat up very straight in her captain's chair—"I told that man to get out. That he was unwanted. I said, 'You're a mosquito.' The gall of those people. Twenty-five years we've lived here, and then someone buys one of those boxes across the street and tells us we have mosquitoes!

"That whole crowd, Mr. Stone—I don't like them at all. Now the people up the road—they're human. Good friends of ours. Bought their house before those boxes went up. But the people in that development—why, it's as if they're living for the day when their bosses come over for dinner. Nothing must be out of place. Every shrub, every blade of grass—everything's got to be perfectly trimmed. No imagination, Mr. Stone—they have no imagination. Everything's got to be in perfect order. Well, I don't doubt you could say the same thing about Disneyland."

Huskily, Mrs. Wentworth laughed. "If Mickey Mouse worked for the Department of Commerce, he'd live in Sark."

"Mrs. Wentworth," I said, "I'd like to talk about what happened in that garage."

Susan Wentworth looked me right in the eye—as if to add a little exclamation point ahead of her statements about the events inside Duke Odysseus's garage.

"We don't know for sure," she said.

"Fred Green says."

"Fred Green says a lot of things." Mrs. Wentworth protested.

"So it wasn't murder?"

"I'm not saying—either way."

"But the way the garage slanted, and the way that sign was apparently moved—well, you'd think."

"You can think whatever you want, Mr. Stone," Mrs. Wentworth said. "I'm just saying I don't know it was murder."

"How much did your husband know about the contract board?"

"Presumably as much as Fred Green told you. Robert and I, we talked it over—everything he'd tell Green."

"You mean to say he talked about his work that much with you—"

"Sometimes, Mr. Stone, a marriage vow is more binding than a security oath."

"Well," I asked, "who in the Agency might want to murder him?"

Mrs. Wentworth shrugged. "It could be any number of people. Let me think about this. No! I'm not giving you any names."

"Just the observation that your husband worked with potential murderers."

"That's your conclusion," she said sharply, "not mine."

"I know this is a time of grief for you"—Jesus, if I had to sound like a mortician, couldn't I be less banal about it?—"but wouldn't you like to know how your husband died?"

"What's that going to do—reincarnate him?"

"But if he was murdered."

"Don't you see, don't you see?—there are some things beyond knowing."

"But you're a fighter, aren't you? Why, you were just telling me about that Health Department man."

"Mr. Stone, we're not dealing with people fearful of mosquitoes. It's very easy to murder in the name of national security."

"You mean national security mixed in with a little corruption," I said. "To get Solomon those leases."

"If you haven't any concern for your own life, at least think of my husband."

"But he's dead."

"His reputation, Mr. Stone. We're not talking for quotation, are we?"

Reluctantly, I shook my head.

"Then, Mr. Stone, I'll tell you the truth. My husband was an alcoholic."

"Meaning?"

"Well, the obvious. The autopsy. It showed enough alcohol in the blood to suggest that maybe—Well, you understand now, don't you?"

"Well, not quite," I said. "Lots of people are alcoholics. It's no disgrace."

"Well, it was to him. He was quite touchy about it. No morality. Just pride. And you're got to remember the survivors' benefits. I've still got three children in college."

"And you're suggesting that the CIA might take away the benefits?"

Mrs. Wentworth nodded. "Mr. Stone, would you please leave now?"

"But your husband," I said. "Don't you think you owe it to him to find out the truth?"

"I owe him nothing but to stay alive and well and keep collecting those benefits for our children. Good day, Mr. Stone."

My back was aching somewhat when I arose from the Victorian love seat. Its cushion had seemed as hard and firm as its owner.

୫୦୯ଓ

My car's air-conditioning wheezed out on me as I was returning from Sark. Perhaps a real ecology fiend wouldn't have minded, but it was a hundred degrees at noon, the asphalt was shimmering, and I was sweating like a Saint Bernard in the middle of the Sahara. The Founding Fathers should never have let the capital be built on such uninhabitable real estate.

I found myself warming up to memories of my favorite syndicated columnist published in the Marseilles paper. Dr. George Washington Crane was a chipmunk-faced old reactionary who, despite his rants against welfare mothers, had some very sound ideas. One of his best was to move the capital to Colorado; no longer would congressmen be tempted by the evil distractions of the East. I supposed that skiing, if diverting, was at least wholesomely so.

When I got home, I was still feeling relatively immortal, so once again I defied the nutrition editor and good sense and started heating up another TV dinner.

I was looking upon carcinogens and cholesterol the way Mrs. Wentworth scorned mosquitoes; they wouldn't dare—I'd live to be 101. A few decades into the next century, the president would sign a bureaucratproof Freedom of Information Act, and I'd try not to dodder too much when the TV cameras panned in on me at the ceremony.

As a centenarian, I'd finally be old enough to feel respectable and comfortable. It would all follow in the great tradition of Upton Sinclair's being wheeled into the White House for a presidential benediction. Ah, the glory. Then I began laughing. Imagine looking forward to being fawned over by a politician; I must be senile already.

The phone rang. If that was Eddy Bullard issuing the White House invitation ahead of time, he had better watch it. I wouldn't go unless he cleaned up the leasing program.

୫୦୯ଓ

An angry New York accent greeted me. "Why didn't you check with me?" Fred Green raged. "Mrs. Wentworth called."

"I did talk to her today."

"Why, Jon?"

"My investigation—what else?"

"What investigation?"

"Why, the buildings and the garage," I said indignantly.

"I thought it was through."

"I never said that."

"Didn't McWilliams call you off the story?"

"He can call me off the story—he can call me vile names. But that doesn't mean—"

"What's the fucking point of it all? Why'd you bother Mrs. Wentworth? You knew ahead of time it wasn't going into the paper."

"Was she upset?" I asked.

"She was crying."

"She seemed to answer the questions fairly calmly."

"Lay off!"

"But you're the one who helped get me into this! You encouraged me!" I took the offensive: "And furthermore, I'd be interested in knowing if you have any other leads in mind."

"I don't do casework," Green said.

"What the fuck?" I protested. He was treating me as if I were a crank complaining about a late Social Security check.

"You've already said your own paper won't touch the story. So why should I help you?"

"Because we've known each other for years."

"And I'm supposed to grant you special favors?"

"I'll publish it freelance if need be."

"You know how McWilliams feels about moonlighting," Green said, and abruptly hung up.

80C03

I tried to reach Margo repeatedly over the next few weeks. But I might as well have been seeking to interview the administrator of GSA about how Bullard had blackmailed him.

When I called her house, she was never the one picking up the phone—which was strange, considering that she liked to curl up on a couch near it in the living room and devour old gossip about

Charlemagne. In a perverse way I was pleased. At least she was thinking about me enough not to answer.

I went there on several evenings and knocked without a reply, even though the light in the peephole briefly darkened. How long until Margo forgot about me and settled down to marriage with her Nixonian friend? Maybe they'd already picked out a house in Sark.

After a while, I retreated from Complex Women, again—in fact, from everything and everybody Complex. I went about my zoning stories in a nice robotic way. And during my off-hours I began to live and think like a mortal instead of a *Telegram* reporter.

I even started dating women in the Raggedy Ann vein—a dental hygienist, a lingerie saleslady, and a grocery clerk—and I decided there were no Simple People, just less pretentious ones.

Several times I went tavern-hopping with a buddy from the back shop of the *Telegram*, Clay Bronski, who was old and bent and outwardly had nothing in common with me except that we were both Dodgers fans. I had *almost* been of a contrary enough nature to root for the Dodgers during games with the Senators long ago.

Both teams were often underdogs, but the Dodgers always seemed calmer about it. Washington is never a good town for losers.

My friend Bronski would nod when I raised that point; then he'd cut short my learned analysis and return to his own Dodgers arcana, such as whether Preacher Roe had thrown as many spitballs as he'd confessed. Clay could tell me everything; he had been a Dodgers shortstop before his legs gave out. I might soon be reaching the point in my own career where I could empathize all too well.

Clay had lost heavily in a bowling alley franchise, started over again as a printer, and was doing fine until his eyes began deteriorating like his legs. From time to time he'd summon me to the back shop, and I'd help him with the pasteup sheets when his supervisor wasn't watching. I'd have thought that McWilliams would have cherished Bronski. Yet he never looked upon him as an old Dodger, just a bumbling man who was a nuisance on deadline.

McWilliams might have been from Brooklyn, but he was committed to Winning. Socioeconomic climbing wasn't the only reason Mac had moved away from there—he'd always said he felt better cheering for the Yankees.

Chapter 29

Roxland County had tucked the press quarters away in the attic under one of the courthouse cupolas. Lighting and air-conditioning were feeble, and the dominant furnishings were nineteen-forty-ish armchairs and Eisenhower-era couches. Roxland's press room reminded me of the courthouse hacks themselves, somnolently stuffy.

To keep awake and informed, the room's regulars tuned in police calls on a portable radio. And it was through the little Motorola, rather than the sleepy flack at the courthouse, that I learned of the collapse of Vulture's Point.

I sprinted out to my Valiant and drove past the hamburger stands and pizza parlors of Roxland County, past the pseudo-Colonial homes—my stomach nauseous over the thought that I might never again see Margo, and hug her and kiss her, and help her forget about the moon rock and the three-piece denim suit and the Greek cathedrals and every other syllable of our argument.

And then I started remembering another event, a News Event, Kent State, which was really a private event, too, since the dead boy from Marseilles had been just a few years younger than I. The paper had asked me to write the obituary and interview the parents after they'd learned of their son's death from a clumsy-tongued rewrite man. All over Ohio, people had argued the worth of Life vs. Property. Kent's ROTC armory had been burned down, and a number of Marseilleans favored the latter.

My mind returned to that funeral and the way it had changed me. Once again I recalled the mourners waiting in their Fords and Chevies for a Norfolk & Western train to rumble out of the way. A school bus had stalled there the next year, and later an old man had died when a wire shorted in one of the warning signals. Then came the mayor's promise that a bridge would rise over the tracks, then delays and delays and more delays, and finally silence, except for the soft, purposeless rustle of paper in some feckless bureaucrat's office.

So Vulture's and Skyline would not be the first times I'd seen Life lose to Property.

And yet, hurrying toward the Point and the gore there, I resolved to try to show Seymour Solomon whatever fairness I could summon up. I remembered how one of the dead boy's acquaintances had wandered into my newsroom. He'd filled up a cassette tape, talking about the National Guard firing at the students and the Marseillan flinging rocks toward the guardsmen just before a bullet blew his skull open. I'd asked the survivor to elaborate on the rocks, and he'd backed off and said his memory must have fuzzed.

I'd looked at his greasy sweatshirt and torn jeans and decided he was not a man to weigh his words. And after that, I had mistrusted everything else he'd told me, and the tapes had ended up in my wastebasket rather than in an archive.

The following day, after the janitor had collected the trash, I'd marveled at how easily you could throw History away, except I knew in his case that I'd consigned not it, but slander, to nothingness. Suppose the survivor had come in with immaculate clothes—and without a stammer and an air of uncertainty. Suppose he hadn't recanted and I'd printed his tale of the rocks. And suppose that I would be wrong about Seymour Solomon and the reasons for the collapse.

ଞୠ

As if guided by an automatic pilot, I sped along—so caught up in my remembrances that I could have easily smacked into a telephone pole—until once more I could smell the sewage plant. Sirens were rrr-ing from ambulances somewhere. How many bodies ahead? As I screeched around a curve, I nervously glanced at a cluster of tall oaks in the direction of the noise. What an odd horizon; something was missing.

Then a second later I hurtled over a hilltop and saw through the trees the surviving half of Vulture's, from which ragged pieces of floor, supported by tangles of reinforcing rods, were drooping over the rubble. Vulture's looked as if a sloppy giant had split it apart with a meat cleaver and trampled on the northern section.

I left my car beside a "Welcome to Vulture's Point" sign, then dashed toward the ruins—flashing my press pass at the cops along the way. Shaking, obsessed by Margo and her fate, I plunged into the rubble at the northeast corner. All around me I could hear the moans and "Oh my God"s of people trapped amid the concrete. I began thinking the most savage of thoughts about Life versus Property and wishing that somehow Margo's survival was worth X number of dollars, so that I might know what sacrifice I could make to assure her return to me.

Then I heard more moans and saw arms and legs protruding from the edges of fallen slabs, and a tax man with his innards spilled out, and file cabinets crushed like tin cans in a weightlifter's grip, and some tax forms being scattered by the wind. Just briefly I imagined the bureaucracy punishing Solomon not for the collapse but for violating the sanctity of tax forms.

For the first time in my life I was covering a tragedy that someone I loved might be a part of, a major departure from the past.

I recalled the Saturday night in Marseilles when the police radio had sent me to a wreck on the High-Level Bridge over the Black River. All our photographers had been busy chronicling scheduled mayhem on the football fields at the local high schools. So I'd taken along my Pentax and eagerly photographed the bloodied face of a five-year-old girl, who, even in her agony, had been pressing a doll against her cheek, lending a special poignancy to my picture.

Flaunted at the top of the front page, it prompted a spate of angry mail from parents empathizing with the mother of the girl.

But the photograph won an Associated Press contest, and I spent the remainder of my career in Marseilles ready again to flash my strobe in the face of a dying stranger.

ଚୠଔ

"You! Leave!" A policeman with a prognathous jaw had seen me climbing one of the fallen slabs. "Leave, before I arrest your ass."

"I'm looking for someone," I said.

"Leave it to us."

"But you can hear the people—"

"They'll never get to them without cranes and dozers."

"But I have a friend there."

"Mister, you can't."

"I can do any fucking thing I please," I protested. "I'm a *Telegram* reporter."

"Just come down from there." He climbed up the slab and hammerlocked me.

"Look," I said, "I'll show you my ID."

The policeman let go, and I pulled out my Roxland police pass—complete with a photo that made me look more arrestable than ever. I'd frowned impatiently at the clerks processing my papers.

"Christ," I said, "I warned Solomon about that building two months ago. You take my word, he's the one you ought to lock up."

"Then how come it wasn't in the newspapers?"

"You'd have to ask my editor."

"You really know someone in the building?"

"A woman named Margo Danialson."

"See that little table near the pumper?" He pointed, and I nodded. "They're starting a list of survivors."

Running toward the pumper I almost tripped over a white sheet whose bulge hinted a corpse. A search-and-rescue man scanned down the survivors' list and read off the closest surnames to Margo's: "Dainlow, Fesserman, Gerwin. No, sir, not so far." More mourner than reporter, I started sobbing.

Someone tapped me from behind, and I wheeled around to see a white shirt with a beer belly pushing against it.

"Hey," said Lucky O'Brien, "you're crying. Big, tough reporter."

"I knew someone in the building," I said. "Just tell me, O'Brien. How come you had the luck? How come *you're* alive."

"Me and the boys, we were leaving to have lunch with ... Hey, you won't tell no one, will you?"

I was too dazed to care.

"Hey, God helps those who help themselves," said O'Brien.

Then he told me how the building had collapsed just when he was pulling out of the parking lot on his way to steak with a GSA landlord.

"What'd it sound like," I asked, groping for my reportorial role, "when it fell?"

"Kinda like *Earthquake*." The disaster movie. If the world ended, O'Brien would die summoning up allusions from Hollywood.

I rushed off to interview other survivors. The word was that just before the collapse, an explosion had instantly ripped apart some of the building, before other sections tumbled and rumbled. From the same area I could see a blaze from an almost surely related fire.

A Papudoian terrorist at work? Punishment from Jehovah? Of whom? I could think of a number of likely suspects.

Then I saw a gas company truck, asked a few questions, and learned that the cause of the explosion and fire might be more prosaic. The eruption had come out of a utility area on the first floor. A gas-powered boiler and an emergency generator with a huge oil tank *had* sat there. No need for Papudoians, despite all of Bullard's rhetoric?

Dark smoke was snaking up. I could smell the stench of burning oil, apparently ignited by flames from the gas, and I saw police ropes around the immediate area. Might another explosion follow?

Fifteen minutes later, I felt another tap on my shoulder, from Margo. "Jonathan!"

"Thank God! Guess who I've been looking for. Where the devil have—"

"With the search-and-rescue people," Margo said as we hugged, then clung to one another. "I know the building layout. So I can help track down the survivors."

"You'd better get back to it. Are your friends safe?"

"I don't even want to think about that," Margo said. As we discussed plans to get together later, she brushed dust from my pants and shirt. "You need a bath."

"All I need is for you to be alive."

"Thanks to you and Little Taverns," Margo said. "A friend and I, we were going out to eat there. Thank God the cafeteria here stinks—stank." We gazed at the rubble in that general direction.

"Little Tavern? I thought you didn't like that stuff."

"Which is why we were going. I mean, it's the most creative form of junk architecture I've ever seen."

"You never made up your mind, did you?"

"Jonathan, it's horrible," Margo said, gazing off. "People trampled to death. Those stairs. If I'd left for lunch just a few minutes later—"

In midsentence she stopped to watch a green Maverick zigzag

around the parking lot. A dark-haired man was driving and gaping at the ruins at the same time.

"Oh my God," Margo said. "He'll kill someone."

"He already has," I said, and watched Sy Solomon speed off.

I put my arm around her shoulders. We cared not the least, or I didn't, who saw us together.

"What about your friend, Mewley, Newley, whatever?" I asked.

"Oh, he's at Headquarters today. I think."

"That's good." I didn't ask her to elaborate on the "I think."

"I guess the marathon runner had his coronary," Margo said, and I remembered our conversations about the chances of a collapse. "Now, here's the crazy thing. I think I actually know what happened—well, maybe."

She paused, and we watched rescuers calling out to survivors and lowering microphones into the ruins.

"So," I asked Margo, "what's the theory du jour?"

"Rain. Lots of rain last week. Which caused the building and the fill to sink a little faster. Just enough to rupture the gas lines. Which blew up. Which set off some oil in the tank of an emergency generator."

Oh, the syllogism Margo was creating here. Spinoza would have been proud.

"But shouldn't there have been a nice sturdy firewall between the oil tank and the gas lines?"

"Except that Solomon was his usual cheapskate self with the firewall materials. Which the explosion did in anyway."

"And," I asked, "that took out a column or two?"

"Exactly," Margo said, "with a little help from the burning oil set off by the gas. Which weakened the steel, which—well, you get the idea."

Sure enough, Sy had stinted on the insulation protecting the building's steel frame against fire. At just 650 degrees Fahrenheit, the steel would have started softening.

"And it happened near the base," Margo said with a frown severe enough to make me wish that Solomon were within scolding distance. "The worst possible place for failure. All those flimsy floors above."

I recalled GSA's quotidian mission as the government's house-keeper, and its reputation as a haven for political hacks willing to bend over for their masters—the lowest form of bureaucratic life despite many stellar civil servants like Margo. Yes, a definitely weakened base.

We watched men in red suits follow search-and-rescue collies into the ruins away from the areas near the explosion, and that made me think of the human canines in the CIA area.

Just what had become of Pointy Nose and the other Dobermans with machine guns? All the armament had been futile against tiny raindrops en masse, the real cause of the collapse, beyond Solomon's corner-cutting that had made it possible. I just hoped that Wire Rims had survived.

Margo returned to her rescue-related work, and I began reflecting on some clips about Ronan Point—the London housing project that a gas explosion had also sundered. I remembered, too, the slogan at the headquarters of the National Archives, part of GSA. Engraved under a statue outside was a quote loosely borrowed from *The Tempest*: "What is past is prologue."

Inspired by the Bard, I ran to a house across the street from the sewage plant. Then I commandeered the phone for a call to the *Telegram* and dictated the facts about the concrete slab, the twisted rods, and the corpses under the white sheets.

None other than McWilliams himself came on the line and rasped, "Good job, pal."

"Thanks."

"Garst and the others, they'll be there any moment now."

"But isn't Garst National?"

"We're a team, pal, a team. Just get ready to pass the ball when the time comes." Click.

When I returned to the ruins, I saw a large station wagon pull up with a parabolic antenna atop its roof. A television crew jumped out, and a bushy-haired reporter started to flit about in search of witnesses for First Witness News.

So frantic was the man that he almost knocked over a doughnut table. Then I recalled who he was: Ernie LaGassie, a professional klutz who worked for a television station The Other Paper owned.

Previewing "Your Washington Weekends," he'd made a career of tipping over canoes and falling off horses. The *Telegram's* TV reviewer pronounced him "our local Charlie Chaplin"; his detractors considered him a very successful flack for the National Park Service. Margo had once speculated that he was actually an Olympic gymnast who liked to fool people.

Within three minutes a secretary was trembling before LaGassie's camera. "Tell our viewers," said Ernie. "How did it feel?"

"How did what feel?" the woman asked.

"Why—to be in the building that was falling."

"Oh, I was in the safe part." She was a drawling, heavyset woman, the kind who probably chewed gum in church and devoured the gossip in the supermarket tabloids. She seemed almost catatonic under the circumstances. "I mean, I just walked out of there."

"But surely you felt something," Ernie persisted.

Anxiously I waited. Maybe a spring would snap inside the woman's head, and she'd say something wildly out of character, like, "Horny!"

"The terror—the terror of it all!" Ernie kept up in a, voice suggesting a one-hundred-point headline. "Imagine. Trapped with a whole building falling around you."

"But I got out, see. I'm all right now."

"And hundreds—hundreds must have perished before your eyes."

"But the other girls and me, we're all right. Everyone in our office—"

"But the guilt. To think you survived while hundreds died." Would that Ernie would stick to covering tipped-over canoes!

I turned and walked off, as tempted as I was to linger and take in more of the absurdity. Vines of honeysuckle climbed some trees near me. The fragrance mingled with the stench from the oil and the sewer plant, and the combination seemed about as believable as the unfortunately named Ernie LaGassie.

Chapter 30

I was about to tour the ruins further—or at least get as close as I could before the cops shooed me off—when I spotted a stooped little man in a seersucker suit.

With a gold-plated pen he was scrawling away on a yellow legal pad. It was— "Stonewall!"

"Well, if it isn't my reporter friend! Been crawlin' through some muck, I see."

I brushed part of the mud off my pants.

"Well"—Stonewall chuckled—"just so it's muck-crawlin', not muckrakin'."

"Who're the notes for?"

"Well, an old client of mine."

"Not Sy Solomon?"

"I'm not ashamed of it. No, sir. Not at all. A true gentleman. I've worked for him for years."

"Zoning?"

"He knows who's best."

"How come I haven't seen you at the hearings for him, then?"

"Well, you know," Stonewall said, "I'm sorta working quietly behind the scenes. You know me—too modest to take credit."

"I guess he respects your knowledge of the area."

"Why, sure," Stonewall said.

"You're familiar with, er, local conditions."

"Why, sure."

"Like which building inspector wants to send his son to a fancy school."

"What?" Stonewall raised his eyebrows, as if puzzled, but the pitch of his voice rose enough to convince me he was more scared than curious.

"I guess I'll have to wait for an answer until the statute of limitations has expired."

"You're not suggesting ..."

I nodded.

"Jon, ole boy, I tell you—Sy's so clean I feel guilty taking his money."

"Listen," I said. "How much do you know about this man named Cox?"

Stonewall scratched his craggy face.

"Who's Cox?" he asked.

"You're sweating," I said.

"It's a hot day."

"A hot day for Cox and his pals," I said. "I understand the boy's doing fine at Harvard. And the sick wife, that was a good turn. It's just that I don't like the way Sy's buildings fall down."

Twenty-five minutes later, Garst swaggered up to me. He looked dressed for a briefing at the State Department, and I wondered how many interviews he'd skip at the collapse site so he wouldn't muddy his Italian shoes.

Garst looked aghast at the dirt on my clothes. "Didn't mean to be late. I guess not everyone knows his way around the boondocks as well as you."

That, I suppose, was his way of smacking his lips over my demotion to the Roxland beat. He always had been good at mixing compliments and insults—sometimes I wondered if he'd taken a course in it at Yale.

"Well, I'll be on my way," Stonewall said, and began walking off.

"There's a guy named Fenton looking for you," Garst told me.

Stonewall's head jerked around. "Is it that nig—that union fella."

"The Supreme Court," I said. "Same guy."

"Yep, that's him. Jon, now I hope you're not gonna let a rascal like that tell you how to write."

"Oh, I don't need lessons from anyone," I said, "especially you."

Just then the rascal himself appeared—his face divided between a smile and a frown.

"I told you the m.f, would fall, I told you, I told you!"

I nodded.

"It heard it on my CB." His Citizens Band radio. "It's all over the CB. They can cover up those cracks, but not this!" Wildly, Fenton gestured toward the ruins.

"Now hold on!" Stonewall said. "It's time for a little more responsibility."

"The government, it's so responsible you've got a couple of hundred corpses on your hands."

"Watch it," Stonewall snarled. "Remember, I'm a lawyer."

"Yes, Solomon's zoning lawyer, and maybe his bagman, too."

I watched Stonewall tap his pen against his legal pad. "Everything you say, I'll take it down. So Mr. Solomon can sue the pants off you."

Lew Fenton didn't even frown at Stonewall—he just laughed. "You fuckin' shyster. The only reason you got this notebook is so's you can think up bullshit to tell the insurance company."

Suddenly Fenton caught sight of LaGassie and a cameraman and cupped his hands around his mouth, and yelled: "Hey, you—come here!" They were within ten yards, but totally absorbed in photographing a white-sheeted corpse. "Hey, you! You with the camera."

LaGassie turned around. Hesitantly, as if trying to decide whether Fenton was dangerous, LaGassie and the cameraman walked up to us.

"I'll tell you the truth about that building," Fenton said.

"I'm warning you!" Stonewall glared.

"What's going on?" LaGassie asked.

"You mean—what went on," Fenton said. "Murder, that's what! Now you turn your camera on, and I'll tell you why that building fell! I'll tell you why those people died. I'll tell you about the cracks and how I warned 'em."

"Who are you?" LaGassie inquired, having regained enough composure to be somewhat condescending.

"The man who told 'em. Who told 'em all—that it was going to collapse."

"You mean you worked there?"

"Better than that, mister. My men built the fucker."

"Your men?"

"My members. Local 2226. Construction Laborers. I'm president. Just turn on the camera."

"And you're really president of—"

"Put that fuckin' camera on!"

"All right," said LaGassie, "we'll tape it and phone the union and check."

"I am the union! Now you turn that fuckin' camera on!"

LaGassie and the cameraman muttered some jargon about lighting and camera angles, and the red light on the minicam glowed. Fenton, at twice his normal rate of speech, complained of Solomon's cheapness with the rebars and most everything else that could help keep a building together. And then, without the slightest warning, Fenton roared into the microphone: "And don't think that the papers didn't know! The *Telegram*, anyway. That reporter standing over there"—Fenton pointed and the cameraman swung the minicam toward me—"he knew everything! And his editors hushed him up!"

"What about this, Mr. Stone?" LaGassie asked in his tabloid voice, and aimed his mike my way. "Is it true, how Mr. Fenton came to you before the collapse?"

Stonewall was still there, a few feet away, scribbling on his pad— as if he were the reporter and I the newsmaker—eager to document my slightest slip. And Garst was betraying a grin, though I couldn't fathom whether it was over my professional embarrassment or over the fact that he wasn't the one on camera.

Off the job, unless participating in interviews or other undertakings blessed by McWilliams, *Telegram* reporters were supposed to be ciphers. Only Mac could bestow glory upon us—including, presumably, the honor of being the target of another medium.

About the only exception to the rule was Wendy Blevin, whom McWilliams could always trust to be responsibly outrageous.

"Mr. Stone?" LaGassie asked.

"Well," I said, still stunned by it all, "that's a matter best fit for discussion with my editors."

"You don't care to comment at this time?"

"Mr. McWilliams will be glad to answer," I said. What a phrase, "glad to." I might as well have been one of the GSA bureaucrats steering me to a nonanswer from Zumweltnar.

ഇരുജ

Metro Desk was proficiently cold toward me when I phoned again with the identities of some of the corpses. The assistant Metro editor swapped none of the usual banter, even when I joked about being on television, or, rather, especially when the topic came up. The news aide who took my dictation kept calling me "Mr. Stone," and her formality unnerved me, since I knew she was mistering not out of respect but out of an eagerness to distance herself from me.

And then, once more, McWilliams's voice grated against my eardrum. "I'm disappointed in you, pal."

"Oh?" I said as casually as possible.

"Letting yourself get trapped like that."

"What are you—"

"You know fucking well what. I don't like my people mouthing off on some dumb-ass TV station."

"Mouthing off?" He'd finally gotten to me. "Jesus Christ, I did a great no-comment act."

"But the whole thing wouldn't have happened," McWilliams rasped, "if you hadn't chummed around with that crazy Fenton. Very unprofessional, pal. I'm taking you off this story. Once and for all!"

"Jesus, you're irrational."

"Pal, you'd better do some fast apologizing if you want to work here. Now get Garst on the line!"

"Yes."

"And get your ass away from there. And don't come back to the office, either. And keep away from your apartment, too. I don't want some asshole trying to interview you there, either."

"All right, I'll be at—"

"I don't care where you're going, pal. Just stay away!"

Chapter 31

Margo's pot fumes drifted toward me, and I found myself on the verge of a wheeze; at least the smell was sweeter than Mac's cigar emissions.

"Please," I said. "My allergist and I would appreciate it if ..."

She tossed the cigarette into her dungeon's solitary ashtray, a miniature castle of clay, and it landed just inside the courtyard near one of the guard towers. The bridge over the moat wasn't that different from the one I'd seen in the Buckingham Manor ad. Maybe Solomon's buildings fell down, but at least his moat bridges were reasonably authentic.

I kissed Margo, both of us naked and sweaty after making love. Some deny humans can or should do this after tragedies, some say it happens as a reaffirmation of the continuity of life; I myself believe that we did it as an act of self-redaction—of the memories of that day.

"I like your 'safe house,'" I said, using the CIA jargon for the places where they stashed away Cold War defectors.

"I just hope those TV reporters aren't as relentless as you."

"In what way?" I'd told her about LaGassie.

"If they were, they'd be boring in here through the walls."

"Or," I was about to add, "knocking on your door again and again."

I didn't say it, though. Having just experienced a disaster, I wasn't going to worry too much about trifles like rival lovers. But I was curious in one way; Margo's friend Tom Newley, had neither called nor visited. Not that I would have enjoyed a confrontation, but I almost regretted his absence—in the sense that Margo deserved as much solace as possible. Surely she must be hurt that Newley wasn't trying to comfort her; I just couldn't believe he had not heard of the collapse; I might yet save her from life in Sark.

Then I remembered Margo's response to my question about his whereabouts: "At Headquarters, I think." There'd been a long pause before the last two words, and she'd spoken them very softly, very hurriedly, and I wondered how certain she was of his survival. Were we talking survival or denial?

"The news!" Margo said suddenly. "Ernie LaGassie, he might be on now."

Her alarm clock said 11:20, probably too late, but we put on some clothes anyway and rushed up the rickety steps to the living room and snapped on the television, which was just slightly less decrepit than mine.

We'd missed Ernie; the sports news was ending. Margo was about to turn the set off when the announcer said the station's "News Guard" feature was next.

"You think?" Margo said.

"Maybe."

"News Guard" was the station's media review feature. Paxley Treadwell, the Guard, had a deep Southern accent and the authoritative ways of a Baptist preacher who knew sin when he saw it.

Old Paxley came on camera holding up a copy of the *Telegram's* first edition, and my eyes just about popped out as the screen filled up with a close-up view of the paper.

Garst had gotten the featured byline on the collapse story, all right; but that wasn't even the biggest outrage.

Right below the main headline was a smaller one running two columns: "Solomon Known for Quality Construction." The Real Estate editor's byline caught my eye. Would Paxley have the gall to criticize a story that would be favorable to a powerful businessman? Then again, I recalled that Sy Solomon rarely used television commercials.

At the same time, I didn't expect Treadwell to lecture the *Telegram* too harshly.

Granted, Fenton had been able to indulge in a blast against us on-screen, in the confusions of the collapse coverage—but normally Channel 12 treated the *Telegram* gently. Our TV critic tended to be both loyal and vengeful.

"One of the more puzzling aspects of today's tragedy," Treadwell was intoning, "is the coverage of it by the *Telegram*. A union leader has been saying the paper ignored warnings of the impending collapse. This may or may not be so. But I was curious enough to buy

a copy before airtime to assess the coverage of the collapse itself.
And now I'm still more puzzled, by this article by Real Estate Editor
James Sherman."

The camera zoomed in on the headline.

"It's several hundred words long," Treadwell said. "It repeatedly
praises Seymour Solomon, the builder of the collapsed building. Yet
half the quotes are anonymous. Sherman simply calls them 'veteran
observers of the Washington construction scene.' Why? Just why
is this anonymity needed in an article defending Mr. Solomon? It's
as if the *Telegram* asked Mr. Sherman at the last minute to do Mr.
Solomon's bidding for him."

"Amazing," I said, as Treadwell vanished from the screen, "simply
amazing! Maybe there's a God after all—I'd better watch what I say
about that moon rock."

"Isn't there something you can do?" Margo demanded. "Some way
to get the truth out. About Bullard and his investment in the building."

"I've already told you—freelancing's verboten."

"No, I'm talking about something really verboten," Margo said.
"Sneaking the story into the paper."

"How?"

"Your friend the layout guy. The one you were telling me
about."

"And get him fired? No thanks!"

"Not if you take credit for it afterward. Tell them you fooled
him."

"Wait a minute! What about character and characters? The hero
routine—haven't we already been through it before."

"But Jonathan," Margo said, her voice rising, "don't you remember
when Bullard invested?"

I recited the dates.

"Which proves," she said, "that he was an owner when the building was going up—when they were stinting on the foundation."

"But how much would he have known?"

"Who's to say? Just remember—hundreds dead, and he was an
investor when it mattered."

I mangled an old truism: "Freedom of the press is for people who own 'em."

"Well, if you can't own a press, at least steal one."

"Gotcha. Wait! The computers, the VDT. Maybe there's hope."

"Then do it, Jonathan, do it!"

Instantly, I arose from the old sofa in front of the TV. "Well, then, good-bye, and wish me luck for the final edition."

As I put on my shirt downstairs, I chuckled crazily to myself. Yes, yes, Reverend Treadwell, I knew just the story I could rip out to make room for mine.

Chapter 32

I swiveled my head back and forth—like a security guard in front of Vulture's Research Assistance Section—as I walked out to my car.

Hmm. If the spooks didn't get me, maybe the muggers would.

Margo had said the crime rate near her house wasn't that bad, but in the dark I thought myself brave just the same. It was eighty-five degrees even at night, and my skin felt moist from heat and worry alike. We were in the middle of the kind of summer when city workers go around turning fire hydrants into showers so there won't be a riot.

Briefly I wished I were back in McLean. Someday, however, I suspected Margo's neighborhood would undergo a little blockbusting in reverse, and "nice" whites would move in from the suburbs, and the muggers would have a choicer selection of victims.

And through it all, the real estate types would keep smiling; for the displaced had to go somewhere, and why not the garden apartments that the builders were still flinging up in Prince George's County? God forbid what the watershed would be like a few years hence; perhaps the new homes and apartments would wobble atop stilts.

When I reached my car, I saw I'd left the windows rolled down. Jesus, I was growing sloppy—I would never have done it in Marseilles in my poverty-beat days.

Back then, however, my Valiant had been new. Any thief who hot-wired it now would have to be either incompetent or charitable enough to spare me a trip to the automobile junkyard.

I turned the ignition key and steeled myself for the corner near a gang hangout—where the light always took forever to turn green.

Then I started trying to grasp why McWilliams had let me investigate Solomon for a while yet had so brazenly protected him with the "Quality Construction" story. Mac was brilliant, and he knew it, and that might very well have been the reason for his slipups.

Sometimes I wondered whether McWilliams shouldn't be wearing a moustache and holing up in a hotel in the Bahamas. He was that much like Howard Hughes in his conviction that his will and intellect would spare him the pratfalls suffered by the rest of us. I remembered the giant wooden seaplane that Hughes had built and abandoned to the hangar. Had McWilliams been richer and not so caught up in his newspaper and his museum of a home, he might well have undertaken similar projects in his weaker moments.

ଧ୍ୟଓଷ

"Mr. Stone," the guard at the *Telegram's* entrance called after me, "would you come here a moment?"

I'd already set one foot in the elevator, and for a second I considered pretending that I hadn't heard him. Maybe he would forget about me and return to the adventure magazine he'd been finger-reading.

Suppose, however, that McWilliams had formally barred me from the *Telegram* offices. No one would forget then.

I turned around and started walking back to the guard. He was a short but powerful man with a revolver and an insistence on "mistering" even copy aides.

"What's wrong?" I asked.

"Just sign here," he said, handing me a clipboard.

"But I work here."

"It's expired, your ID. I just noticed"—he pointed to a list of names on his desk.

I restrained a sigh and scrawled out my name with the leaky ballpoint pen chained to the clipboard.

"Ask Editorial for a new card tomorrow. We gotta follow the rules, see?"

"Sure."

"Good thing I noticed." The guard appeared to be so impressed by the rules that he seemed considerably less fearsome. He could have been a jittery clerk. I remembered a story I'd once written about an unemployed circus giant. He had let little secretaries and bureaucrats intimidate him, so he couldn't collect unemployment checks until my article embarrassed the District government.

As the elevator doors were shutting in front of me, I took one last look at the lobby. Victoria Simpson had turned it into a museum of sorts for tourists and Scout troops, and now a rickety Linotype towered above the guard desk. She'd borrowed her machine back from the Smithsonian.

Behind glass were old copy pencils, green visors worn by editors in the *Front Page* days, and an antique Remington typewriter that had escaped being melted down for scrap during the Depression.

It all seemed so ancient now, so different from the video display terminals starting to show up elsewhere in the building. I thought of a science-fiction movie where mysterious forces tried to re-create a motel room for an earthman. Were Hildy Johnson to step out of *The Front Page* and appear alongside the Remington, he'd probably feel as out of place as the earthlings must have.

For a few seconds I lingered at the bulletin board by the elevator, as if I'd just dropped by to mosey about the city room and tidy up a few odds and ends of work. I hadn't the slightest desire to seem hurried.

Looking over the city room, I could see that the night crew was larger than usual that evening, and I wondered if McWilliams had assigned extra people to do last-minute collapse stories. Maybe Mac was going to put out a special Solomon supplement full of praise and real estate ads.

I was about to sit down at my just-installed VDT when I noticed Hubert Raymond, the Night Metro Editor, pacing up and down the room. Raymond was thick in the gut but had a mean, taut face and a military-short haircut, and I recalled his Green Beret days in Vietnam. Might I end up the Viet Cong of the moment?

What was Mac's city room but a military organization at the core, despite the personal eccentricities and dramas of the journalists—a machine like a Japanese whaling fleet, the Chicago police force, or a global oil company? The wheels and belts needed to be in alignment lest typos creep in or careless skepticism offend the wrong advertisers. Just as with our thunderous presses—tons of steel, myriads of moving parts—nothing major could slip out of place. Bloody injuries might otherwise result. And yet the most gifted reporters were compulsively curious, the very trait that must evaporate whenever the bosses of the word mill wanted it to.

From my drawer I pulled out a notebook filled with indecipherable scribbles. Then I began my labors at the video display terminal.

The terminal looked like a cross between an electric typewriter and an overgrown portable TV whose screen was too small. Even though I'd quickly mastered the basics, I felt less than comfortable with it. I might as well be a seal trainer forced to tame a giant duck-billed platypus. There was something reassuring about the clacking of typewriter keys and the sudden and permanent appearance of ink on paper.

Even the IBM Selectrics, the gizmos with the little type balls that zipped across the page, left me feeling in charge. But the VDT hogged half my desktop, and it wouldn't even recognize my existence until I spelled out a series of instructions in computerese.

My first story of the evening wasn't for the *Telegram*. It was for Raymond, in case he ambled by and asked what I was doing. There were controls on the terminal with which I could skim over my prose electronically and select the words lit up on the tube. If Raymond came too close to my desk, I'd simply shift from my piece to the imaginary zoning story glowing before me in khaki green. For the sake of novelty, I had written up a case where a shopping center owner clearly deserved a variance.

At last I was ready to start tapping out my exposé, but I didn't reach into my desk for my leasing material—not only because of Raymond but also because I'd memorized all the facts after having argued so often with my editors.

I looked across the room. Raymond was bent over his desk, pencil in hand, nitpicking away, presumably, at the third edition. He was just as much a stickler as E.J.—he must be no less vigilant about gaffes in the *Telegram* than he'd been about snipers in Vietnam.

By JONATHAN STONE

Already I'd crossed a Rubicon of sorts. I'd given myself a byline instead of letting an editor bestow it on me.

President Bullard, secretly and apparently illegally, invested $90,000 six years ago in the huge building at Vulture's Point south of Alex-

andria where at least three hundred Internal
Revenue Service employees died yesterday in a
collapse.

I stopped writing a second and gazed at the two CLEAR keys on the VDT. It had more than one, just like a missile launch control, so you wouldn't accidentally wipe your story off the screen. No, it wasn't too late to zap.

Bullard sold his half-percent interest in the
building five and one-half years ago but was an
owner at the time of its construction.

Again I paused. How thoroughly could Mac have me blacklisted in the newspaper business? Would the Marseilles paper take me back? I remembered how the dust from the steel mills had kept me coughing half the time I was there. Well, maybe I'd hack it as a stringer for one of the tabloids peddled at the checkout counter of the A & P. I'd go out West and spot UFOs often enough to bring in rent money.

The president invested in the name of a
partner in his Chicago law firm.

Jeez, I hadn't written that the statute of limitations ran just five years and would let Bullard off the hook. I shuffled around some words in the second paragraph, then glanced up from the screen. Sergeant Raymond was still at his desk and out of the way.

At the time of his investment he chaired the
Senate Governmental Affairs Committee, which
oversees the General Services Administration,
the federal agency through which the IRS leased
the fourteen-story building from the Vulture's
Point Limited Partnership.

Yes, my lungs and I would appreciate Arizona or Colorado more than Marseilles.

Bullard was one of a number of politically or
socially prominent investors in the partnership formed
by Washington businessman Seymour Solomon. He is
founder, chairman, and president of Seymour Solomon
Companies, the large construction and management
firm.

How soon in the story until I mentioned Luci Elkins?

*Among the other investors was Congress-
man John Boynton, who, because he invested
through an incorporated company, his family
real estate firm, did not violate the law involved.*

Damn. I should have put the Boynton part closer to the top.

*Bullard, however, may have broken the
law, Section 431 of Title 18 of the U.S. Code,
which bans congressional ownership of feder-
ally leased buildings (it carries a maximum fine
of $3,000). He invested personally, through a
trustee, in the unincorporated company owning
the building at Vulture's Point. As a partnership,
it lacks the kind of legal isolation that a corpora-
tion affords investors.*

Was there any way to say Bullard had blackmailed the head of
GSA? I supposed not; the proof just wasn't there; that was one trans-
action you'd never find hinted in the partnership papers.

*Marvin Forester of Pensler and Magnus-
son, who was Bullard's trustee, told the Telegram that the president's investment had been
an accident. "This man Solomon has a number
of partnerships," Forester said, "and he simply
forgot that Eddy Bullard was an investor in the
building. Mr. Bullard, of course, left the partnership just as soon as he found out who the tenant
was."*

Should Forester's side go in an earlier paragraph? The line was
dismayingly thin between fairness and wishy-washiness.

Forester said ...

ഽⱮഽ

I heard footsteps, Raymond's, it turned out, and he was coming
my way. So I pushed a few buttons and started lighting up the screen
with a new paragraph of the zoning story.

The quote there was real even if the surrounding facts weren't.
Eloquently, old Stonewall was spewing out his normal bullshit

about "the need to cultivate a healthy business climate in Roxland County." Could you "cultivate" a climate? I supposed you could always seed the clouds with money from plain white envelopes.

"It's going to take a lot more than this to get you back to National," Raymond snarled.

"What?" I managed to look as if caught in the middle of the most engrossing of projects.

"I don't care if you work twenty-four hours a day," Raymond said. "You're not coming back to National. Not after the way you fucked up that investigation."

Raymond didn't just kick people when they were down; he stomped on their faces again and again.

"What about the building?" I asked. "It's down, isn't it? So much for your respect for my predictive powers."

"Yes, I saw you on the news." It was an angry, matter-of-fact statement, not in the least way a funny one. If I'd been in boot camp, he would have assigned me eighty push-ups.

"Some people say I looked pretty telegenic," I said.

"Your aunt must have been drinking," Raymond growled. "Now finish and get out! You know McWilliams wants your ass out of the office!"

"But the Zoning Board is—"

"Just finish up and get out," Raymond said, "or he won't let you come back!"

Shaking his head, as if in disgust at me, Raymond walked back to his desk. I waited. Yes, he was once again lost in his front-page nitpicking. I restored the Bullard exposé to my screen, added some more of Forester's bullshit, sneaked in a few careful references to the Research Assistance section at Vulture's, then listed some of the other investors in the building.

Upon reaching Luci's name, I paused. Should I remind the world she was George McWilliams's girlfriend? Perhaps not. Throwing in that detail might suggest a personal grudge, and there were so many more decent ways of acting unprofessionally.

As fast as I could, I summarized the Solomon interview—making it clear that Sy was a lovable crook. Then I glanced toward Raymond again; the chair was empty. Suddenly, twenty feet off to my right side, I again heard his growl; "Stone! I want you to clear out in five minutes, or I'll call the guard!"

"All right," I said. "Just let me get a printout so I can work on this some more at home." But first I added a final paragraph, deadpanned in my most professional way:

> *Solomon called Bullard "a man of character ... The first thing Eddy tells me when I go to his house, he says, 'Sy, I'm a senator. I must not put my money in anything crooked.'"*

Chapter 33

Raymond glowered once more as I walked by him on my way to the machine that would print out my tappings.

"Stone, I've got to admit you've distinguished yourself tonight. It's been a long time since anyone around here worked so hard to get fired."

"You know me," I said. "I never shirk from anything."

"I'm watching you, Stone. I'm not going to take my eyes off you till you step into that elevator."

I punched a few buttons on the printout machine, then glanced back at Raymond. He was still peering at me; I don't think he blinked once, at least not at that moment, and I realized he'd probably be McWilliams's equal if they ever got into a staring competition.

Normally the machine took just fifteen seconds or so to spew out two stories, but with Raymond shooing me away, it seemed as if I were in a slow-motion movie, and the projector kept jamming. Then I started trying to calm down.

I was bypassing the usual step between the terminal and the printout—the editing—but that wasn't suspicious in itself. Raymond, after all, thought I'd be taking my copy home for changes.

Of course in a way it really was going home to its natural destination, the back shop of the *Telegram*.

The paper rolling out of the machine was a long strip about the width of a newspaper column. It curled a little like a freshly developed picture, and I had trouble thinking that this floppy thing could be taken seriously by the back shop and turned into part of a newspaper. The images were sharp, the ink just as black as could be, and yet I looked on the strip the way a child does on a caterpillar—would it ever become a butterfly? And I wasn't even trying to make a whole butterfly, just a little piece of wing.

"Stone!"

"I'm through. Good-bye!" Then I hurried to the elevator and sped up to the tenth floor to await the best moment to smuggle the Bullard story into the *Telegram*.

The tenth was the executive office section, a part of the building that would be deserted at that time of night. Our overlords had softer schedules than those foolish reporters whose union they had housebroken.

All my surroundings were pitch-dark, and as I wandered around the hall, I brushed against something prickly and felt still edgier.

Perhaps it was a leaf or needle of one of Mrs. Simpson's giant potted plants, for she was a fanatical horticulturist, who believed that the presence of vegetation ennobled anybody.

A few cacti bristled even in the city room, near Mac's office. Had McWilliams chosen them, or were they simply standard *Telegram* issue?

I found a large, soft couch and sprawled out on it and started hoping I'd timed my smuggling right. If I showed up in the back shop before Raymond left for the evening, he might see me and obtain authorization to fire me. If I was too late, I wouldn't get the story into that day's paper.

And there was a problem heaped atop all the others; as part of my rebellion against Mac, I wasn't wearing a watch that night, with or without a glowing dial.

Having avoided one as a little protest against his Rolex-driven news bureaucracy, I was hampered in my efforts to fight the organization.

I was tempted to turn on some fluorescents and look for a clock, except that in my fright I envisioned a *Telegram* guard strolling down the street and glancing up and wondering why the lights were on. Soon there'd be footsteps growing louder, and I'd hide, but in vain. The guard would point his gun at me, and I'd feel like a Nixonian caught in the middle of a black bag job at the Watergate.

But I wasn't spying; I wasn't stealing; in a few minutes I'd in fact be making a solid journalistic contribution; I wouldn't even charge the *Telegram* overtime for the Bullard piece.

How smug I felt with the story in my hand. It was printed out on the long strip ready to be slipped onto Clay Bronski's pasteup sheet for the rough equivalent of a photograph. Several processes later, the images would be on curved plates that rolled against newsprint eight hundred thousand times.

Solomon and Bullard might be safe in the white-collar part of the *Telegram*, in the editorial and business offices where people knew and protected them. But not in the back shop, at least not when all the important supervisors had gone home.

How I'd enjoy seeing my story on the way to the presses. It would almost be as if the plates were pressing against Solomon and Bullard rather than the newsprint. And it might well happen just as I'd planned. For the final edition of the *Telegram* was only lightly proofed. Probably the story wouldn't even get a cursory glance since it presumably had shown up in the paper's earlier versions.

I'd even be sneaking it in under the original headline: "Solomon Known for Quality Construction." Ah, if only I could see the look on Sy's face when he opened up his *Telegram*, expecting to find at least one positive story there to offset the disaster news.

What magnificent subversion. What fine industrial anarchy. I remembered Juan Garcia, a malcontent of a steelworker in Marseilles. Back in the early seventies, he'd tampered with some machinery at U.S. Steel so that a sadistic foreman became part of a twenty-ton ingot shipped to a Chevrolet foundry.

And what about the Luddites in the *Telegram's* back shop who had blithely sabotaged the VDTs as part of their union's last spasms of defiance against Vicky's managers?

Then again, I might not be anarchistic at all; I was just helping the *Telegram* do its real job, which supposedly was to tell the truth about Solomon and Bullard.

For fifteen more minutes I must have lain on that couch—alternately worrying about the guards and falling asleep. Mrs. Simpson herself might find me, for she always arrived at the *Telegram* before 7 A.M., to fool herself into thinking she was needed. Then she'd flee at noon to attend to her charities the rest of the day.

If Vicky discovered me asleep, she would summon up the wrath of which only rich, imperious old ladies are capable. She might even break off a cactus needle and keep jabbing it into me until I awoke. I'd mumble a few words of apology, but Vicky would snap, "Young man, I'll never invite you to a *Telegram* tea again!"

Finally, I began descending the stairs to the composing room. The steps were metal, and no matter how softly I trod, I seemed to hear loud echoes. All the lights in the stairwell were turned out above the eighth. Vainly I fumbled for a switch. Could I sue if I tripped and plunged downward in the dark? Would the *Telegram* have to pay damages to a journalistic anarchist?

On the fifth floor the stairwell opened up between the newsroom and the back shop, so I wouldn't have to venture there and increase the possibility of Sergeant Raymond's finks' seeing me there. He himself normally did not pace that often through the shop, preferring to confine his sentry duty as much as possible to the newsroom.

Years ago, Raymond had missed an important deadline and traded obscenities and blows with a 250-pound printer, who bloodied his nose to protest Editorial's "fuckin' meddling."

The *Telegram* had gotten rid of his assailant, but not of the grudges that some other workers still harbored against Raymond. Indeed, the fisticuffs were even said to have helped cause The Great Strike, the one where Linotypists cheerfully smashed in the picture tubes of the company's very first VDTs.

I had scabbed along with most of the other reporters; we had been good white-collar workers—as protective toward Property as toward our jobs. We'd swallowed both our liberal pride and Vicky's bullshit that she would respect our newsroom union.

Then some printers had spat on reporters walking through the picket lines. Management had set up a helicopter shuttle to the rooftop, high above the strikers' shaking fists, and I'd felt quite proprietary toward the *Telegram* even if the ownership actually was in the other direction.

ಬಿಂಬ

Emerging from the stairwell, I glanced around and saw that Clay Bronski wasn't at his pasteup table.

Well, I could always try to sneak in the story myself and hope that the supervisors wouldn't notice me doing his work. I felt the back of my head to see if my hair was in place, then patted down a cowlick. A good story-smuggler ought to be well-groomed.

A quarter of the way to Clay's table I heard a loud, female voice call out my name. I twisted my head and saw not a boss but Nancy Huggins, one of the pasteup people.

"Hey, Jon, how'd you like to write about fireflies? Our 4-H project."

"Sounds interesting," I said, "but I've got this story to take care of."

"The kids," she said, oblivious to my impatience, "they've been catching 'em to go to the national convention. This company—it pays for the fireflies!"

"Fine—we'll talk about it when—"

"So that's how we're gonna get to Omaha. They pay a dollar for every seventy-five you catch."

"Sounds great, but I've got to—"

"So you'll write about it? Here I thought I could depend on you! But I can see now you're just like the others—too stuck-up to be interested in kids and fireflies."

"Well—when I can."

"Oh, Jon, you know how newspapers are always saying bad things about kids. I thought that just once—"

"We'll get together about it next week."

"This company—it even gives them special boxes to send the fireflies in."

"Great."

"Of course some people say it's cruel—letting the fireflies die in there. But you know what I tell them, Jon? I tell them it's all in the interest of science. Just so them chemicals are preserved when they get to Chicago—the ones that glow in the dark."

"What's it all for?" I was curious, not just feeling a touch of guilt over my brusqueness.

"The scientists," Nancy said. "They use them to see if there's water pollution. I just want to emphasize one thing. Them fireflies don't feel a thing in the boxes."

"I believe you," I said, turning my head.

"It's absolutely painless, there's no doubt. The boxes, they just dry 'em up and save the chemicals."

Once more I said good-bye to Nancy and hurried over toward Clay Bronski's table.

A men's room door opened nearby, and I saw him step out. His legs were no longer fit for the Dodgers, but he still walked with a good, spirited lope, and though he bumbled in his work, it was because of his eyes, not his mind.

Clay had a crafty, poker player's brain, with which he could have gotten quite rich if he'd wanted, but somehow he stayed almost resolutely unlucky and poor. I never saw him cheat anyone except a man in a tavern who told bad Polish jokes.

On the job, Clay suspended his intelligence and was a nice, tractable factory worker—meaning that he'd automatically slip into the *Telegram* anything that I asked him to.

"Jon, my man." Clay said as he sat down at his stool.

I was feeling so illegal I could hardly believe someone at the *Telegram* was happy to see me.

"Hey, Clay!"

"Didn't think it was your night." His bifocals were slipping, and he adjusted them: the old-fashioned, horn-rimmed kind with glass as thick as heavy windowpanes.

"Well, that collapse story. Metro said I should work—" Christ! That was all I needed—to call too much attention to my illicit story.

"Some game yesterday!"

"Wasn't it!" I said, and Clay's sports patter started pouring out as if I'd dropped a nickel in a jukebox: "Now you take Jim Rice—it's unfair—that run in the fourth. Why, you'd think he'd be slowing down now. Been at it how long?"

Not that Clay wished ill for anyone, but he was always alert for signs that younger players would be just as prone as he to the debilitations of age. He'd never been able to stop feeling remorseful about having to give up baseball early.

"While we're talking," I said, "you mind if I slip this stuff in? For A-1." Clay shook his head as I rolled out the Bullard story to its full length. "Last-minute piece for the final. Goes here."

I gave Clay directions and happily watched him as he leaned over his table and ripped away the text of the original version of "Solomon Known for Quality Construction."

Then I noticed that another pasteup man several yards away was giving me some mean looks.

"Hey, gotta be running now," I said, "but you'll take care of it for—"

"Only if you come over next week for the Orioles game," said Clay.

"Deal."

"Hey, you got the form? You know—authorization for this change."

"Relax," I said. "I'll forge something for you next time around." Bronski laughed. He was just as down on bureaucracy as I was. "I bet you two bucks on the Orioles," I said.

"Naw—I wouldn't want to take advantage of a friend."

Somewhat discomfited by Clay's words, I said good-bye and hurried down the stairs and into the lobby and reached for the clipboard on the guard's desk.

Then I scrawled in my departure time and scratched out my entry in the "Company" column of the visitors' records.

For "*Telegram*," I substituted "Self."

Chapter 34

Before sunrise I saw a morgue, not a newspaper one but the Roxland County Medical Examiner's.

Margo tarried outside the body-viewing room, drumming her fingers against the tiled walls of the county hospital, while a police sergeant waited for us.

"You're sure you want to do it tonight?" I asked.

She nodded.

"We might be able to find someone else to do it," the sergeant said—which made me like him, for I knew that many policeman tried to rush friends and relatives into identifying corpses, so the cops, too, could finish up the unpleasantness.

"But suppose you don't," Margo said. "How'd you like to go to sleep knowing you might have to do it the next day?"

A yell startled us as we walked into the viewing room. Inside, a large black woman had fainted—a nurse began shaking her back to consciousness. I saw a window and behind it the body of a young man with an Afro. We turned around. The sergeant shut the door and shook his head: "I'm glad I got the farm."

"What?" I asked. He seemed too pale-skinned for a farmer; he must have bought it recently.

"Tennessee—I'm going back soon as I get my next paycheck. They better be glad they ain't in Tennessee. We'd go after them with a shotgun—putting up a building like that."

"We'll just wait here," I said.

"I didn't know we had that one ahead." The sergeant disappeared to wherever a policeman goes after he's shown people one more body than necessary.

I held Margo's hand, but neither of us looked at the other.

Rather, I stared at the green walls outside the viewing room—a familiar green, a hospital green, the green of the curtains behind the corpse in the window, and the green, too, of the walls of my elementary school.

I remembered the air-raid drills and my teachers' assurance that
we'd survive the Russian children if only we learned to crouch in the
right position.

Perhaps institutions should set up coordinating committees to
discourage gratuitous green. It muddled memories of hospitals and
schools and post offices so you couldn't enter one without thinking
of the others.

"I still can't believe this," Margo said finally. "Do you realize we
were still fighting it out with Father?"

"Huh?"

"Over Tom's job. He said I was marrying a clerk."

"A GS-15 who majored in—"

"I don't think he'd want me to be anything less than Norman
Mailer's wife."

"An Episcopalian priest?" I asked.

"As if I want to be famous anyway."

"Gotcha."

"I'll marry J. D. Salinger instead. Secretly."

"You and reporters."

"Let's not bring that up again," Margo said.

I nodded.

The nurse walked the black woman out of the viewing room,
then returned with our sergeant; and we went in again.

A new body was in the window, Tom Newley's—wrapped up,
except for his head, in a heavy black bag with a name tag on the
zipper.

"Is that him?" the sergeant asked, but Margo was gazing toward
the door, her hands above her eyes, sobbing.

"That's him," I said.

"You knew him well enough to be sure?"

"Yes," I lied.

I was almost sure. The bag covered whatever might have remained of the three-piece suit, but I could see a few patches of the
crew cut encrusted with dried blood.

Both ears were missing. One eye was gone and the other looked
ready to pop out. It was just part of a face, actually—less face than
skull—and the skin was the color of weathered aluminum. More

than ever I wished immortality for myself; I was too vain to die.

Wordlessly, the sergeant led us back into the hall. I glanced out a window and saw the lights in the parking lot reflecting off a huge refrigeration truck.

"More?" I pointed.

"Yeah."

A few doors down we entered a room with a large steel-topped table where I saw the contents of Tom Newley's wallet, including an emergency card with Margo's telephone number on it

The sight touched me, except that I also saw a seven-hundred-and-fifty-dollar gift certificate from a travel agency in the Abraham Solomon Building. I wanted to tell Margo she'd probably misread his character, but I didn't, and not simply out of compassion, for he was dead and beyond future crookedness. So I didn't expose Tom Newley, not to Margo, not to the policeman, not to GSA, not to the *Telegram*; especially after I recalled the talk of the Greek honeymoon. I resigned myself to tolerance and silence.

Well, if nothing else, there were different levels of corruption.

Seven hundred and fifty dollars was more than a hundred-dollar lunch but a speck of the probable size of Eddy Bullard's profits from his illegal investment.

Then I thought of a lecture from my UVA days, a little story that my professor had told about a distinguished colonial in India in the middle of the nineteenth century. He'd made off with a few rubies from the vast coffers of a rajah. And yet he had won acquittal by convincing the judge he was surely an honest man because he stole so little.

૪૦૯૪

I lie naked on the autopsy table and feel a sting as a scalpel starts slicing through my chest.

"Stop!" I yell.

"Quiet!"—the rasp is familiar—"we already have your brains in a jar."

I hear guffaws.

"Please!"

More laughter.

I turn my head.

"You can't see us," the voice says. "We've already taken out your eyes."

"The fuck I can't!"

It is no doctor at all. It is Sy Solomon and Eddy Bullard and George McWilliams, laughing and cutting together.

They aren't wearing normal gowns—just old newspapers.

I protest that they're violating city health regulations.

Sy chuckles. "The commissioner, Jon, he's an old friend of mine. For this I give him a big share in my next partnership."

Vicky is watching through a window and pleading over the intercom for Mac to speed up the autopsy, so she and Sy won't be late for a board meeting of her concert pavilion.

She's smoking a huge cigar. E.J. is standing next to her and coughing.

"Hurry," he tells a photographer. "We might be able to make the final edition."

Vicky's cigar turns into a flash attachment, and a burst of light blinds me permanently while I hear the camera click.

"I don't understand," I say. "It's noon. You don't even have the first edition out yet."

"The business people," E.J. says. "They keep moving up our deadlines."

"Well, then," I tell Mac, "don't carve me up until tomorrow."

"Quiet, pal!" he says. "I'm the one making the decisions around here."

"But you'll kill E.J.! The deadlines … his heart."

"Shut up! We've already cut out your vocal cords."

I hear this strange sound, this ringing, and I—

೮೦೮೫

"Jonathan!" Someone was shaking me.

"Leave me alone, damn it! I'm dead."

"Oh, Jonathan—it's me, Margo."

"Tell them to stop! Please, pickle me. I promise I'll keep till tomorrow."

My vision was still terribly blurred, and my limbs felt as if rigor mortis had set in.

"Wake up! The paper's on the line!"

I groaned my resentment that someone was interrupting my nightmare.

"McWilliams," Margo said.

Immediately my full alertness returned; it was as though I'd been jabbed all over with Vicky's cactus needles.

Margo handed me the downstairs extension.

"Like my story?" I said.

"Get your ass down here—now!"

The phone clicked dead.

I turned to Margo. "How the fuck could he have known where I was?"

She shrugged.

"The son of a bitch wants me back at the office. How do you feel?"

"Much better," Margo said.

"Mind if I go out for a while?"

"Tony and Jane are back."

"But they weren't supposed to return …"

"The collapse," Margo said. "As soon as they heard about it."

"You do look better, a lot better now."

"I'm almost embarrassed. They interrupt their vacation, come back as fast as they can—and you're already taking care of me."

"Just don't go back to the way you were last night," I said.

"Tony says he'll call the funeral home."

"Then I'm off for a while. I think I'm gonna enjoy seeing Mac mad. What can he do besides fire me?" I kissed her. "To hell with journalistic niceties. I'll be a terrific stringer for *The National Enquirer*."

Chapter 35

My confidence waned as soon as I began reflecting on the ferocity in Mac's voice.

No—I just couldn't have sneaked that exposé into his paper. Clay must have caught on to what was happening the moment I slipped away. Which perhaps was for the better; for if Mac wanted someone canned, I'd rather it just be me.

Driving to the *Telegram*, I almost cracked up my car, I was so determined to keep my eyes away from the news racks—I mustn't remind myself of my failure.

Normally, Margo's neighborhood never seemed to have enough vending machines, but suddenly I was convinced I was seeing them at every corner.

I wondered where I might freelance the story after Mac finished bad-mouthing me around town. Perhaps I could get it into a super-market tabloid between the saucer sightings and the cancer cures.

At the *Telegram*, the midday guard was on duty, a friendly sort who had never demanded to see my ID, and I smiled hello and started signing the visitors' records.

"Why, Jon," he said while I was still on the J, "you work here, don't you?"

He was a little, round-shouldered fellow, a Social Security pensioner. Probably he had taken the job less for the money than for the chance to greet people. Somehow he reminded me of a white-haired woman who frequented the lobby of my apartment building and insisted that everybody call her Granny. Must I disappoint him by breaking up our camaraderie over a bureaucratic trifle?

So I didn't mention the "Self" I'd written in the "company" column of the records the night before.

"You need a rest, fella, that's what you need," he said. "You've got bags under your eyes."

I nodded and gave him a good yawn.

"You ask your boss for some time off," he said.

"Oh, I've got myself a long vacation coming, that's for sure."

On the fifth floor one of the surlier copy aides walked up to me and slapped my back. "Gotta hand it to you," he said, "the way you shoved it to those bastards." I thanked him without knowing if he was praising a successful story or an aborted rebellion.

Straight ahead, Mac was standing in the door of the Shark's Cage, arms akimbo, and he was yelling at me as though summoning a servant. Half the city room seemed to be watching as I entered the Cage; were people awed at my luck or pluck?

McWilliams motioned toward a hard-backed chair in the Cage. Once more he was frowning—enough to make me think that his temples might soon become as well creased as Eddy Bullard's forehead around the whiskey-line region.

I almost felt as if he had a hand on my shoulder and was shoving me down.

"You chicken shit," he said, "you thought you could put one over on me, didn't you?"

"Fuck you, McWilliams," I said. "That's the only reason I'm here. Just so I can say—"

"Jesus, Stone, what more do you expect—my job?"

"I don't follow you," I yawned.

"Christ, we gave you half the front page."

I rubbed my eyes.

"Pretty good play, if you ask me," Mac said.

"A two-column head?" I said. "If I weren't such a modest bastard, I'd have made it the lead."

"You don't even read your own paper, do you, pal?" Mac reached into his wastebasket and pulled out a *Telegram* wet with coffee stains. He slapped it so hard across my knee that I almost yelped.

"Here! Read your own fucking paper!"

I unfolded it and saw my Bullard story stripped across the page—displayed almost as well as the collapse itself.

Within the present version, however, I noticed one difference: the insertion of an assurance from Eddy Bullard that his investment was indeed a most unfortunate accident.

"You mean you called Bullard in the middle of the night?"

"Not quite, pal. I'm not as rude as you. What happened was—"

The phone rang, and Mac answered in his customary way: "You're talking to him." He excelled at certain details; he would neither insult the grammarians with "That's me" nor offend the small-d democrats with "This is he." Not that Mac had to worry about upsetting that many people; he'd long since reached the point where he could compile a big shit list and enforce it.

"Exactly right," Mac was saying. "There aren't any friends in the newspaper business."

He cupped his hand over the transmitter and rasped to me: "It's Reuters asking why we took on Eddy Bullard."

"Yeah," Mac said into the phone, "it was a group effort. Stone did the legwork, and E.J. and I pointed him in the right direction ... Of course we're proud. It's a Pulitzer for sure... Nope, he's our Housing reporter. We had him on the Roxland beat a while, just something temporary to help circulation out there."

McWilliams presently hung up and turned to me: "It's the fifth call I've gotten from them today. It's on all the radio stations, UPI, Tass, AP."

Again he answered the phone:

"... No, not at all ... I don't see any connection ... Do what you want, pal. I'm just saying that's the biggest piece of crap I've heard since I last talked to you." Slam.

"Who was that?"

"It's nothing," Mac said. "Just some crazy Japanese reporter asking if this solves the Kennedy assassination."

"Listen," I said, "about what you were telling Reuters. Someone's getting promoted back to his old beat, you say?"

"To save face," Mac said. "Yours."

"Yours, you mean."

"Christ, Stone. If I'd been on the ball, I'd have canned you before all this happened."

"Bullshit. You printed the story because you knew I'd take it elsewhere. And to convince yourself of your own honesty."

"Of course," said McWilliams, reaching for a cigar, "I can fire you now."

"You wouldn't dare."

"Try me."

"And that strip across the top—I've got to hand it to you," I said. "It's a first-class job—how you co-opted my story."

"Co-opted? Who the fuck authorized it?"

"And pulled me off."

"Because you were doing a piss-poor investigating job," Mac said. "I was about to turn it over to Garst, as a matter of fact. So we could get it done right."

"Bull."

"Of course we're promoting Garst," McWilliams said.

"From Housing?"

"What else? He's too good for it. And you—you didn't even bother to get Bullard's side. If the night crew hadn't phoned me... Don't you have any scruples? I mean, if you do a story on the zoo, you at least try to interview the animals."

"Then how'd it get in the paper?"

"Because I talked to Eddy Bullard," Mac said, glancing at his Rolex.

"But," I protested, "you said you didn't call him."

"Last night."

"You mean you had the basics pinned down and withheld the story until now. When you could get in on my hero act."

Again the phone jangled, and I heard Mac snarl to a secretary:

"... No, no, I don't ever want to speak to that murderer again ... No! Tell Solomon he's through! ... No—not Bullard, either!"

൙൫

O'Brien managed to shamble past security into the city room one day with his beer belly sticking out between his pants and a sweaty T-shirt.

His breath suggested he'd been drinking something stronger than Budweiser. I almost picked up the phone to call a security guard, and not the friendly one at the front door.

"I see GSA's let up a little on the dress code," I said.

O'Brien made a fist.

"A bad joke," I said, "okay?"

"Some joke—turning me in to the feds. The lunches. They found out about the lunches."

"But not from me," I said.

"How do I know?"

"Because I'd have nothing to gain by turning you in."

O'Brien moved his fist closer to my face.

"Christ," I said, "who'd want to talk to a fink reporter?"

"Feds been through here? Searching your desk and all?"

"No, that's one scene you can't include in the movie."

"Well, they must of found out somehow," he said. "They're going after everything. The lunches. The football tickets. The Christmas gifts. Everything. And of all the times. I'm never gonna be able to pay for that camper."

That was a month after the collapse and amid some mutterings on the Hill about impeachment.

₧₧

What followed was a flood of distracting leaks from Zumweltnar to The Other Paper—engrossing revelations of misused credit cards and stolen plumbing fixtures and Kotex missing from GSA supply stores. President Eddy Bullard expressed great outrage against corrupt bureaucrats. He considered their removal so important, so worthy of a special prosecutor inspiring the highest trust, that he appointed one of his former law partners.

Some of the wilder attorneys at Justice talked of taking Solomon to court for putting up a building that fell down. But the special prosecutor sensibly pointed out that GSA had inspected Vulture's Point when it was under construction and that therefore the government itself was at fault—which was to say that no one was to blame. Nor could anybody help it, after thinking things through, that Sy Solomon was generous at lunch.

For a while I thought I was onto something else, corporate connections between the administrator and other landlords. But that investigation was just another fart in a windstorm. It was like trying to take apart microscopic Chinese boxes. And so I contented myself with rewriting the rewrites of the leaked audit reports, until GSA ran out of scapegoats, and the administrator resigned—only to resurface at a New Jersey waste disposal company owned by one of Bullard's contributors.

McWilliams and Luci Elkins broke up over her loyalty to Solomon, though I suppose it would have happened anyway. She'd never liked Vivaldi, even in Mrs. Simpson's presence, and Mac was getting tired of the famous hairdo.

ဆဟ

Amid all the other diversions created by damage control from the White House, Donna Stackelbaum and Hilton Kahn went to prison in a well-timed nuclear scandal.

Prosecutors made nary a mention of Hilton's equal gifts for real estate dealings. Instead, the feds zeroed in on the "regulatory adjustments" that had led to the cooked bass and weakened radiation precautions at Quad's massive riverside plant.

I was thankful I'd walled myself off from the messier details of Donna's government work. Two other "love buddies" of hers sang before grand juries about the career brags she had made between orgasms. Poor Donna. I'd always said she was test-smart, not Machiavelli-smart, but never had I expected that her life would come to this.

Donna and Hilton ended up in his-and-her penitentiaries, so to speak, within a quick drive of each other. Alas, the bureaucracy at the Bureau of Prisons was deaf to Apple and Foster's eloquent arguments on behalf of their sex lives. Not once during Hilton's and Donna's time behind bars, two years each, would BOP schedule conjugal visits.

Chapter 36

"You look thinner," I said to Fred Green at the Little Tavern. "Here—have some potato chips."

My leakaholic friend pushed them away. "Liquid protein diet," he said. I remembered his line, "Every time I talk to you I gain two pounds." Maybe there was something symbolic here; Green hadn't been in touch with me for the past two months.

"This better be good stuff you're giving me," I said. "'I don't do casework.'"

"What?" Uncomfortably, Green laughed. "Oh, that. It was just a busy day."

The Little Tavern man brought my main course, and I tried to recall an article about McDonald's and Little Tavern. Which had the less carcinogenic way of cooking hamburgers?

"You see The Elephant column yesterday?" Green asked.

"Is that why we're here? Jesus, do you really believe the crap about Wendy having an affair with Sy Solomon?" It wasn't that much to believe, really, just six lines of type near the beginning of The Elephant: "Wendy Blevin Is Flying Out of the Cuckoo's Nest to be with her friend Sy Solomon at a ritzy estate near Wellwater, Maine. How naughty, dear. Elephant promises not to tell unless the mansion falls down."

Green yanked a napkin out of a dispenser and started twisting it into a phallic shape. Perhaps it was his subtle, subconscious way of suggesting what he believed had transpired between Wendy and Sy.

Imagine the Freudian potential: Sy Solomon as a Morrison Blevin replacement! But although I remembered the incongruity of the coupling between O'Brien and the society snob, the Morrison possibility was simply too much of a stretch. The idea of even a platonic relationship between Wendy and Solomon seemed risible, with or without his millions.

Or was it?

"Didn't you say she could have been leaking your investigation?" Green asked.

"Which she might have been doing," I said, "but Solomon's an old man. Why the fuck would she mess with him? Not that he's ready for a nursing home."

"Maybe he's into goat's glands."

"And his money," I said, "I bet she could buy him out twice over if she sold her MTB stock. It's sort of like saying she's screwing Ted Kennedy. I mean, this is deepest bullshit territory."

"Then maybe I'm wasting my time trying to get you to believe the rest of what I'll say."

"You sure you don't want some chips?"

"Ever heard of Jesus Sanchez?" Green asked.

I nodded. "A member of the Papudoian junta. Didn't Wendy do a People Page piece on him once?"

Green nodded.

"The one where he came across as Clark Gable?" I asked. "I still don't get it."

"What if people told her how to write it," Green said. "Especially Solomon."

I remembered the bulletin board notice, the way Mac had complimented Wendy on her "objectivity and total professionalism."

"She might be a snitch, but a puff artist?" I asked. "Wendy? Terror of Georgetown? A columnist who speculates about the length of Henry Kissinger's penis?" Not in print, of course—just discreetly by implication at party-parties.

"Then maybe it has something to do with the length of Solomon's," Green said.

"But why would Solomon want her to puff Sanchez?"

"Well, to be more direct, why would the CIA?"

"Oh, no. Not another of your grand conspiracy theories."

"Except that it's true." Green reached for one of my potato chips. "Sanchez wanted glory, not just money."

"What money?"

"The two-million-dollar bribe. For making sure the others in the junta didn't snuggle up too closely to the Russians."

"It's still something of a right-wing junta," I protested.

"*Something,*" Green said. "You might think of the two million as a way to encourage it to become right-wing entirely." Then he discoursed on the exact circumstances of the bribe.

"And Solomon comes in somewhere?" I asked.

"By way of his buildings," Green said. "As safe, profitable places for Sanchez to invest his money via automatic deposits. With a few middlemen in between. The Drivers' Union, they have the Sanchez money blended in with a unit of one of their pension funds. In fact, you might almost say Sanchez was a CIA landlord. Not just a business partner."

"Cozy."

"Through Vulture's Point and other places—through the pension fund arrangement there."

"But why all this investment stuff? Couldn't the CIA just stash his money away until Sanchez wanted it?"

Green sighed. "Well, put it this way. Once the foreigners we bribed had a touching faith in the dollar. But not now. Swiss francs, real estate, you name it—anything but the dollar itself. And you know spooks. Pragmatic as well as patriotic. So they arranged for Solomon and Sanchez to get together. A very nice deal for everyone, considering that the CIA has already been subsidizing Solomon. And benefiting from the resultant cash flow."

"Not to mention those hidden microphones in the buildings the government leases," I recalled. "So how does Wendy figure in all this?"

"The puff piece," Green said. "Wendy was part of the deal. Helped consummate it."

I raised my brow.

"For Sanchez's ego and peace of mind. For assurance that the spooks could handle things well—that they could throw some weight around if a newspaper found out what was happening."

"But what's the logic here?"

"If you can get a nice story in the papers, doesn't that suggest you might be able to keep a nasty one out? And as for the ego—well, even Papudoian butchers need to think they're loved."

"I don't know about keeping nasty ones out." Not that the *Telegram* didn't cover up. I just didn't like the implied syllogism.

"I do," Green protested.

"Who's your source for all this?"

"I think I'll order a hamburger."

"Mrs. Wentworth?"

"By the way," Green said, "McWilliams knew what was going on. Not that he did anything. He just permitted it."

"Once CIA, always CIA?"

"Well, in his case, sort of," said Green, and I began having some extravagantly paranoid notions about how Mac had tracked me down at Margo's. "I mean, come on. It's his life, his fortune."

"You mean Mac's embezzling from the CIA?"

"Who needs that? You don't know about Mac, do you, pal?" Green mocked. "You don't know what he really did during World War II, do you?"

Along with most of the town, I was ignorant. To that day Mac and friends had been resolutely vague about his wartime work for the OSS, the CIA's spookish predecessor. Was it all one big hoax?

"So," I asked, "he actually wasn't with the intel people?"

"Oh, but he was. Mac was one of the main brains behind currency destabilization. The more trouble for the mark, the less money for tanks and Messerschmitts. There was only so much to be done, but Mac did a lot with what he had to work with. Not just with the Germans but their friends. So the boys remembered him."

"'The boys'?" I asked.

"Let's just say the Network."

A beacon switched on inside my head. "Tips from his old job? So that's how he made his pile?"

"German, French, the Brits," Green said. "If a clerk in the Exchequer's office farted too much in the men's room, Mac was about the first to hear about it."

"What a great way to outwit the rest of the traders."

"You might want to make that present tense," Green said. "Through straws."

"You'd think that the *Telegram* was enough to keep him busy."

"But what if it's just another Network thing? What if the Network someday will own the *Telegram*? A nice long-term quid pro quo."

"Excuse me, please, but does Vicki know this piddling little detail?"

Green shook his head. "Nope, just the amount he and the Network are gonna pay her in a buyout."

"But isn't the *Telegram* going public?" I asked.

"The whole thing's a big sham. The press'll just think it's politics when the deal collapses. Nice little distraction, then the Network permanently controls the *Telegram*."

"The millionaire as a mole, kinda?"

"It's a great arrangement," Green said. "Imagine: the financial desk as Tip Paradise for the Network. Not to mention the benefits for the alma mater. Remember, the CIA can honestly say it doesn't own a share of the *Telegram*. Who's to know that it's really the alumni? On top of that, they can blackmail Mac right up to the gills if he steps out of line."

"Would he?"

"Hardly likely. He's one of the Network's top people."

So Mac's famous maverick side, small m, along with his eccentricity, helped to conceal a solid establishmentarian, at least on the things that counted?

I nodded: Green actually made sense. Most everyone at the top in D.C. might well be in one big secret society together, regardless of all the feuding within.

Power People had no other choice in this city of traded favors.

I remembered all the gossip, true and untrue, about Skull and Bones and other secret societies at Ivy League schools, and how you could worm your way to power through premade holes.

Mac was hardly that kind of clubman. But metaphorically he could well have lain down in a coffin or stroked the skull of a dead Indian chief. How the regulators and taxmen might have feasted on Mac's subterranean financial life had their bosses been more curious! At the same time, from the CIA to the Securities and Exchange Commission, Mac exercised no small amount of control over the world's perceptions of various and sundry bureaucracies.

Imagine, then, some spooky friends and family of the CIA, so to speak, preparing to buy out the paper whose editor was the city's ultimate arbiter of news. Such was life in Washington—a seamy chain of alliances, where you'd be mistrusted if you stepped outside the circle.

I remembered the first day I'd met a colleague of Fred Green's. Within two minutes, he was holding forth on a female congressional staffer's enthusiasm for anal sex. Did that little vignette not capture the spirit of the place?

"So," I asked about Mac's networking, "are we on or off record?"

"Off, off, off."

"But what makes you think he'll print the Blevin story, at least?"

"Nothing," Green said, "except that two days from now I'll be giving AP a press release."

"AP" was another way of saying Al Bergmann. He was a hiking buddy of mine, as I've mentioned earlier—one of a string of reporters who had built their careers on Green's loquaciousness.

"Oh, and by the way," Green said, "there was a little accident. The general actually fell in love with Wendy. Every week he sends her roses."

So that explained it—the muscular, foreign-looking men who came to the desk near the Shark's Cage, bearing the bouquets of giant white roses. "Background only about the roses," Green said. "Not even for Mac. Particularly not him."

I nodded.

"Too close to home," Green said. "For you, not me. Not one word about Wendy and the roses. The Solomon angle's safe to go with, and the rest of the Sanchez info. Just keep the infatuation stuff out of print."

"So," I asked, "she's messing around with both?"

Green shook his head. "Just Solomon."

"But she accepts the roses, doesn't she?"

"Let's just say she's flattered and tactful and eager to avoid a diplomatic incident."

"With a little encouragement from the CIA?"

"Understandably. The general was inclined to believe all those nice things she wrote. And Wendy can't go too far in backtracking privately. Which means that Solomon had better be careful around construction cranes."

"Ah! What's one more corpse?"

"Exactly," Green said. "Sanchez's been waiting long enough. Either Solomon dies on his own, or eventually the general will hasten the process."

"Oh, to be able to print this," I said, watching a still-plump hand grab another potato chip.

"Kind of touching in a King Kongish way. A would-be relationship between Beauty and the Beast. He's terribly protective."

No, I wouldn't write about the unrequited love that Wendy was drawing from General Kong. But Green had still left me free to scoop my friend Bergmann at the Associated Press. I could be the first to tell the cosmos of the CIA-Sanchez-GSA-Solomon relationship and the agency-influenced People Page story—the alleged fruit of her supposed affair with Solomon.

Should I do the piece before Al did? Or wait?

If Kong's Brown Suits had something in mind, ideally they would kill off the competition rather than me.

But Al was not just competition in the abstract. He was the guy I hiked with up the Appalachian Trail, and with whom I shared Dylan albums and pulpy old spy novels.

So screw personal caution and scoop Al for his own good, if the facts held up.

Besides, if there had to be a corpse, and I hoped there wouldn't be, maybe I could somehow take advantage of fate and let it be neither his nor mine.

Chapter 37

"What's 'The Capital Connection'?" I asked, intrigued by the slug line on the story Wendy was tapping out.

"Classes for social climbers," she said. "I really can't see the harm, dear. It's only nine dollars to enroll. It's right next door to a dance studio."

"How do you Climb?"

"Party-crashing, of course. Just hold a glass and pretend you're on your fifth Scotch. Then back in the door, and they'll think you've been there all evening."

"I suppose the students practice before a special row of doors and mirrors."

"Or you can sneak past the doorman saying you have some earth-shaking news for the ambassador."

"Sounds like a bargain for nine dollars."

"Of course, dear. It's even taught by a PR woman from Cincinnati."

I wondered how the PR lady accommodated students who wished to befriend the president. Did she give poker lessons so they could crash the most exclusive party-parties in the Free World? Would the students know the right brand of tennis shoes to wear?

"They even teach you how to tattle to The Elephant," Wendy said, "so you can get your own name in. Working for peanuts, you might say."

Why had she mentioned The Elephant, of all things? Perhaps it was her way of saying she didn't care about the previous day's column.

"Have your peanuts arrived yet?" I asked.

Wendy laughed. "I suppose that's the part of the class *I* should be teaching. No, they haven't, and when they do, I'll send them back because I don't think I've earned them very honestly."

"You mean it's crap—that item about you and Solomon?"

"It was silly yesterday, it's still silly today, and it'll be just as silly tomorrow. Unless I do decide to have an affair with him. Then I'll ask Ida if she wants to go out with you."

As Wendy spoke, she fiddled with her hair, and I studied her eyes for a suspicious number of blinks. It had to be true, the theory about blinking and lying; a journalism professor had written his thesis on the topic. The doormen of Washington might even take lessons from him to expose the PR woman's Climbing alumni.

The only problem was, I myself was a miserably inept blink-counter. But I fuzzily remembered something that might help me learn the truth about Wendy—something that O'Brien had spilled out between his beers.

Sy Solomon had an insane son who was currently insane in Maine. And The Elephant had said, "Wendy Blevin Is Flying Out of the Cuckoo's Nest to be with her friend Sy Solomon at a ritzy estate near Wellwater, Maine."

"Excuse me, dear. I've got to get back to telling our readers how to Climb."

"Hurry up and write it so I can learn all the tricks."

"My, we're modest today."

"No," I said, "I'm just thinking of it for Business Page stuff. That idea of backing through doors with a Scotch in your hand—it's just the thing to crash stockholders' lunches."

⁊⁃

The name "Wellwater" kept teasing my memory. It was one of those sheer hunches, like my feelings about the Chicago address on the partnership papers for Vulture's Point.

And so I went to the *Telegram* library, the morgue, and started searching through the clips and pondering whether Wendy would really sell out the People Page, the way Green had depicted her to me.

She wrote on the frivolous, but did it ever so seriously; she was one of the few people in town who, it seemed, could always separate integrity from respectability. If she went to Solomon's parties, if she were still friends with Bullard, she at least had professional justifications.

Wendy might be a gossip, she might even have set back my investigation, but I could not see her as being aggressively corrupt.

If indeed Wendy had glorified Sanchez for Solomon, she might have had romantic reasons—which wasn't to say I completely accepted that possibility.

However old her father at the time of her birth, I still wasn't Freudian enough to consider seriously the chance of an attraction between her and Solomon based partly on his age.

And from the start I'd dismissed the question of money.

I thought of social standing, too, and laughed at myself for doing so. Solomon's was a fraction of hers among the Old Money crowd. Wendy would have had to commit a triple ax murder before the Green Book tossed her out.

The only thing left was Power, of which I was certain Solomon had less than before the collapse, but then I reflected on the GSA cover-up and Bullard's steadfastness in defending his old friend. Solomon still went to the poker games at the White House. Might that have been a motive of Wendy's—access to a Power Player?

Never mind. Mac himself had played poker at the White House up to the time of the collapse at Vulture's Point.

Such thoughts coursed through my mind as I rummaged through the clips, looking for possible sell-out stories beyond the Sanchez piece.

But I found nothing else of interest in Wendy's byline file in the *Telegram*'s morgue.

And so I continued my search in other places: elsewhere through the W's ("Wellwater"), through the M's ("Maine," "Mansions"), until I discovered a cross-referenced possibility under the E's ("Estates"), a story Wendy had done on Christopher Marns's mansion near Wellwater.

The robber baron Artemus Marns had built it as a summer home, and his descendants had named their legacy Our Country Place, causing Wendy to observe that "sometimes the very rich cannot decide whether to be droll or pretentious.

"I drove along a straight road for almost ten minutes before seeing this neo-Greco-Roman creation, which looked less like a house than a monument. There were deer, ducks, all kinds of native life, including third-generation servants, who later glared at me if I got too close to the Rodins in the living room."

But did the People Page piece show she was thick with Christopher Marns and Seymour Solomon?

Obviously quite the contrary. She had even indulged in some unflattering speculation about the origins of the Marns crest above the marble mantel, and she had questioned the authenticity of the Renoir in the den.

I could hear the indignant murmurs of the real party-party people, feel Wendy's terror as the reprimand came down from Mrs. Simpson herself (maybe Wendy hadn't always been *responsibly* outrageous).

If the article had appeared while Wendy was spending her weekends with old Sy, Christopher Marns might have called in all of Solomon's loans.

Then I looked at the date stamped on the clip—just a few months after Wendy had started working for the *Telegram*, when she must not have known Solomon except perhaps vaguely through Sidwell Friends.

Even so, I remained skeptical of the gossip. What about Ida, dear old Ida, the sharer of the overheated apartment, the apartment without a radio? I could hardly imagine her whiling away the weekends by screwing her plastic surgeon. An affair between her husband and Wendy seemed utter fantasy.

As much as I believed in Solomon's guilt in the building collapse, I believed in his venerating himself as a good family man when it was convenient. Solomon's son, the one you never read about on the People Page—might not Sy be resolutely philanthropic and pureminded not just to immortalize the family name but also to mitigate what he perceived as divine punishment?

It was almost like Andrew Carnegie or Artemus Marns endowing libraries to get into heaven, but Solomon wasn't Christian, and if he had been, I supposed he would have been a tad more honest and given St. Peter an outright bribe.

Then again, Solomon might bargain with whatever angels and ghosts took care of real estate men regardless of faith. He might find an angel somewhere with a good eye for real estate deals; then he could kindly extend a loan for an interest in a government-leased building where the angel could invest after proper consideration about whether to be listed in the partnership books.

Perhaps Solomon would ask Christopher Marns to arrange a
trusteeship; even Jehovah might not be omniscient enough to find
out what was happening at the Lincoln Trust Department.

Then my thoughts returned to Maine, and to the son, whom
I imagined Solomon dutifully visiting—a very possible reason, I
believed, for going to Our Country Place.

With that in mind, I called up a licensing board in Maine and
learned that a home for rich, young psychopaths adjoined the
grounds of the estate. I still harbored my doubts, however. There
were Accidents, there were Coincidences, there were many detours
between Suspicion and History.

The better the story, the more outrageous the scandal, the less
chance it existed.

I wondered, too, why The Elephant hadn't noticed a Marns connection, except that the gossips couldn't care less about the difference between Suspicion and History.

For all I knew, the whole item might have been based on just
a few whispers overheard at a Georgetown bistro. The Elephant,
unlike some other gossip columns, did not always trouble itself with
calling its victims for confirmations and explanations. All too often
it just sucked up whatever malarkey came its way, via the twenty-
four-hour tip hotline or otherwise, and printed funny apologies
later.

So I went down to the newsstand in front of the *Telegram* and
bought the first edition of the evening paper and looked.

There was no apology, funny or otherwise, just the casual addition
of the fact that Solomon and Wendy had been visiting Our Country
Place—along with mention of the gift of an Afghan that Solomon
had bought her in Wellwater.

And somehow I began believing that Coincidence might coincide
here with History.

Chapter 38

I returned to Wendy Blevin a few minutes later and backed into what was obsessing me.

"Have you ever seen this man?" I held up a file photo of Sanchez, with his Neanderthal forehead and bulging eyes.

"Of course, dear. That profile I did." She was acting as you'd expect many of the smarter journalists to behave at first under the circumstances. She was readily conceding the obvious.

"That's quite a flattering piece. That aura of romance. The way you put it, he'd give Clark Gable a run for his money."

"Of course," said Wendy. "But why are you so curious?"

"Tell me—how'd you get the inspiration for that article?"

Wendy laughed, a little nervously; I didn't count the blinks. "If you'll tell me how you got the inspiration for your questions."

"It might affect the validity of the answers."

"What are you doing, dear—a sociological study of the romantic tastes of the People Page staff?"

"Well, the photograph. It hardly bears out the contents of your article. He's, well, a little on the homely side."

"Sanchez photographed terribly. Just a bad picture, that's all. Copy Desk didn't complain."

"Taken during his visit here?"

She nodded.

"Who introduced you?"

Wendy shrugged and averted her eyes. "I really don't remember."

There was a pause, then an addendum spoken an octave higher than the earlier words: "The embassy, I guess."

"You don't recall who there?"

"No." She glanced back at the screen of the VDT, as if to say I was in the way of her work. "What's this leading up to, dear? Are you at least giving up on Solomon?"

"Maybe, maybe not."

"No, I don't sleep with Sanchez either. And don't dare repeat that to The Elephant. Next thing you know, they'll have me flying every weekend down to Papudo."

"Your Sanchez story," I said. "Can you remember step by step how it developed?"

"Dear, I really can't figure you out. You're not moonlighting for a journalism review, are you?"

"Just tell me, step by step."

"It's really none of your business. How would I remember? It's been months and months."

That was a sensible enough response for somebody in Wendy's place. If she volunteered the whole story piece by piece, I might pick it apart; we were past the point where Wendy could blunt my curiosity by way of a selectively loose tongue.

Then I showed her a clip of the new Elephant column.

"What about it?" she said. "I've already denied everything."

"To The Elephant?"

"Why bother? They'd just keep on lying."

"So you've never been to Our Country Place—not with Solomon, anyway?"

"No, dear."

"Well," I bluffed, "that's news to the gardener."

"Which gardener? They have sev—"

"So you've been there, *are* going there," I said, and watched her quiver.

"Oh, for God's sake, can't we have any privacy?" Wendy's trembling yell left not the slightest doubt that Solomon was half of the "we."

Hands over her ears, as if that could forever block out nettlesome questions, she ran for the stairs.

ഇരേ

Wendy's scream was unnerving enough to make me feign bewilderment when others started gawking. Blithely, I returned to my desk and started a memo on Jesus Sanchez's fondness for flattery and safe real estate investments.

I hadn't typed more than two short paragraphs when I felt McWilliams grabbing my collar and heard him rasp once more:

"What's going on, pal? What were you two talking about?"

So I told him the story, most everything on record that Green had revealed in the Little Tavern, then what I'd pried out about Wendy's weekends. Mac kept his thin lips together until I triumphantly mentioned the inevitability of the press release.

"What? That can't be, damn it, that can't be! Christ, we had an agreement. National security."

"With Green?"

"No, with—Never mind!" he said, and raced back into his glass booth, shut the door, and grabbed his phone.

Between the building collapse and all the wild rumors, not to mention Green's impending release, the Solomon scandals had reached a tipping point—toward an even more diversionary exposure of the fringe players. Wendy qualified.

I wondered about Solomon, too, and whether he would finally be a main course, succulent meat, for the prosecutors. Or was the cover-up machinery well enough oiled for this not to be of concern? Just how bipartisan might the affair be?

Might Solomon look forward to a pardon over the CIA-related aspects of the scandal, no matter who sat in the Oval Office—assuming that the prosecutors went after Wendy's man in the first place? How quiet would she herself keep, in view of a possible action from the Justice Department and on the Hill? Thankfully, she'd usually been discreet in reporting the wanderings of married senators.

An hour later, McWilliams called me into the Shark's Cage and thrust a notebook at me.

"Take it down," he said. "Take it all down, everything I say—it's all confirmed."

"Who through?"

"It's confirmed, period. Now—we'll want to flesh things out." Mac rattled off dates and places and other mundane facts about Solomon, Sanchez, Wendy, and the spooks. "And of course there's the dog."

I was intrigued, so I said nothing and looked as dumb as I could.

"Wendy's, up in Maine—this Afghan hound. And not just your run-of-the-mill Afghan. He's a four-thousand-dollar dog. And a gift, Solomon's."

"Which she received when?" I asked.

Mac told me.

"That must have been a year before her Sanchez story."

"What do you expect, pal—a contract saying, 'I, Wendy Blevin, do hereby agree to flatter your friend Sanchez in return for an Afghan'?"

"Not really, but—"

"You think Solomon's bribing? Well, he's not bribing—he's investing. Financially—with campaign gifts. Socially—with the parties and the affair."

Only, Mac had turned himself into a write-off.

He squinted at my notes, and I worried about myself; how could I rise to the very top of my profession if I couldn't read scrawls upside down?

"It's long-range," Mac said. "No chicken-shit quid pro quo with the people who really count. Well, perhaps on big stuff like the loan and the interest in the building. But for the most part just friendly favors and plenty of patience. The parties, they're the big thing."

An old saying from American Lit tickled my brain cells: Ralph Waldo Emerson's wisdom about consistency being the hobgoblin of little minds. I knew Mac was a genius. "But," I almost felt like flinging in McWilliams's face, sarcastically, "he even drives a Maverick."

"And," McWilliams said, "you know our policy, don't you—against gifts?"

"Sure." The idea was to refuse anything you couldn't eat in one sitting; it was a good way to allow for continuing feedings in the form of party-parties. Who could forbid you from dining again and again with the respectables of the moment? Of course the ban might include Afghan hounds unless they were cut into little pieces and served with the hors d'oeuvres.

There might or might not have been an exemption for White House poker games. Outside my meanest imaginings, I hadn't any idea how much Mac had won.

"So," he said, "we're running a sidebar about Wendy. We have a responsibility, a professional responsibility—we've got to level with our readers. And I hear Solomon's not her first. You name it—if it has two legs and a pair of pants, she's been to bed with it."

"Wendy? I don't believe."

"It's in court records."

"Where?"

"Alabama. When she was covering some sit-ins against the reactor there. A married man. The poor son of a bitch—he was divorcing his wife. Except that he died of a heart attack. One of these degenerate good ole Southern boys. And then there was a gas station attendant, a telephone repair man, a teacher—"

"Interesting," I said, "but is this relevant?"

Prudence—fear of reprisals against me from Sanchez's ever-watchful Brown Suits—mingled with decency.

"Relevant? Christ, Stone, this woman has a track record. No doubt she's Ms. F. Scott Fitzgerald, but she's a pretty poor excuse for a reporter."

"But you're the one who made her what she is."

"Stone! Are you or aren't you doing the story? She fucked our paper, damn it—your paper, your investigation!"

"I still don't understand how you know all this dirt."

"Are you or aren't you? You've got the facts. Now write!"

"'It's been learned that'—is that how you want me to attribute it?"

"You got it, pal, except for what Green's putting in the release."

"But we've got to confirm—"

"Stone! We've got to get this out before the competition. Especially about Wendy." He shook his head in disgust at me and, almost reflexively, looked over his shoulder at the shelf where the mitt was sitting. "Christ, our credibility's at stake."

"I'm not writing it."

"Suit yourself, pal," McWilliams said, and bellowed across the newsroom for Garst.

୫୦୧

Margo was hitting and jiggling me. "I'm not awake, I'm not awake!" I rolled over on the mattress and yawned.

Little did Margo understand what she was up against. Years ago some fanatic of a Metro Editor had insisted that all his reporters attend weekly staff meetings at eight o'clock in the morning—to which foolishness I'd responded once by showing up in pajamas.

"Please," I groaned now, "it's Saturday."

"How can anyone sleep after what you've done?" Margo said.

"Which of my many sins?"

"You lied! Oh Jonathan, how could you?"

"But it *is* Saturday."

"The story—you promised you'd have nothing more to do with it."

"Well, I didn't, did I?" I said, glancing at the Kafka poster and wondering how Franz would have dealt with the *Telegram*'s bureaucracy.

"Then how come it's out with your byline?" Margo stuck the Saturday paper in front of my face. "Look." My name appeared with Garst's over both the Sanchez story and the Blevin exposé.

"I—I don't get it. I told McWilliams to fuck off. The moment I finished with the notes."

"I almost feel like calling Wendy Blevin and apologizing for you," Margo said. "What right, just what right have you to snoop into that poor woman's private life?"

"Goddamn it, I didn't write it!"

"The hypocrisy, that's what puzzles me," said Margo. "You screw one of your sources. Then you crucify another woman for a 'conflict of interest.'"

Margo gave the Blevin exposé a nasty jab. "Look what it says: 'Observers believe she may have committed one of the most serious of all professional offenses—writing a story to accommodate hidden personal and business interests.' And then this sanctimonious bullshit from your friend McWilliams on how he was so shocked to find it had happened. Sure, Jonathan, sure—after all you told me about Luci Elkins and that bunch. The parties, the White House, and yet Wendy—"

"A scapegoat," I agreed.

"Who's next," Margo asked, "me? For leaking information to you."

"Then GSA would make you a scapegoat—not the *Telegram*. That's GSA's job."

Margo shrugged.

"What's the difference," she said, "it's the same game. Look! All this about the divorce suit and the private eye. And then the rest. About, quote, 'her unusual sexual preferences.' My God, Jonathan."

I nodded in sympathy with both women—Margo in the room and Wendy in her despair, wherever she must be drinking or weeping, or whatever heiresses do when their reputations founder in a sea of toxic black ink.

Wendy had been wild in public and private, but always with style and within the bounds of the randier studs and mares of the standard Washington party circuit.

No one before had accused her of Sapphic acts.

So were the crazier of the rumors true, the dirt that the *Telegram* should have shunned even *if* court records had beckoned? I neither knew nor cared. The whole spectacle on the front page made me want to go from, "Just don't frighten the horses," to, "Where's the real sleaze here? In the sex acts or the gotcha laws that crooked corporations and politicians use to control the rest of the planet?"

Not much of a barrier stood between sexual politics, so to speak, and the Washington variety.

Very likely Bullard had entrusted GSA pork to Harold Jones because of Jones's secrets, not in spite of them. And potentially most every political reporter in town had been part of the tacit threat, an unwitting enabler for the blackmailer in the Oval Office. Baruch de Spinoza needed to come back to life with the right syllogisms to guide me through it all.

"But," I told Margo, "I just did the *notes*. Just raw background—because he ordered me. Nothing I wanted in the paper. Beyond which the extra sex garbage was news to me."

"So why's your name on the story?"

"Used without permission," I said. "I just chucked my notes back at Mac and said I didn't want to touch the stuff. I thought Garst would get a single byline on the sidebar."

"And yet they still used your name?"

I nodded. And imagined the words between Mac and me on Monday: "Christ, Stone, you were bitching we'd co-opted your stories. So I thought I'd give you some extra credit this time."

৪০০৪

"No, dear," Wendy said when I called to apologize for the smear and explain the unwanted byline, "I'm not going to hang up on you. In fact, I'm going to invite you to my party."

"Party?"

"My party to celebrate your story about me. You'll come, won't you? Tomorrow for dinner?"

"Look," I said, "I just want you to know I didn't write that story."

"It's a buffet," said Wendy, ignoring me, "nothing too formal."

"Mac tried to trap me—dictating some notes."

"Of course, dear," Wendy said, with all the conviction of an astronomer who'd been told the sky was green.

"McWilliams, he just turned over my notes to Garst."

"Please, dear, I've been around. What's there to deny?" Wendy said. "I loved that man. I still love that man."

So it had been a definite lie, everything she'd said about not having an affair with Solomon, and I searched for ways to ask Wendy for an explanation. Might there be some exculpatory details, some way of mitigating History? Once more I thought of Marseilles, of the long-haired spreader of the rock story, of the discarded cassette. And right then I just wished I could dismiss all the Solomon scandals as Coincidence and toss the *Telegram's* entire press run into the can.

"But the part about being a lousy lay," Wendy said after a pause, "what do they know? Anonymous sources, dear. Not that you weren't trying to please Mac and do your job, but in all the time you've known me, have I ever made up quotes?"

"It didn't come from me. I told Mac I wanted nothing to do with it."

"Of course, dear, of course."

"Garst, he just wrote up the crap Mac told him."

"So you're coming, dear? To my party?"

"Sure."

"You'll love the canapés. I've asked Cozely's to send over their best people."

Cozely's was normally booked weeks ahead, but I supposed that the caterers might show some deference toward the right party-partiers.

"I'll be there, promise." At least in person I'd stand a chance of seeming credible.

"I've got this super old movie I thought everyone might watch if they're in the mood," Wendy said. *"Guess Who's Coming to Dinner."*

"What time?"

"And bring a friend," she said. "Bring a friend, bring a friend of a friend, bring a friend of a friend of a friend! I want the whole world to come! We can always knock down the wall of the next apartment."

"Just give me the time," I persisted.

"I might even put an ad in the *Telegram.*"

"Just tell me the time."

"You'll like it, dear—it's going to be quite a show."

"If you tell me the time."

"Eight o'clock," said Wendy, "and don't stand me up. I promise this is going to be the last word."

"On what?"

"On parties, on everything! And to think they fired me! God, what I'd give for a chance to write this up!"

Chapter 39

Wendy had sounded frantic enough to wear anything at the party: I'd envisioned her in transparent jeans and a blouse with a neckline fit for a tip-hungry barmaid. But her actual attire was Rich Girl Modest, a long, white dress of cotton, the kind she might have worn to please an elderly uncle. It was as if, through her appearance, she were trying to calm down those who had worried about her the day before.

She kissed me lightly me on the cheek, treating me more like a relative than someone whose byline had appeared above an exposé of her sex life. I scanned around the room for any stray Brown Suits who might happen to wander in at the request or command of General Kong-Sanchez. So far, so good.

"Here, let me take your coat." As she spoke, her Afghan bounded up on me. "Down, Thackeray, down!"

"Why not Dickens?" I suggested, pushing the dog off.

"Because," Wendy said, "Afghans are stuck-up enough as it is. So why name him after the best?"

I took in my surroundings more fully. Wendy had furnished her place in High-Tech White, with gleaming tables and cabinets that looked as though they'd come from some medical supply house. A huge television screen hung from one of the living-room walls, and a videotape recorder was built into another.

Washington abounded with such gadgetry, especially in the homes of journalists and politicians, some of whom were rich and narcissistic enough to own three machines in case they made all three networks while away at a dinner party.

Thackeray barked, and I gingerly patted him.

"Shake hands, Thack," said Wendy.

Her dog stuck out a well-trimmed paw and began smiling at me as if he'd been training in Maine for his Washington social debut.

"Actually I wanted to name him Isaac," Wendy said, stroking Thackeray's back, "but Sy said we ought to be careful about Singer and his demons. They might take it the wrong way."

While she was putting my coat away—I saw no help other than the normal catering crew—I glanced at the Roman numerals on her electronic clock. I was ten minutes early. But already some two dozen people were milling around, and I wondered how many would have come that early if they had been slumming among their peers in the middle-class suburbs.

"I know you've got your party," I told Wendy, "but I just want to say how rotten—"

Wendy put a finger to her mouth. "Ssh. Let's all have a good time."

"Mac deserves to burn."

"Please, dear. Let's not be so negative."

Rich Girl Modest or not, Wendy was starting to give me odd, uncomfortable premonitions. I wished Margo were around to share my fears with, but I'd warned her not to come lest she encounter the wrong people from work.

"Who's that man over there?" I asked Wendy.

His face was Lawrence-Olivier-aristocratic, his gray hair curly in just the right places, and he was wearing a tuxedo. He looked splendidly oblivious to the fact that most of the other men in the room were dressed as if for a business lunch.

"That's Waverly Weinblatt."

"The automobile dealer?" I remembered the name from the television commercials.

"Only in Washington," Wendy mused. "Every hunting season, he rides to the hounds in Middleburg."

"Is he in the Green Book?"

"Not yet, but he and his friends made the Blue Book from the very start."

"Blue Book?"

"You haven't heard of the Blue Book? They started it."

"Just like country clubs, I suppose. When ostracized, start your own."

"Don't act so superior," Wendy said. "I doubt they'd let you in. Besides, the Weinblatts are home-grown nobility. They started out in the carriage trade here—the buggy kind. And I'll grant them this: At least they do something. The real Middleburg types, they're such bores. Egotistical enough and secure enough to be ignorant. Which horse is fastest at which track—that's their version of current events. At least Waverly can tell you if a Morgan accelerates better than a Pinto."

"Pinto" made me think of another Ford car, the Maverick, and that set me thinking about a Maverick owner named Seymour Solomon. Where was he?

Wendy glanced toward the caterers. "Excuse me, dear. The caviar, I want to see if we have enough."

I nodded, and reflected. The last time I'd heard the word "caviar" had been a week or so ago when Margo and I were with one of my more colorful friends, a stringer for the tabloids. When he wasn't poking through celebrities' garbage, he was writing government waste stories. Among his classics was an exposé of the way diplomats from impoverished countries whooped it up at Washington parties—indirectly, it seemed, through the generosity of the American foreign aid program.

"They all serve caviar, don't they?" his *National Enquirer* editor had asked.

"I guess," my friend had said.

"We've got to make sure—top priority, boss's orders. We've got to say somewhere in the story, 'Dollops of caviar.'"

I went to get myself a drink from Wendy's bar, but instead stopped to overhear two fat women in mink stoles. They looked like clones; even the folds in the double chins matched. Both wore Elkins hairdos.

"It's absolutely disgraceful, the way she carries on," Mink Stole Number One was saying about an unnamed person.

"You've heard the pony story, haven't you?" asked Two.

One shook her head.

"It's sort of ancient," said Number Two, "but it gives you an idea of why she's so mixed up. She fell off this pony one day when she was little, and the family didn't even see if she was hurt. They just ordered her back on. Tough, demanding people—both parents. She must have been starved for affection. So you can see why she's so mixed up."

"I'm glad she's not mixed up with my daughter," sighed Mink Stole Number One.

"I bet she's on drugs."

I was about to think it might be Wendy when one of the husbands materialized and presently asked whom the women were gossiping over.

"Why, Caroline Kennedy."

"You know her?" asked the husband, a small, timid-sounding man who belonged to Number One.

"Well, not exactly," said Number Two. "But you hear things."

I'd spent years in McLean without meeting one Kennedy, and yet this woman spoke in the tones of a disapproving next-door neighbor. I wondered which tabloid was the source of her malarkey.

"Don't I know you from somewhere?" Number One asked Number Two.

"You seem familiar, too," Two said. Perhaps fat women in minks were like the Chinese as depicted in racist fiction. They could tell each other apart even if the rest of the world couldn't.

"Do you know Julie Bowmar?" Two asked.

"Oh!" In a lowered voice: "The Capital Connection."

"I almost didn't recognize you," said Two. "You wore stretch pants to class, didn't you?"

"Girls!" said the husband, who seemed as attuned to the nuances of bitchiness as the women were.

"Hush, Edward," said One.

"What I can't figure out," said Two, "is why we're here."

"We simply must have made a good impression," said Stole Number One. "She quoted me in the article. How about you?"

"She said I hoped to get to a party at the White House. Well, this isn't the White House, but it's close."

"I feel sorry for the poor thing—the scandal she's been through."

"Well, I'm still very pleased I could come," said One.

At that very moment I heard fierce pounding on the door and subhuman bellows: "Hell, Wendy, you hiding from me? Let me in, lemme in!" Blithely, as if the bellows were everyday sounds, Wendy had looked up from the silverware she was rearranging: "Someone let him in, please." Her newest guest, however, by then had made such formalities unnecessary.

"Oh, Paul," Wendy said, as though greeting treasured company, "I'm so glad to see you."

"What's this," he slurred, "an apartment for pansies? You know damned well the honest people own homes."

"I'll grow a little lawn on the balcony."

"I bet this place cost you a pretty penny—how much your daddy leave you?"

"Who needs Daddy?" Wendy said coolly. "I made my pile writing about you crazies on the Hill."

Paul Merton was crazy, and he was on the Hill, if not the wagon, for he was a congressman—a former truck driver who'd risen to be Majority Whip without turning effete.

"Glad to be here! Where's the eats?" The question was pointless, however, because he was already staggering toward some roast at a buffet table.

"The goblets!" cried Mink Stole Number One. "Oh, he mustn't knock over the goblets—they're such lovely goblets!"

But Merton was too busy decimating Wendy's roast to care. He had the face, bulk, and appetite of a giant sea turtle.

"Can't anybody stop him?" said Stole Number Two. "If there's anybody I hate, it's a party-crasher."

"He's a congressman," Wendy said.

"That's right," roared Merton, and tossed a bone toward a Jackson Pollock at the other end of the room.

He removed his shoes. Then he slumped sleepily into one of Wendy's swivel-based armchairs—ready to doze through the rest of the party.

"Isn't anyone going to call the police?" asked Mink Stole Number Two.

"I told you," said Wendy irritably. "He's a congressman."

"But a very drunk one," said a hard-faced woman in a sequined dress with a plunging neckline.

"It's all right," said Wendy. "He just thinks he's Davy Crockett. It's his act, you know. Come down to Washington from the hills of San Francisco."

As if inspired by the congressman, Thackeray suddenly snatched a slice of meat.

Wendy pulled her dog away from the table and lightly hit him on the nose. "Bad Thackeray," she said in the tone she'd used with Mink Stole Number Two. "Bad Thackeray."

"I have one myself," said the sequined woman whom I recognized from a People Page picture. "Same way exactly. An aristocratic thief."

"Not Thackeray. It's just a momentary lapse in judgment." Affectionately, Wendy looked him in the eye. "You won't do it again, will you?" She patted him as if he were a delicate baby, and Thackeray gave a respectful whimper.

"I could swear, they're the most contrary animals," the sequined woman drawled. "Mine won't eat unless I hide his food." With so strong a longing for the forbidden, her Afghan would have made a good social climber.

Wendy wandered off to check up on the connections for the videotape recorder on which she'd be playing *Guess Who's Coming to Dinner*. The sequined lady turned to a bald, solemn-faced, lawyerish-looking man: "I can't figure her out. All these people, and she's just showing an old movie? And that fellow over there, the one serving the punch, he says she let her maid go. She's nuts, that woman. Just who's going to do the dishes?"

"The Cozely people?"

"No," she said, "I've already asked them. Still, I guess I'm enjoying myself. Except I'm a little worried."

"About Ms. Blevin?" the lawyer inquired.

"I'm very disturbed that she doesn't have any Arabs here," said the sequined woman, a lobbyist for a petro-rich dictator with four hundred wives and a predilection for beheading his enemies. "The fate of our country, of the world—it's in their hands. It's quite serious, these parties. You leave out the wrong people, and you might start World War III. When I go to a party, I stand in front of a mirror ten minutes just checking my hair. And I'm not vain, not at all—only careful. You come across the wrong way, they might cut off our oil."

The man silently sipped his drink, and the sequined woman babbled on:

"It's a bad time for the country, the trouble Bullard's having in Papudo. And I could cry over Taiwan. All we need is for that to go. Of course I miss the Iranians, but no one comes close to the Nationalists. Especially that birthday party, the one honoring Chiang. They gave us each of us a fortune cookie with a hundred-dollar bill, but I ate mine before they told us what was inside."

A Broadway tune, from *The King and I*, was wafting around the room, and a few couples were off dancing in a corner near one of the quadraphonic speakers.

I approached a young blonde wearing a bright orange skirt and a blasé expression. She looked as if she spent her days tooling around in a Corvette with a bumper sticker from a rock-'n'-roll station.

"Want to dance with me?"

She shook her head.

"You like disco more?" I asked.

"Most of the time. I work for The Buck Stops Here." It was a cafeteria near the Home Loan Bank Board, until late in the afternoons when the bar opened. I could just imagine a tipsy banker fretting over interest rates and stumbling out of there with martini stains all over his funereally dark suit. He might even join Merton at the Blevin party.

"Please look me in the eye when you talk," the girl said. "I'm reading your lips, I'm deaf." An occupational injury? "Wasn't it simply dreadful, the hatchet job they did on her?"

"Not everyone at the paper went along with it," I said, "if that makes you feel any better."

"You work there?"

"Bland stuff. Housing beat."

"Yeah, I figured that," Ms. Disco said. "You don't dress very on time."

"Well, this suit may not be the latest, but who cares?"

"Excuse me," she said. "I've got some people I want to meet."

"Actually, I'm the nephew of the editor of *Variety*."

"You *are*?" she said in a semishriek.

"If you want me to be."

"You're really not very on time," she said. "I don't know why I came—hardly anybody here is."

"What? Most of the people were early."

"Don't you know what 'on time' means?" she scolded. "It's like 'cool.' You know—'with it.'"

"Well, then," I said, "if I'm so ignorant, I'm 'behind time' for sure."

"You don't know nothing from nothing," she said, and turned her back on me.

Nearly everyone in the room was like the disco girl—a name-in-the-paper guest, not a party-party one; it was as if Wendy had gone out of her way to invite social climbers.

Except for the congressman and the disco girl, I didn't see any crazies there. And that was a surprise, for Wendy's invitation had led me to think that half the partygoers would be motorcycle hoods and cocaine dealers. Either Wendy had wanted her party to be somewhat more sedate than she'd hinted, or else she had chosen her guests for their shockability.

If she were planning to expose herself, I wished she'd get on with it. That's all I hoped her craziness would be, nothing more.

Chapter 40

Carrying some cold cuts, Wendy lured Thackeray into her kitchen and placed them in a small silver bowl. She was aristocratic to the extent that the use of the bowl didn't seem gauche. Thackeray attacked the food as if he were still imitating Congressman Merton.

I'd followed Wendy there, but she didn't even notice me at first, she was so attentive to her dog.

"Oh!" she said, startled. "I guess he's a little messy tonight."

Cold cuts littered the floor near the bowl.

"You'll just have to teach him to use a knife and fork."

"He's smart enough, aren't you, baby?" Wendy cooed. She patted Thackeray, and he acknowledged with a loud, immodest yap. "Oh, how I love that dog! I don't know what I'd do if something ever happened."

"If what happened?"

"Well, if—if the Watergate said we couldn't have dogs."

"Couldn't he simply go back to Maine?" I asked—confident that The Elephant would have gossiped about Thackeray if he'd been in Washington very long,

"Why'd you say Maine?" asked Wendy.

I shrugged.

"Somebody would take care of him," Wendy said. "I know they would."

"Listen," I said, "you've got to understand that Mac—"

"Please, dear, haven't you twisted the truth enough?"

"I just want to—"

"Don't make a scene."

We left the kitchen, and I drifted over to a chair near the sofa where Mink Stoles Numbers One and Two were jabbering away. I enjoyed the irony. Imagine their eagerness to meet Society, and yet now that they were at the Watergate, they were squandering half their time on each other.

"And when I went in I saw a bidet," I overheard Number Two say, "and the plumbing was gold-plated."

"What's a bidet?" Mink Stole Number One, in the parlance of the disco girl, obviously wasn't "on time."

"It's this little bowl near the floor, sort of like a water fountain, except you use it for washing off your privates."

"Why not use a regular bath?"

"It's supposed to be more convenient. They have 'em in Europe. Owen and me—when we went to France we had one in the hotel. Well, I told him to see if we could buy one and take it home, but he wouldn't stand for it."

"Too expensive?"

"No," said Mink Stole Number Two in a near-whisper, "he was worried I'd have an affair. He kept saying if you could wash up so quickly, it'd be too easy to mess around."

"Men!" said One

"For heaven's sake," said Mink Stole Number Two, gesturing toward a six-and-a-half-foot Redskin and a short, balding man. "Look who Owen's talking to!"

Jack Terkins played tackle for the Skins and was president of Jack Terkins Toyota for Waverly Weinblatt. He weighed three hundred and fifty pounds. I couldn't see how he could fit in a Japanese car, much less "run" a dealership selling them.

"Stone! I don't get it!" Nor did I. When I turned around I saw Larry Zumweltnar, the flack at GSA.

"Didn't you write that story?" he said. "Why'd she invite you?"

"I'm still trying to puzzle that one out myself." I told him about the unauthorized byline. I still hadn't fathomed the real reason for the invitation, except that apparently I was supposed to chronicle a spectacle.

"I believe you," said Zumweltnar solemnly and more than a little drunkenly. "Anything bad about the *Telegram* I can believe."

I took a moment to glance at Merton; he was still snoring away.

"What are you doing here?" I asked Zumweltnar.

"I live here."

"At the Watergate?" Just how could I ever know the truth, one way or another? Maybe Zumweltnar wasn't on the take from a GSA contractor; perhaps he had a rich, dead uncle or was secretly overpaid enough to afford life amid the elite.

"I just thought I'd drop by to help her through this crisis."

"I'm sure she appreciated it," I said amicably.

"You know, Stone," said Zumweltnar between sips of Scotch, "I don't know why we're always fighting. You and I, we're both parkers."

"What's a parker?"

"An old expression of mine," he said. "The world, it's divided into right-steppers and left-steppers and parkers."

"So who's what?" I asked.

"The subway, the escalator," Zumweltnar said. "The people on the right, they're the ones who let the others pass. Now the left ones, they're the ones in a hurry." It was an accurate description of local Metro etiquette. "The left ones! They're the ones who're trying to run the world!"

"What about the parkers?"

"They're the ones who already have it made," Zumweltnar said. "That's why they can afford to park and not take the subway. You and I shouldn't be fighting. We're both parkers."

"But I need a car for work," I said, "and sometimes I ride my bike."

"It makes no difference," Zumweltnar said gravely. "You work for a company that pays the parking for you. So we won't fight, okay?"

"Of course." I was astounded. Wendy's Scotch had changed Zumweltnar from a rude PR man to a friendly drunk.

"Abe Lincoln was a parker, okay? So was Washington. Remember that, Stone. Anybody who was anybody was a parker."

"But didn't Lincoln free the slaves? That wasn't a very parkerish thing to do. Property rights."

"Doesn't matter. Abe Lincoln was in the White House. He was a parker, okay?"

"Like Franklin Roosevelt?"

"The smartest parker of all. He had the parkers give up a few things for the right-steppers before they revolted."

"But doesn't revolution require a certain amount of initiative—drive?"

"So they'd be left-steppers. But the wrong kind."

Zumweltnar droned on and on, while I sat in tactful silence, wishing I'd had my cassette recorder with me to preserve the phenomenon.

"Bullard's going to win big next year," he said. "Your common man might be a right-stepper, but he knows quality when he sees it. Eddy Bullard is a born parker."

I remembered Zumweltnar's past encomia to Nixon. You couldn't fault parkers for lack of loyalty to the bosses of the moment. Everyone in Washington had a boss or bosses; that much was clear. Bullard's just happened to be his campaign contributors.

"Take your seats, everyone," Wendy announced jovially. "Time for *Guess Who's Coming to Dinner.*"

"The movie?" slurred Zumweltnar.

Wendy nodded.

"It's a bad thing McWilliams's done to her," he said, stumbling toward a cushion on the floor. "We parkers got to stick together."

Wendy dimmed the lights slightly; the woman in the sequined dress yawned.

Sidney Poitier appeared before us in color as good as that of a movie theater, and the sights looked otherwise convincing. Jack Terkins, the statue-sized Redskin and Toyota-endorser, covered his eyes when Spencer Tracy had an automobile accident. He must have been as susceptible to movies as to reliable compensation from Waverly Weinblatt.

Paul Merton woke up around the time Tracy was learning his daughter might marry a black man.

"Where am I?" Merton demanded.

"Shh!" Wendy said. "We're watching a movie."

"Who cares?" Merton slurred. "The honest people own homes."

"Lord!" Mink Stole Number Two couldn't help saying.

"Hush!" Wendy scolded. "I keep telling you—he's a congressman."

She restored the lights to full brightness: "Intermission time."

"But we haven't even seen the first half yet," the disco girl protested.

"Presents, you've got presents, all of you," Wendy said, and we followed her into the bedroom, where she pointed to a huge pink cardboard box on the floor. "Open it, Jon."

I did. It was full of vases, apparently the ones that had held the giant white roses from General Sanchez.

"Everyone, grab your own! There's plenty to go around! Waterford, finest Waterford."

The two Mink Stoles and the rest of the guests oohed with delight and nearly trampled each other to grab their crystal vases. No one even bothered to ask about the reasons for the Waterfords—these people were more Talkers than Thinkers. Clearly in their minds they merited Wendy's generosity.

"Jon," Wendy asked, "don't you want one?"

"I'll pass," I said uncomfortably.

"All right, everyone, now back to the action," our hostess said, and we reconvened in the television area.

Wendy picked up a little silver TV camera resting atop a hospital-white cabinet. I couldn't believe how small it was—perhaps an experimental model sold at an exorbitant price to the party-party crowd? She turned toward Merton: "You know what this is, don't you?"

The congressman nodded dumbly. I remembered his *Telegram* profile and some old talk around town; he was supposed to be as intelligent when sober as he was stupid when drunk. But the newest scuttlebutt was that the two states were becoming less distinguishable.

"Just keep watching me," Wendy told him as she changed the tape in her video recorder.

With the camera still in her hands, she walked over to her window and opened the curtains. Across the Potomac I could see the lights of Rosslyn, Virginia, one of the places that Solomon and friends had turned into mini-Manhattans.

Some of the Watergate's residents had complained when a forty-story skyscraper spoiled their view of the Virginia hills and Roosevelt Island

The *Telegram* had reported their grievances—politely unmindful that a few of them owned shares in ugly high-rises elsewhere .

"All you do," said Wendy, "is point the camera at what you want to show."

"I don't give a hoot," Merton slurred. "The honest people own homes." Then, still shoeless, he staggered out of her apartment, slamming the door.

"Mr. Zumweltnar," Wendy said. "How'd you like to operate this for us? I'll show you."

"I don't see why not," Zumweltnar said as he staggered toward her. "You're a parker, aren't you?"

"What?"

"I believe in Freedom of Information, okay? So I'll run your camera for you."

Wendy flipped a switch on the camera. "Look, everybody—look at the screen."

Her guests gasped in awe. Far smaller than the usual minicams, the camera produced pictures more real than TV stations'.

I didn't see how. Her video gear must have been experimental, so new it hadn't even been written up yet in our Business section. Maybe the party-party people had some special "in" with the electronics companies.

The camera even had a sniperscope mode that could turn night into day. When she aimed her silver box toward Rosslyn, it was as if we were gazing through her window in the middle of the afternoon.

Wendy's guests kept oohing, even the most blasé.

"But how do you focus?" Mink Stole Two's husband finally asked.

"It's automatic."

"What f-stop?"

"Quiet," said Mink Stole Two, as if annoyed her husband could ask such a banal question amid all this magic.

"No f-stops, either," said Wendy.

Excited, childlike murmurs were still coming from the guests. I looked over the crowd of jowly lobbyists and jaded PR women and pondered the silliness as well as the mystery.

There was Wendy Blevin, the party-party girl, the local Daisy, entertaining a roomful of stodgy, would-be Gatsbys without the guts to set up a still.

Wendy strolled over to Zumweltnar and handed her camera to him. "Just keep it on me. Everybody else watch the screen." But the guests instead were shifting their eyes back and forth between it, Wendy, and Zumweltnar.

Somewhat shakily, he aimed the camera as Wendy had asked. She opened the door to her balcony, and a chilly December wind whistled into the room.

"What's happening?" Mink Stole Two demanded.

"Just keep the camera on me!" Wendy ordered Zumweltnar. "Don't dare get me out of sight. Closer—move closer."

"Anything to help a parker, okay?"

Suddenly Wendy ran toward the barrier on the balcony, screaming, "Last word, dears!"

The lawyerish-looking man and I bounded toward her, almost knocking over Zumweltnar, but it was too late.

As Wendy climbed over the serpent's teeth, graceful to the end, despite the long white dress, I heard a loud thud and an unnerving tingle, but I could not take my eyes off the sight of her plunge.

The light was just bright enough for me to see the dress afterward, six stories below. I glanced around. Jack Terkins had apparently hurled himself into her television screen, and in the confusion, Zumweltnar had dropped the magic camera, its lens now shattered.

I rushed to Wendy's phone to call an ambulance, but for two minutes I couldn't get through, hearing nothing but the buzz of a busy signal, and finally a tape recording.

Once again I cursed bureaucracy.

Zumweltnar, meanwhile, had rolled himself into a fetal position and was weeping like an infant: "How could she? Why can't parkers learn to stick together?"

"Hurry up!" Mink Stole Number Two shrieked at me.

"No, I was here first," said Number One.

"I'm doing the best I can," I said.

"Well, get finished," shrilled Number Two. "I've got to call The Elephant."

߷ঙঃ

On the legs of my Dynamic Executive suit I can still see the vestiges of the stains from that dazed night. I forgot about mundane worries like rust spots and let the suit hang on a damp old water pipe just outside Margo's door.

Then I entered her room and removed my shoes and fumbled in the darkness toward the mattress.

I yelled out my pain when I stepped on the edge of the ashtray— the jags reminded me of the Watergate balcony.

Margo, awakened, said in a soft, calm voice, "It's all right now, isn't it?"

"Just clumsy me stepping on your castle."

"Wendy, I mean. She understands."

I wrapped my arms around Margo and kissed her.

"She understands, doesn't she?"

"About what?" I asked pointlessly, trying to delay the news.

"About the smear," Margo said. "The notes, the byline."

I kissed her again.

"Jonathan, is something wrong?" I felt her head turning toward an alarm clock with a glowing dial. "My God, it's two in the morning."

"Something happened," I said.

"What, Jonathan, what?"

"I had a story to write."

"What kind of story?"

"A suicide," I said.

As we both reflected, Margo stunned for now into silence, I couldn't help but think of what I had not written, as a conscientious nonshrink. I remembered a stray paragraph in the London *Times* article on Wendy, the quick aside on the "fall" of her grandmother from the Calvert Street Bridge. Had the curse returned? Oh, the imponderables here.

I could imagine puzzled strangers saying that Wendy was too rich, too hard a bitch, to kill herself. Couldn't she simply have laughed off the scandals and retreated to the 300-acre equestrian estate that the Blevins owned in the hunt country near Middleburg? But she had still jumped.

Even her $150 million could not drive off the demons that had softened her up for the *Telegram's* gratuitous demolition job—far harsher than anything I'd have written.

I recalled those mysterious weekends when Wendy was lost to the world, to the party-parties, not just the name-in-the-paper variety. Might she have been publicly manic, privately depressed? If so, how did Solomon fit in?

Just how had they complemented each other, until finally 72-point headlines separated the two and loosed her demons to go public?

಄ఌ

"I'm just sorry Mac wasn't around," I said, as Margo and I hugged each other, there in her dungeon. "I'd have pushed him off."

"And you couldn't stop her?"

"Another man and I, we tried, but we had to get around Zumweltnar." I told Margo about the bizarreness, the drunkenness, the eagerness to help a fellow parker.

"The paper, though, they're making it up to her, aren't they? Your story?"

"The best I could do. What happened at the party, and then Raymond let me do the obituary. And I wrote it Blevin-style, too. No sap. And a quote toward the end—exactly what she'd have wanted."

Wendy had spoken the words amid the clinking of the vending machines in the Pierre L'Enfant Room two weeks before. A minor Chinese diplomat had been banished back to Peking for being too candid with Wendy about Mrs. Bullard's hairdo—prompting her to say, "Really, dear, I can't figure out why these people talk. I'd never let myself talk to me."

Chapter 41

Before dawn, I bolted out of bed to see what my efforts looked like in the City Edition. I filched a robe from a graduate student upstairs and ran out of the house, down the street, to a news rack.

My suicide story was on the front page, sure enough, but hardly recognizable, so extensive was the condensation. Nor did I see all of the long, lovingly detailed obituary that I'd also rapped out for that edition—just 578 words, 40 percent shrinkage.

And the *Telegram* had struck from both articles some disturbing paragraphs about Wendy's motives for the jump from the balcony.

"Compassion, pal," McWilliams explained later at the office. "You've got to show compassion."

"And that's compassion—exposing her sex life, then giving her this shitty little obit when she kills herself?"

"Her family," he said. "Why rub it in? A thing like this, you want to help them forget it."

"I suppose you polled all her aunts and uncles. You know exactly what everyone wants to read, don't you?"

"I think I know just a little more about this business than you do," said McWilliams, puffing his cigar toward me. "That's why I told the night crew to clean up your mess."

"Oh, yeah—then how come it's the lead story on the radio? And yet you stuck it in the lower left-hand corner. And with all the details bled out. Hell, there's not fifteen inches left."

"Learn to write tighter," said Mac.

"An embarrassment, that's why you downplayed it. So people would forget faster that it was the *Telegram* that did her in."

"The *Telegram?* Just who the fuck thought up the story idea, the Maine angle? I didn't kill her, Raymond didn't kill her. You did. Which is why you should be grateful I saved you from making a greater ass of yourself."

"Just as Garst should be," I said, "the way he embellished my facts. And at your suggestion."

"What are you talking about, pal?"

"The notes you gave."

"What notes?"

"That garbage you dictated to me about her sex life. And I don't mean the stuff about Solomon and the People Page. I'm talking about all the extraneous stuff."

"I don't get you, pal."

"I'm talking about the stuff that came from you," I said.

"From me?"

I nodded.

"I didn't give you anything, pal, I just told you where to look."

"'It's all confirmed,'" I mocked Mac. "Which is how Garst seems to have treated it."

"In other words, you're impugning his integrity along with mine," McWilliams said, gazing at his Rolex.

"It would be nice," I said, "if you'd follow up tomorrow with a full-length appreciation in all editions. Do you think there'll ever be another Wendy?"

McWilliams just kept looking at his watch. "You'll never be great in this business if you don't learn a little compassion."

"But the wires," I said. "You can't kiss off the story. It's on all the wires."

"You'll never get anywhere without compassion."

I agreed, though not about Mac's interpretation of that word as applied to Wendy.

When Paxley Treadwell, the media critic, called me the same afternoon, I did not wimp out about Mac.

Once again, decency toward Wendy mingled with prioritized prudence. Maybe, just maybe, the Brown Suits watched Channel 12's media criticism segment.

∞☜☞∞

"I don't ever want you in this building again," said McWilliams after summoning me back into the Cage the next day.

"Treadwell called me," I said, "not the other way."

"And you told him I tricked you with the notes."

"Because he repeated your lies about me. You said they were in my handwriting, and implied—"

"We'll mail your severance check," McWilliams said. "Just start clearing out your desk and leave all your files here. Of course, they're probably not that valuable, considering your record for veracity."

"Apparently Wendy Blevin wasn't enough of a scapegoat for you. Now, what about Garst? What's happening to him?"

"He'll be getting a promotion soon. To Seoul."

"Because," I said, "he's a better flunky than me."

More than ever I was wondering how much difference really existed between the *Telegram* and *The National Enquirer;* survival at each depended on a willingness to act and write for the boss. McWilliams might as well be placing orders with his reporters for "dollops of caviar."

"He didn't even go to her party," I said, suspecting that if Wendy had invited me, she'd have done likewise with Garst.

"Because he's more professional than you. He doesn't compromise himself. By the way, I know you've been fucking that girl at GSA."

"We're talking about Garst."

Mac shook his head. "We're talking about you, pal."

"Jeez, she's going back to grad school next month. I mean, do you really think a GS-7 could tell me what to write?"

I could have said more, a lot more, about what Margo meant to me. Someone else I might have told about the way she leaned against my shoulder during Hitchcock films. I could have bragged of her wordplays, her Charlemagne jokes, her inventive brain from which had sprung the just-steal-the-press idea.

But "GS-7" was the language Mac best understood and which best served me at the moment—just a quick little reference to her place in the hierarchy of our white-collar factory town.

Margo, both loving and Midwestern-practical, would have wanted me to respond to him exactly as I did.

So just how long had Mac known about us; what other occasions had he been saving this scrap of information for? Under the same rule against bedding down sources, Mac could have fired a dozen reporters, but instead it existed as simply another way for him to boss his word-mill help around.

"I could can you for that alone," Mac said, like the mind-reading shark he could be at times.

"Now about Wendy," I said. "That's pretty good. First you blame me for the suicide. Then you say I shouldn't have gone to her party."

"A good reporter doesn't pal around with the wrong people," Mc-Williams said.

"What about Solomon?"

"So I was conned. I thought he was respectable."

"It took you long enough to find out."

"I was conned," McWilliams repeated, and I looked for some trace of uneasiness, a tiny quiver of a hand, a flick of an eyelash, but I saw nothing—not even a slight relief from his rock-hard stare.

"I thought he was a friend, a pal," Mac said. "Sy and Shelly Philips and I—we'd walk along the Canal Path and I'd forget about my fucking newspaper and whether Russia would nuke us if we invaded Papudo. Don't you see? He and I were friends. We'd talk about the grocery store where his father worked, and how they'd argue with the shochet. You don't know what a shochet is, do you, pal?"

"Well, I've read—"

"Well, I've lived. And that's what makes it tough—thinking you know it all, then finding your friend's a crook. But I'll say this for him. He believes it. He really believes he's an honest man. Which makes him better than you."

"Now just a minute."

"All his crap, he believes everything the moment he says it. It's a hell of a lot better than naked lies."

"What naked lies?"

"Kicking me in the ass on TV, trying to save your fanny! That's some thanks, pal. Some thanks after all we've done for you at the *Telegram*. And if you're shitting on me, you're probably shitting on the whole world, because I've done nothing to deserve it."

I left my chair and started toward the door of the Cage.

"Just as I thought," said McWilliams, "no guts."

"Guts? That's why you're firing me? Why, that's how I got into trouble in the first place."

"No—for simple lack of decency. There's no substitute—in newspapers, in politics, in friends, in anything. It's what Solomon said all the time, and he was right, Stone. Don't you have *any* decency?"

"I guess you can kiss the Pulitzer good-bye," I said.

"What?"

"For my work."

"We'll just use the paper's name."

"Never," I said. "Besides, you've got the Treadwell interview to explain away."

"It was a team effort," Mac persisted.

"Including that sleazy sidebar on Wendy?"

McWilliams nodded.

"Not bad—a Pulitzer for a smear job."

"What smear? You're the one who told me about Sanchez."

"But that sidebar," I protested. "My God, I could win a Pulitzer investigating you."

"To hell with the Pulitzer! All I want to do is run a decent newspaper."

So went the very last conversation between Mac and me, outside my dreams, nightmares included.

Chapter 42

The next day, a small bomb exploded under the seat of Mac's gray BMW in the *Telegram* parking lot when he turned the key.

A Latin-looking man, dressed in a brown suit much like those worn by the deliverers of Wendy's roses, was seen in the area by my friend Clay Bronski.

The bomb made surprisingly little noise but blew off Mac's legs and an arm, causing him to die a painful death from massive bleeding. He proved preternaturally resistant to the trauma that would have blacked out many a mortal. His last words were to the ambulance crew, delayed in traffic: "Christ, you're slow fuckers." Still strapped to the severed arm, his Rolex kept on running.

Mac's one living relative, his disabled sister in Brooklyn eking out $6,000 a year as a seamstress, fought briefly over his estate but could not claim a dime beyond the token dollar he had left her. Every other penny was to go for care and maintenance of his econo-Versailles.

A few years later, the bulldozers finally caught up with that part of Montgomery County, Maryland. Through legal legerdemain, dazzling even by the standards of *Bleak House* and Washington lawyers, some builders were able to get the mansion razed to make way for tract houses built like miniature Mount Vernons.

General Jesus Sanchez, McWilliams's killer as Fred Green and I both saw it, fled Papudo upon the overthrow of the junta, the same week Mac died so horribly. Today, he is alive at seventy-six and in prosperous retirement in a Spanish villa on a high cliff overlooking the Mediterranean.

Thackeray vanished amid the confusion and sorrow from Wendy's suicide, but he is said to be thriving in Spain. The rumor is that he sired thirteen puppies by an Afghan bitch the general bought for the dog's pleasure.

Lives and memories go on. Bouquets of giant white roses still come to Wendy's old desk near the Shark's Cage.

Recalled after three months in Korea to be a top deputy to Mac's successor, a Skull and Bones man from the Boston *Globe*, Rexwood

Garst claimed the desk. He learned to tolerate the flowers as just another annoyance of the job.

Cleaning and security crews had tried to stop the bouquets from coming. But like determined rats chewing through plaster, the general's men almost always succeeded.

Vicky Simpson finally threw up her hands and ordered the vases sent to a local charity shop on whose board she sits with a major real estate advertiser. They are much cherished—along with the persistent gossip about Mac's demise—among both the party-party and name-in-the-paper crowds.

In the wake of Mac's death, the *Telegram* and most every other respectable American daily pronounced the murder an unsolvable mystery despite the never-ending flow of roses and a flood of speculation in the European press about Wendy and the general. None of McWilliams's newspaper friends could bring themselves to do a full-bore investigation, given the unsavory details that might have tainted such an essential profession. The civil servants in Eddy Bullard's Justice Department felt the same way about theirs.

I managed to sneak a few of Fred Green's unconfirmable revelations about Mac into an alternative weekly, but no one in power would believe me or Green. Drained, I left newspapering and moved to Los Angeles, where today I write up history disguised as conspiracy movies.

From time to time, I dabble at revisions of my memoirs, without in the least upsetting my wife, Margo the publicity-hater, who is convinced that no one at present will publish them as fact. Even my father-in-law won't believe us. I suppose he thinks it's more "literary" for the most astounding of these events to be depicted as fiction.

If I tell the whole truth, my own parents and sister nod politely, then change the subject. They love me, rejoice over my Hollywood earnings, and are content to regard my memories as pragmatically creative imaginings.

The big compromise between Margo and me is that *The Solomon Scandals* is to be sealed for a full century upon its completion. In the late twenty-first century, it is to be opened by the Virginia Historical Society and sent to our families. A friend of hers works there as an archivist and has made arrangements in perpetuity for my manuscript's preservation.

I won't tinker with *Scandals* forever. You see, I've almost always thrived on deadlines, my own included; and I'll soon type the last words. It's 11:05 P.M. Eastern Time on the tenth anniversary of my first day at the *Telegram*, a continent away. That is just perfect for a "-30-," in the jargon of the old-time reporters.

Don't ask me why they ended news stories with "-30-" in the Smith Corona days and often still do. No one can agree. Some say it's because the first story sent in Morse Code had thirty words. Others insist the number is in memory of a telegraph operator who dropped dead after spending thirty hours tapping out news bulletins. An employee of Mac in another incarnation?

Whatever the history of the number, I love its finality. So does Margo. Next week we'll fly back to family and friends in the Washington area, drive down to the society's Ionic-columned building in Richmond, entrust *Scandals* to the Manuscripts Department, and *try* to move on.

Perhaps the world in time will be more receptive to the entire truth. I won't settle for publication of anything less, my ultimate act of insubordination against George McWilliams.

Both Big and Little Mac still swim through my mind despite my efforts to exorcise McWilliams and the memories he has wrought as a hell-worthy editor. No true hell exists in classical Jewish theology, alas. Just a waiting room where souls are purified and where the maximum wait is generally said to be no more than twelve months. Mac needs to draw twelve hundred as timed precisely by his Rolex.

If hell is real in the fire-and-brimstone sense, may his treatment of Wendy Blevin make the flames burn all the hotter for him. Not a day goes by when I don't reflect back upon Wendy and the snowy evening when she charmed me into her Mercedes for a drive to the National Christmas Tree despite my boredom with pageantry.

Some extraordinary people I mourn when they die, and others I marvel about, consumed even more by awe than by love or hate. Over Wendy, I mourn and marvel; over Mac, I marvel.

-30-

Afterword for the Seventh Edition:
Comfortable Obscurity and Beyond

By Rebecca Kitiona-Fenton, Ph.D.,
of the Institute for the Study of Previrtual Media

Readers will recall Uncle Jon's telling Aunt Margo: "Promise. You're neither famous nor infamous. Just comfortably obscure."

He kept his word, and they lived a quiet life in the Hollywood hills.

Uncle Jon prospered as a scriptwriter and director without either the challenges of true fame or the Washington-level moral dilemmas that his father had faced in "public affairs."

Margo the publicity-hater had won Uncle Jon over. His best screenplays often appeared under pseudonyms. And as a director toward the end of his career, he remained determinedly media shy, letting the actors enjoy the publicity void he had created.

By the time of his directing, he was too old, too gray, for the tabloids and gossip columnists to bother writing much about him anyway. It gave Uncle Jon great pleasure to dine in restaurants without sycophants pestering him for autographs. He'd always been a little touchy about his abysmal handwriting.

A mere handful of people outside Uncle Jon's family knew of the existence of *The Solomon Scandals* manuscript. In comfortable obscurity, his beloved Margo having succumbed several years earlier, he died in his sleep at ninety-seven, with a short but respectful item appearing in the main VR feed of *Variety*.

Meanwhile, as hinted by the "Fenton" in my name, our family had turned multiracial, reflective of changes in American society at large. I myself am Jewish-Samoan-WASP-African-Hispanic. My children and I carry more than a few drops of the blood of Queequeg, Melville's savage from the South Seas, the sailor who harpooned so well. In an era when humans and machines have melded, how bizarre it now seems that Uncle Jon once could not even have seen himself marrying a *Caucasian* gentile.

In his later years he and his family were more open-minded. The first interracial marriage actually happened as one of the many after-effects of the scandals.

The son of Lew Fenton, the African-American union man, had earned a scholarship to UCLA and excelled in the film school, where Uncle Jon lectured on occasion. Friendship between the two blossomed around the powerful, shared memories of the Vulture's Point collapse. Peter Fenton's marriage to my great-great-uncle's niece, my grandmother, followed.

Peter and Alicia had met at a Southern-style poolside barbecue where Margo the food fiend was the solo cook. Uncle Jon never, ever, learned to enjoy preparing or eating pork.

The brilliant young Fenton wanted to collaborate with Uncle Jon on a script about his investigation of the scandals. But in keeping with his dislike of publicity, my uncle declined. Hollywood, moreover, would almost surely have passed. No longer was the material so controversial, so beyond accepted belief; rather, the story faced a far-less-surmountable barrier—no one would have cared.

Especially with linear, single-medium books on the wane, including the electronic ones, the same would have applied to Uncle Jon's actual memoirs, even had they been on the market. George Mc-Williams was winning. The whole truth was just another fart in a windstorm, as Larry Zumweltnar, my uncle's foe at GSA, would have put it.

All this changed after the Virginia Historical Society unsealed *Scandals* and sent a copy to Aunt Erica, who, knowing of my interest in previrtual media, promptly mailed it to me. I arranged for the publication of Uncle Jon's memoirs out of family pride as much as anything else. Up to the last edit, I couldn't decide whether *Scandals* was a major historical find or just an old family heirloom to be cherished like an ancestor's gold-plated wedding ring. Would anyone read *Scandals* beyond a few of my fellow academics? And then only in the most halfhearted and dutiful of ways? I simply put the file up on the Institute's server, VR-mailed a few friends, and held my breath.

Well, I don't have to tell my readers the rest. Like *Moby Dick*, ill suited to the literary commerce of its time but a staple among the classics of the century that followed, *The Solomon Scandals* belatedly found its way into the mass consciousness. It was as if explorers had run across a talking, impeccably preserved caveman, or an articulate mastodon.

Academics seized on *Scandals* as a Rosetta Stone of sorts, a way to decrypt the Washington of yore. First *Scandals* was an electronic book, then actually a paper edition, one of the very few that our institute was publishing, and the acclaim among socially aware reviewers was nearly universal.

Here is a partial transcript of the lengthy review from *New York VR*, the virtual successor to the old *Times*:

"Rebecca Kitiona-Fenton's foreword to *The Solomon Scandals* is uncannily apt in likening George McWilliams, the obsessed newspaper editor, to Captain Ahab in *Moby Dick*.

"McWilliams, though short in physical stature, is an Ahab indeed—more than a shark, the comparison that investigative reporter Jonathan Stone, narrator and main protagonist of *Scandals*, makes without a full historical perspective.

"To enter the city room of the *Washington Telegram* is indeed to step aboard the *Pequod* and sail off into a world of Melvillean good and evil.

"Some might call McWilliams an anti-Ahab, with certain Leviathans spared or pursued only in a halfhearted way. But a little sagacity is simply tempering his fervor.

"An Ahab he can be—when he wants to—in the thrill of the chase. Just ask all the politicians bloodied by his crewmen.

"He entices his lookouts and harpooners with a shower of gold doubloons in the currency of the day: pickups by other newspapers and fawning mentions in the press sections of the newsweeklies.

"Other parallels are ineluctable.

"Most all of Washington shows up in cameos at the least, from the political elite and society matrons to corrupt little clerks and the First Lady's hairdresser—a spectrum of memorable characters worthy of Dickens or Tolstoy.

"Some readers may also think of the works of Dante as we descend into Stone's *Inferno*.

"Almost everyone is among the betrayed or betrayers or a mix thereof, and the worst of the offenders are bound straight for the Ninth Circle of Hell, even if they freeze up in newspaper archives rather than the ice of Cocytus.

"Stone is uncomfortable with the ethos of both Washington and the newspaper that reflects the metropolis around it, and worse, he finds he cannot separate Work from Life.

"Donna Stackelbaum, his lover and old family friend, is caught up in a nuclear-energy scandal that the White House uses to distract the media from the Solomon Scandals. Can Stone avoid testimony to a grand jury?

"And just how should he write up the suicide of Wendy Blevin, a much-feared, much-loved gossip columnist and colleague whose reputation foundered 'in a sea of toxic black ink'?

"From historians to sociologists and sexologists, academics will revel in Stone's memoir-cum-confession from the dark heart of the fourth estate.

"Along with laypeople, they will find themselves drawn into a powerful allegory in the collapse of Vulture's Point, a shoddily built complex where hundreds of tax and intelligence bureaucrats perish.

"Is not Vulture's the ultimate stand-in for putrid government programs that just don't work out, ill-conceived wars included? Where are the lookouts and harpooners when we need them?

"The *Telegram's* Ahab on occasion is so busy inventing slayable monsters that the real whales sometimes swim away unseen, only to return later to kill and maim the unsuspecting.

"Stone's direct boss, *Ezekiel* Rawson, as coincidence would have it, is a good man. But he is too blinded by gold doubloons to bear even the remotest resemblance to the biblical prophet.

"As a true tale of corruption, deceit, betrayal, and suicide, *The Solomon Scandals* haunts us with a multitude of questions. Most notably, a century later, is society more or less evil than in Stone's time? And are politicians as likely to abuse power?

"We are led to recall the fate of the old Internet, quietly born even before the Solomon Scandals.

"Optimists in time envisioned 'the Net' as opening up government. In fact, all kinds of Web sites sprang up to track political donors and even match them with the names of government contractors and businesses regulated by federal agencies.

"What's more, other sites were created to monitor the press and encourage it to do its duty—in effect, to avoid cover-ups of the *Telegram* variety.

"But corrupt politicians still resisted adequate campaign finance reform and went about committing their usual crimes, often with the help of rogue business executives and the apathy of most of the press.

"That wasn't all. Countering reformers inside and outside the media, Congress passed insidious legislation.

"New technological measures reduced the freedom of the Internet and enabled Washington to spy constantly on citizens' movements through cyberspace. The legislators had mixed motives. But one was to discourage activists and journalists from acting and speaking out against corruption and other crimes.

"Thankfully, those measures were mitigated or repealed, and in many other ways, too, as Dr. Kitiona-Fenton often notes in her lectures, Americans are now beyond blackmail.

"And yet corruption, abuse of power, and other crimes are still with us, as, for instance, the Wozlinski Scandals show.

"How outrageous that multimillionaires have been systematically bribing government and corporate researchers to enjoy early access to the very latest genetic enhancement techniques and cyborgic technology!

"Consider, too, the sellout of nanotechnology secrets to foreign defense contractors. Or the impeachment and conviction of President Welton five years ago, the result of his secret, ongoing ties with his old hedge fund.

"For today's Stones, the people who would expose such wrongdoing, life is not always simple. The FBI and other law enforcement agencies can use neuroscans to read the minds of the journalists and other troublemakers.

"Without specific authorization from courts, law enforcement agencies can even require chips to be embedded in the reporters' brains.

"Judges have ruled that the agencies must have ample reason to scan the brains of journalists or insert Reporting Chips within them, a powerful temptation in the era of cyborgs.

"But in practice, law enforcement agencies do not always play nice with the First Amendment.

"The result is that the government can track the identities of the people the scanned journalists talk to. In effect, Washington can render investigative reporters worthless as revealers of corruption.

"Let's hope that the use of Reporting Chips against journalists remains rare—well, rare to the best of our knowledge, considering the law that prevents the scanned from publicly disclosing the existence of their unwanted implants.

"All in all, good weighed against bad, we are probably no better, no worse, in terms of corruption and the related abuse of power than America was in Jonathan Stone's time.

"To learn about Stone's Washington is to learn about our own—about how far we have come, and how far we need to go. He has performed a public service in arriving at eternal verities and inspiring us with his own courage.

"Eddy Bullard, Seymour Solomon, and George McWilliams live on, in many skins, many shades, in America and elsewhere. One would hope that enough Stones are around to thwart them.

"Read this book if you care—it could change your civic life."

Praise of *Scandals* in *New York VR* was just the beginning. A torrent of commerce ensued: docudramas, text sequels on Uncle Jon's career in Hollywood, biographies of Wendy Blevin, even rebuttals from pro-McWilliams academics.

They suddenly came out of the woodwork, only to be sullied by disclosures of unsavory connections between them and a think tank Mac had secretly endowed—an independent entity apart from the physical and financial estates.

Bulldozers had leveled McVersailles, but not the think tank, created partly to resurrect McWilliams in the public mind and besmear the names on the McShitlist long after Mac and his fellow corpses had rotted. Mac, it turned out, had not kept the list just in his head.

In the end McWilliams and Uncle Jon both won. Mac had sought immortality; Jon, the promulgation of the truth.

After *Scandals* conquered the media world, I was especially heartened to see a massive revival of interest in books, paper and electronic, and even the return of the old *Times* in text form online. Faithful re-creations, both actual and VR, appeared of the newsroom of the *Telegram*. Rights were purchased from Mrs. Simpson's estate, and as part of a libel settlement, the result of lies against McWilliams's living foes, his operatives cannot interfere with us.

Today, schoolchildren can visit the *Telegram* Museum and hear a robotic Mac and Jon square off against each other, then see in the next room a re-creation of Margo's stone-walled dungeon. After which they can head off to a VR rendition of the collapse of Vulture's Point.

I myself write the scripts. My skin color may be many shades darker than Uncle Jon's, and I am of another sex and time. But I definitely seem to have inherited some of his stylistic quirks, which I happily exploit, the better to serve the cause of previrtual literacy.

More than 70 percent of the earnings from these memoirs and related properties are going to my Institute, the Museum, and the previrtual section of the New York Public Library. No small amount of the remainder is destined for the public library in Washington, D.C., at the urging of Wendy Blevin's great-grandnieces and -grandnephews. Even members of the Solomon family have donated lavishly to our various library projects.

In his fixation on Mac and Wendy at the end of his memoirs, Uncle Jon never told whether Sy and Ida remained a couple, so, while we're on the subject of this remarkable clan, let me fill in the big gap and also give him his due. He and Ida stayed married despite the scandals. Contrite, Solomon agreed to her demand that all the hospitals, community centers, and scholarships would henceforth be named in honor of *her* parents. What he did, putting up his rickety building, was utterly unconscionable, but we must also remember the filial piety that drove him to see Vulture's Point erected.

I made my peace with the descendants of his nieces and nephews. However tragic the collapse, and however deserving he was of the eluded punishment, they have been wise stewards of the fortune he created. The Solomons have even conceded the truthfulness of *Scandals* despite their fond memories of Seymour's better sides.

Last week at the Cosmos Club, I dined with Suzy Feldman-Alvarez, the great-grandniece of Sy and herself a history buff, like so many of the old rich. "I think of Andrew Carnegie and the hundreds of men shot during the Homestead Strike," she remarked, as we lingered in the summer dusk beside the cast-iron fence bordering the Townsend Mansion. "What if he hadn't put a union hater in charge of the mill? You can't deny the past or bring back the dead, but you try to do your best with the money left behind. Seymour had his blind spots, tragic ones, but he loved books, and would surely have supported previrtual literacy."

I was equally pleased by the open-mindedness of the descendants of Eddy Bullard. Having examined private records at the Bullard Presidential Library in Chicago, they admit that the Vulture's Point transactions reeked of foul dealings.

Just as Solomon got off the hook, the courts never did catch up with Bullard, but Americans eagerly voted him out of office after his first term.

Never mind his laudable efforts against poverty and for better housing and education for the poor. Who can ignore the tragic and telling ironies of his death? His private jet would never have crashed if his White House hadn't rammed through a law—at the behest of campaign contributors—to relax oversight of aircraft maintenance.

Today, one of Bullard's great-grandchildren sits on the Institute board, and together, aided by computer scientists, we have also embarked on a new government integrity project. It will use powerful search engines to sift through VRcasts and government documents, looking for patterns of corruption that might otherwise elude activists and prosecutors. Thank you, Uncle Jon, for writing your book and setting in motion the events that bought Joan Bullard and me together.

Among the other members of the Institute board is a Yale professor named Martin Kahn, the great-grandson of Donna Stackelbaum and a veritable whiz at all things cyber.

But what of Donna and her husband, ensnared in the nuclear scandal used as a distraction from the Solomon Scandals? Hilton Kahn died of cancer some years after leaving prison—the result, his doctors speculated, of his fieldwork for legal clients in the waste division of Quad-State Atomic. He was born with an unusual sensitivity to radiation and happened to have been touring a Quad plant during a well-documented leak.

Sometimes life's endings are too Dickensian, just like Bullard's death by dint of his underregulation of aviation; but those are the facts.

Fate was kinder to Donna. In prison, she gained some of the street smarts she never could summon up in her Nuclear Regulatory job—enough to know she wasn't sufficiently Machiavellian to make it as a big-time sleaze.

Uncle Jon successfully prevailed on his father to get her a civil-service-safe sinecure tucked away within a lobbying firm specializing in atomic issues. Shaken by the probable cause of her husband's death, however, she gave up the K Street life to go to Hebrew Union College.

In time she emerged as a leading Talmudic scholar and a popular rabbi at a Reform congregation in Washington, her abundance safely concealed every Friday night under loose-fitting black robes. Uncle Jon, whenever he and Margo flew into D.C., never failed to delight in Donna's company. Absolutely no one could better explain Spinoza.

Not all the direct and indirect outgrowths from the Solomon scandals, of course, were as positive as Donna's eventual vocational choice. Imagine the anger I felt decades later when Russian mobsters were able to track down a descendant of Thackeray, Wendy's Afghan, and, via neuroimplants and vocal surgery, equip him to sensationalize the scandals. As if the story required it!

The gangsters stole long passages from Uncle Jon's book to give their lies a patina of fact—alas, this was not a borderline transgression. A front company for the Russians put the poor beast on tour in Eastern Europe and on popular Web sites, pocketing millions in download fees.

Our trademark and copyright infringement suits followed. Although normally in favor of permissive copyright laws—do we really need terms "in perpetuity, short of a day"?—I am very gratified that our lawyers crushed the other side.

We won not just a large sum of cash but also Thackeray II, whom we immediately reprogrammed for his work as a guide and performer at the *Telegram* Museum. Children dote on him. They can even choose between the Afghan and the Wendy robot if they want to hear a reading of *Alice's Adventures in Wonderland*. Off duty, our Thackeray doubles as a family pet—just as fond of cold cuts, he tells me, as Wendy's dog was. I'd never have allowed the surgery, but as long as it was done, how could we deprive Thack of his powers?

Except on Solomon-related matters, the Russian biohackers gave him an extraordinary breadth of authentic knowledge, and he cannot resist an old quote attributed to President Harry S. Truman. "If you want a friend in Washington," it reads, "get a dog."[2]

Suzy Feldman-Alvarez, hearing Thack do an uproarious Truman send-up at the Cosmos Club, kicked in another eight hundred thousand dollars toward a previrtual literacy campaign in Anacostia.

Perhaps even Margo the publicity-hater would approve of all the dazzle, all the showmanship—given the felicitous millions raised for libraries and books, as well as large gifts in her memory to Washington National Cathedral.

Serendipity is ever so sly in its disguises. If a Great Twitch exists, and I hope not, and if Wendy's suicide was inevitable, then one can at least rejoice in the happiness of the original Thackeray in Spain and in all the little Afghans born to him and his passionate mate.

No, I wouldn't have wished the scandals on anyone, not even George McWilliams, but I love the puppies that have popped out of *this* bitch.

THE END

End Notes

[1] Except for corrections of typographical errors, we are publishing Uncle Jon's memoirs virtually without changes. May I personally object to the ageism he displays in his crone reference? In fairness to Uncle Jon, he sent these memoirs to the Virginia Historical Society while he was still a relatively young man, and never have I encountered similar prejudice in his other writings—in fact, just the opposite, as suggested by his pro-bono work years later for a multimedia Web site dealing with age-discrimination issues. – Rebecca Kitiona-Fenton

[2] Unfortunately, even Thackeray's omniscience has its limits. As determined by my researchers at the Institute for the Study of Previrtual Media, the actual quote was: "You want a friend in life, get a dog!" Worse, the words were apparently put in Truman's mouth by Samuel Gallu for his play *Give 'em Hell, Harry!* (1975). Source of this information is *The Quote Verifier* (Macmillan, 2006), by Ralph Keyes, who relied on archivists at the Harry Truman Library. I have asked Thackeray to modify his act and have recommended that the *New York Times*, a spreader of the Washingtonized witticism, retract the quote.

Author's Note

1. Individuals, situations, and events are fictitious as depicted here. Same for all organizations. Among other things, I've invented two newspapers, a real estate management and construction company, a bank, a "citizens" group, two law firms, a county, and even a country. Possible overlaps with the names of actual counterparts are coincidental. GSA room numbers for various offices are also fictitious.

2. Beyond the people thanked at the start of the book, let me also express my appreciation to others—especially, in alphabetical order, Carol Anderson, Frank Dobisky, Margaret Engel, Paul Gilster, Nick Lyons (mentor extraordinaire), Jon Noring, Andy Oram, Peter Powers, Bob Rich, Roland Rohde, Marilyn Solarz, Chris Torem, and Beth Wellington.

3. I used the name "Marseilles" for a fictionalized version of Lorain, Ohio, where I'd worked on the newspaper. But I recently discovered online an actual Marseilles, a village of 124 in the same state. Still, my Marseilles was "as large a city as could exist without anyone having heard of it," so I doubt anyone would confuse the two.

4. This version of *The Solomon Scandals* is appearing in 2010, with a list of major characters and other tweaks.

About the author

The Solomon Scandals is fiction, but David Rothman did report on such stories as the secret investment that one senator's "blind trust" had held in a CIA-occupied building in Arlington, Virginia.

"The Case of The Missing Cafeteria" also came to light through his newspaper work. A cafeteria at the Environmental Protection Agency had gone AWOL despite a lease calling for one. It would have cost more than five-hundred-thousand dollars to build.

Rothman's reporting, under grants from the Fund for Investigative Journalism, led to a congressional investigation and reforms in the federal office-leasing program. Both NBC and ABC evening news broadcasted Rothman's GSA-discoveries.

Author of six nonfiction books, Rothman is a native of the Washington area, where he lives today with his wife, Carly.

Visit Rothman on the Web at www.SolomonScandals.com. You can reach him via email at dr@solomonscandals.com. The Solomon-Scandals.com site will include links on related topics ranging from journalism to building collapses.

"*The Solomon Scandals* is a mordantly entertaining book that broadens the cast of the standard Washington novel beyond spymasters and politicians to include real estate barons and federal contract officers. David Rothman's detailed knowledge of the D.C. scene comes through in his satire. *Scandals* is set in yesterday's Washington, but it is about truths behind today's headlines—and about the troubled newspapers that publish the headlines.

"Like *Boomsday* and others of the best recent Washington novels, it amuses while broadening our understanding of how today's government works—and doesn't."

James Fallows, author of *Breaking the News*

"David Rothman's bright, breezy, fast-paced, and funny novel shines a merciless spotlight on greed, skulduggery, and fraud within the government, catching President Bullard like a deer in the headlights. But what resonates with me, as a long-time investigative journalist, is protagonist Jonathan Stone's nightmare in getting his explosive findings into print. Seemingly the *Washington Post* hungered for every syllable Woodward and Bernstein could dig up on Watergate. However, it's not always that easy. Stone's fictional struggle to write and publish his exposé is more than a shadow of the truth."

Bettina Gregory, former ABC News Correspondent.

Order Form

If not available from your local bookstore or favorite online bookstore, send this coupon and a check or money order for the retail price plus $3.50 s&h to Twilight Times Books, Dept. LS0111 POB 3340 Kingsport TN 37664. Delivery may take up to two weeks.

Name: _____

Address: _____

_____

Email: _____

I have enclosed a check or money order in the

amount of $_____

for _____ .

If you enjoyed this book, please post a
review at your favorite online bookstore.

Twilight Times Books
P O Box 3340
Kingsport, TN 37664
Phone/Fax: 423-323-0183
www.twilighttimesbooks.com/

CPSIA information can be obtained at www.ICGtesting.com
260670BV00001B/4/P